I0699900

An Unforeseen Chance

A Novel

Joyce Hanewinkel

QUILL HAWK PUBLISHING

An Unforeseen Chance

Copyright © 2025 by Joyce Hanewinkel

All rights reserved.

No part of this book may be used or reproduced in any manner whatsoever, including to train artificial intelligence technologies under Article 4(3) of the Digital Single Market Directive 2019/790; Quill Hawk Publishing and the author expressly reserve this work from the text and data mining exception. Only brief quotations embodied in critical articles or reviews may be allowed.

Cover design by Ava Wood, Fins and Feathers Designs

ISBN: 978-1-965142-38-7 (Paperback)
ISBN: 978-1-965142-39-4 (Hardback)
LCCN: 2025917611

Edmond, OK

Dedicated to all who struggle within the darkness of trauma. May your inner light illuminate a path to purpose, healing, and freedom from torment.

Contents

Prologue

My heart hammered as I raced up the steps of my daughter's home. In the moonlight, a thin slice of darkness was visible between the door and jamb. Breathless, I hesitated, then eased the door open. A hinge moaned in protest. As I breached the threshold, silence and fetid air engulfed me. My eyes adjusted to the gloom. Diffused light filtering through the blinds revealed Mike lying on the couch, his head on a pillow, and turned away from me. A blanket was pulled to his neck.

"Mike?"

There was no response. I approached with a slow, halting pace. When I reached Mike's prone body, the sight of a hole in his temple stunned me. Frantic, I fell to my knees and searched his cool neck for a pulse. There was none. My hand dropped away and hung limp at my side. *Gracie!* Fear choked me.

"Gracie?" Gasping, I staggered toward her bedroom.

The metallic smell of blood hit me first. Then splashes of crimson drew my attention to the walls, the floor, the ceiling, and finally the bed. "No, no, no. Gracie!" My scream shredded the silence. Black specks dotted the center of my vision. I clutched the door frame for balance. Covering my mouth, I retched as I ran from the horror.

1.
William Arthur Curtis
The Savior

It had been a month since the murders of my husband and daughter. I hid in the shadows of my house in Mounds, Oklahoma. No longer a home or sanctuary, it had become a morgue for my life... before. That was how I viewed my life then, in terms of before and after their deaths.

In front of the fireplace, huddled in a blanket, I shivered and heated my hands on a cup of coffee. I couldn't get warm. The chill stemmed from my loneliness and anguish. Pieces of Mike and Gracie's lives surrounded me—a picture of her atop a pony when she was three years old, a photo of Mike and me with friends in Jamaica.

Until Mike and Gracie's deaths, I hadn't realized heartache could cause physical pain. A powerful constriction gripped my heart. My entire body was stiff. My head throbbed, my eyes burned, and my face swelled.

The doorbell penetrated my despair. I didn't want to see anyone, talk to anyone. I wanted to die. The bell continued ringing. Then a relentless fist pounded, and a muffled word bored through the door.

"Dawn!"

That had to be William. I wished he would go away.

William Arthur Curtis, the man of three first names. His fellow detectives called him Wac due to the rumor that he was just this side of crazy because he worked with relentless obsession and tenacity. He was the lead detective in Mike and Gracie's murder investigation, and he was the best.

William recently lost his wife, Libby, to cancer. She fought with everything she had to live. He battled hard to save her, but she couldn't be saved. He carried the weight of her death with him daily, right next to his guilt as if her death were his fault.

She had no choice, and neither did he. I did have choices, yet I wanted to die. I suspected William knew it and checked in with me on a regular basis under the guise of giving me updates on the investigation. When he was with me, his eyes would search my face. As an empath, I felt the nervous energy that radiated from him.

I think he feared what I might do.

The incessant banging and my guilt motivated me to open the door. Concern etched double lines between William's brows, and his lips formed a stern frown.

"I hope I didn't wake you," he said.

Devoid of emotion, I stared at him. His one hand grasped a carryout bag, while his other hand supported my elbow, leading me to the kitchen. He pulled out a chair for me at the table. I hadn't showered or dressed in days. I wore only a robe. Dirty dishes and trash littered the table and countertops. I should have been embarrassed, but I just didn't care.

After clearing the cluttered table, he searched the cabinets until he found paper plates. The scent of fries enticed me as he set a bag of them on the plate with a fish sandwich. My stomach clenched, then growled. *How long had I gone without food?*

We ate in silence. He scarfed down his meal and left me in the kitchen. I was vaguely aware of running water and drawers opening and closing. Then William was beside me.

"Come with me, Dawn." His firm tone left no room for argument. Numb and indifferent, I followed him to the bathroom. He led me to the tub and, with the gentleness of a man familiar with sorrow, he removed my soiled robe. "Get in the tub."

I slipped into the water and closed my eyes. Numb to everything but my despair, I cried while William washed my hair and bathed me as if I were a child. There was nothing sexual about it. It was an act of unconditional kindness.

He took a professional risk that day. I believe saving me was cathartic for him. He couldn't save Libby, but he did save me.

A bond was forged between us; however, our connection was linked with my grief to the deaths of my loved ones. The gratitude I felt toward William would last a lifetime, but there was too much sorrow in our pasts for us to have a future together. William Arthur Curtis would always be dear to me.

I needed to leave the house in Mounds. I wouldn't survive in that tomb of lifeless memories.

2.

A Chance Meeting
People Cross Your Path for a Reason

I labored for months packing up the house in Mounds. I stored photographs and mementos that elicited pain when I saw them. I hoped someday I would be able to enjoy them again. The estate sale was another level of pain. Watching people walk away with pieces of my life felt as if layers of my past were being ripped away like frayed wallpaper. But I reminded myself, it was just stuff.

So, on a bright September morning, just over a year since Mike and Gracie's murders, I sat in a booth at the back of the Last Chance Café in the Southern Oklahoma town of Chance. Feeling every one of my sixty-five years, I slumped over a cup of coffee. I was still alive, but an uncompromising emptiness plagued me. Peering through strands of hair that escaped my ponytail, I observed the other diners. A whiskered old man in worn khaki work pants and shirt chased egg yolk around his plate with a piece of biscuit. Two veterans, one wearing a sweat-stained Army cap, and his buddy, who wore a crisp new Marine hat, swapped war stories and drank coffee. The clatter of silverware and dishes, and the buzz of conversation, soothed me.

And then, I saw blood in a darkened room. The stench of death invaded my nostrils. My pulse throbbed in my temples, sweat dampened my scalp and covered my body, and I struggled to breathe while locked in the horror of that memory.

The aftermath of those heinous acts broke me. I was unable to move forward, yet impotent to reflect on the past. Floundering in a sea of loss, I clung to my routine as though it were a life preserver—an inadequate one that left me treading water in a desperate attempt to stay afloat, as if I wore children's water-wings in a turbulent ocean.

Would the pain never end? Could I resurrect the woman I was? Would the monster pay for what he did?

A burst of laughter and the aroma of bacon and fried potatoes invaded my trauma and pulled me from the flashback of that day. But I knew it would strike again when least expected.

I took another sip of coffee and studied the breakfast tribe, straining to hear their stories to escape my own. A bank of windows gave me a clear view of the bus station next door. I savored my coffee and studied travelers burdened with battered luggage as they wandered in and out of the bus terminal and scurried across the shared dusty lot. This routine lent a small sense of normalcy to my tumultuous state of mind.

With a wave, the last diner left the café, drawing my focus back to the parking lot where a waif of a girl, who looked to be in her teens, stepped off a bus and into my orbit. She carried an infant on one shoulder and a huge diaper bag over the other. A backpack added to her load. A frown creased her forehead as she struggled under the weight. Her fingers grazed her cheeks as if wiping tears. No doubt, misery was her companion. She scanned the road and parking area, then hurried away from the bus towards the café. Her quick steps were in stark contrast to her drained look and wilted posture.

The bell over the door tinkled as the girl entered the café. She stood just inside the door. The contrast of a black eye against her delicate features made the bruise more offensive. Hoisting the baby higher on her shoulder, her eyes darted around the room.

Cici, the owner of Last Chance, and his brother, Blane, were friends of mine. They watched the girl, too, their protective natures on high alert.

Drawn by the roar of an approaching vehicle and the subsequent sound of spraying gravel in the parking lot, we all glanced out the window. A truck slid to an abrupt halt, interrupting the morning calm. A rising plume of powdery grit surrounded the vehicle. A man jumped out, slamming the door behind him. Hands on hips, he narrowed his eyes and surveyed the parking lot as if he were searching for something or someone. He appeared to be in his early twenties. His rangy, muscular build, tattered jeans, and dusty work boots suggested that he was a manual laborer. With a furrowed brow and clenched fists, he stomped toward the bus station.

Everything about you says you're volatile. I've seen your type before.

My assessment of the man was reinforced by the girl's reaction. She paled. A sheen of sweat covered her ethereal features. Her chest heaved. Rooted in place, her eyes followed him as he thundered into the bus station.

Watching the scene unfold haunted me. The storm of her emotions buffeted my senses. Her panic and fear were a physical manifestation that pierced me and launched me into action. I shot from the booth and hollered at Cici. "If he comes in here, keep him busy as long as you can."

I glanced at Blane and nodded towards the truck. "Flatten a tire?"

He gave me a wink. "Piece of cake, sugar."

I approached the girl. "Come on, sweetheart. Let's get out of here. There's a window in the bathroom with your name on it. My van is parked out back. Cici and Blane will keep that guy busy."

Standing immobile, her eyes darted to the truck, then back at me as she continued to hesitate—her panicked expression unmistakable.

"If he doesn't find you at the bus station, he'll come here. Let me help you," I urged.

She blinked and swallowed her fear. With a quick nod, she followed me to the bathroom. I slid the window open. There was a clear view of the bus station. Anyone coming from there had an unobstructed view of the window, too. I touched her arm to reassure her. "You wait here. I'll watch for him. After he passes the corner of the building, we'll go out the window."

She nodded and pulled her sleeping child closer.

From the dining area, I watched the bus station door close behind him. He pounded towards the café, shoulders hunched, arms pumping.

Once my van was blocked from his view, I rushed to the bathroom. "Let's go!" I hoisted myself up onto the window ledge. "When I'm outside, pass me your backpack and diaper bag, then hand me the baby."

She passed me the bags, but when I reached for the baby, she faltered. Appearing nervous, her luminous eyes searched my face, and she swallowed hard. "Why… Why would you help me?"

Inhaling to calm myself, I told her, "I have experienced devastation inflicted by a violent man. Please, let me help you."

Her eyes roved over my disheveled appearance while she contemplated my answer. She gave a slight nod, handed her child to me, and whispered, "Thank you."

She climbed out and gathered her infant. Hidden from view, we hustled to the van. I opened the side door and helped her inside. "Go to the back of the van. Stay out of sight. I'll let you know when it's safe to get up."

As I drove through the parking lot, I observed Blane walking away from the truck.

"Where are you taking us?" she whispered.

"I live in a cabin a couple of miles from here. You can rest there and decide what you want to do, okay?" In the rearview mirror, I noted the girl's slight nod while a strange combination of relief and concern crossed her face.

Waiting for a break in traffic, I glanced in my side mirror and caught a glimpse of the predator kicking his flat tire. Satisfaction settled in my gut, until his head turned in my direction.

"Stay down!"

His eyes lingered on the van as I pulled out of the lot.

A few minutes later, we neared the turnoff from the highway. It was just a dirt track. Visitors often drove right past it if they didn't know where the turnoff was. I followed the trail into the woods. After about ten feet, the trail transformed into a graveled drive that cut through the dense trees.

"You can get up now. No one can see you here." I drove for about a quarter mile to a nondescript log cabin and parked in the circle drive.

I grabbed the bags and led the girl up the steps to the wood-plank porch. The front door opened into a cozy living area. I walked to the sofa and set the bags on it. The baby fussed, and the girl attempted to soothe her child.

"Have a seat if you like." I gestured to the rocking chair near the fireplace. "My name is Dawn. What's yours?"

"Angi. My baby girl is Sophie, and she's hungry."

Angi crossed the braided rug that blanketed the hardwood floor and eased into the rocker. The look of exhaustion deepened, and the baby's fussing intensified. Angi looked at me with appraising eyes and exhaled as if she'd been holding her breath.

"Are you breastfeeding?" I asked.

Angi lowered her eyes as if to study the rug. "Yes, ma'am." She appeared embarrassed as a light shade of pink colored her cheeks.

"Well, how about I fix lunch while you feed Sophie. Do you like barbecued ribs?"

"Oh, yes, ma'am."

"There's one condition, though. You have to stop this ma'am business. It makes me feel old. I am old, of course, but I'd like to ignore that fact as long as possible. Please call me Dawn."

Angi smiled, crinkling the skin around her eyes. "Yes, Miss Dawn."

"Well, I guess that's close enough."

By the time I got the leftovers heated, little Sophie finished nursing, her diaper was changed, and she cooed in contentment.

I arranged the food on the coffee table. Steam rose from the baked potato, and the tangy aroma of barbecue sauce filled the air. I held my arms out for Sophie. Angi hesitated, then handed her to me and moved to the couch while I settled into the rocker.

That tiny body nestled against mine, as well as the soothing scent of baby lotion and powder, calmed my anxiety. My shoulders relaxed.

"I'll sit right here so you can keep an eye on sweet Sophie. Go on and eat before the food gets cold. It's great that you're breastfeeding—that's good for the baby and you."

She blushed again.

"If you prefer, we can just say nursing instead of breastfeeding if that would be more comfortable for you."

She nodded her head, studied me, and a lazy smile appeared. She devoured the meal and carried her dishes to the kitchen.

I called after her. "Don't mess with those dishes. I'm going to give Sophie back to you, then I'll eat and clean up."

But first, I had a more important task in mind. I handed Sophie to Angi, carried her bags to the guest room, and retrieved an empty dresser drawer. In the living room, I nestled the drawer against the sofa and used a small blanket to form a cushioned liner.

I could see fatigue tugging at Angi. Her eyelids drooped, and she yawned.

"When was the last time you slept?" I asked.

"It's been a while."

Moving to the loveseat, I perched on the edge and leaned forward. "Angi, you can use that drawer like a bassinet. Lay Sophie in there, and you can lie back on the couch and take a nap. It's your choice. I have found that I make better decisions when I'm rested." She hesitated, perhaps evaluating whether she could trust me. "I'm going to the kitchen. I hope you decide to nap." I retrieved the afghan my grandmother had crocheted and laid it on the end of the couch.

After eating, I cleaned the kitchen. When I returned, I found both girls sleeping. Angi hadn't used the afghan. She looked as if she had drifted off while deciding whether to nap. I unfolded the throw and draped it over her, then watched the slight rise and fall of Sophie's little chest. My heart ached for them.

As I considered the opportunities available to Angi—if she would accept help—a sense of purpose introduced a level of energy and motivation I had not experienced in over a year.

I lit the wood in the fireplace and curled up on the loveseat with my Kindle. A smile tugged at my mouth, and for the first time in months, I felt a lightness in my heart that had been so heavy with grief. And as I observed my charges in peaceful slumber, a memory—pure and radiant—consumed me and eased my pain. I put down the Kindle, grabbed the yellow legal pad off the coffee table, and began writing.

Sometimes You Just Get It Right

> *In the quiet hours before dawn, I sit in my grandmother's rocking chair in the near-darkness of my bedroom, the only light ~~coming from~~ seeping in from the nightlight in the bathroom. My three-day-old baby is cradled in my arms, her head nestled against my breast as she nurses.*
>
> *Her breathing is in ~~syne~~ rhythm with my own and it feels as though ~~a cord a ribbon~~ an invisible ribbon has ~~entwined~~ encircled our hearts creating an unbreakable bond.*
>
> *She raises a ~~small~~ tiny, ~~hand~~ perfect hand, and amazingly she pats my breast softly. Her eyes are closed as she suckles, and the hint of a smile*

crosses her lips. We are both content. I am truly blessed.

Writing was a gift. The slow process transported me, immersing me in the joyful experience of my newborn baby. As I wrote the last line, Angi stirred on the couch, and Sophie made noises from her improvised bed. I laid the legal pad on the coffee table and wiped my eyes.

Angi stretched and blinked a couple of times as if to get her bearings.

"So how was the nap?" I asked.

"Oh, I kind of forgot where I was." She smiled, looking almost relaxed for the first time since she'd walked into the café. "How long did I sleep?"

"You've been out for a couple of hours."

Noticing the throw lying over her, she caressed the crocheted pattern. "Did you cover me?" She sounded surprised.

"I did. Even with the fire going, the room can get cool. I hope you don't mind."

Her lashes lowered, and a hint of a smile appeared as she shook her head. "No, I'm just not used to anyone doing something like that for me."

"What about your mother?"

A little snort escaped. "My mother? No. I took care of her for as long as I can remember, until I left...."

I gave her an inquisitive look. I didn't want to pry, so I didn't question her. Sophie began to fuss, and the moment was lost.

Retrieving a clean dish towel from the kitchen, I said, "Here, let me explain a trick that can make feeding Sophie less public." I handed her the towel. "I'll go to the other room. When you get Sophie situated and she is nursing, just lay that towel over her. That way, you're covered, no one can see anything, and I hope you'll feel more comfortable. What do you think?"

"I... I'll try it."

A few minutes later, she called out to me. "You can come back now." As I reentered the room, she smiled. "Thank you. I don't feel so self-conscious."

***

The angle of light across the floor indicated that dinner time was near. A beep sounded. Angi's eyes darted to mine. "What was that?"

"That sound is the driveway announcer. It's about two hundred yards from the cabin and alerts me to approaching vehicles. Living off the beaten path, it's nice to have a little warning. I don't get too many visitors. I suspect Cici is coming to check on us."

I glanced out the window as a vehicle pulled up behind my van. Cici, carrying a couple of grease-stained paper bags, exited the truck and mounted the steps. I opened the door before he could knock and was greeted by the familiar aroma of the best old-fashioned burgers around.

"Cici, you shouldn't have, but I'm glad you did. Come on in, and I'll introduce you to my guests." His bulk filled the doorway as he strode across the threshold. "Cici, meet Angi and Sophie. Angi, this is Cici. He's one of my best friends. He owns the Last Chance Café, where you saw him earlier today and from where these burgers came."

Cici gave a brief nod of acknowledgement. His shoulders were hunched, and I felt his tension as he spoke. "Angi, I avoid getting into other people's business, but you need help. That guy that came looking for you hasn't left town yet. I passed him on the highway just now. You need to stay put."

He looked at me, and before he could say more, I answered. "She can stay right here with me, no problem."

Angi watched our exchange, then asked, "What about your husband? Will he mind?"

Cici glanced at me. He knew I wouldn't want to speak of Mike, so he waited for my cue.

My breath caught, and my heart clutched. Looking away, I cleared my throat and forced a smile. Turning back to her, I answered, "No, he won't mind. He won't be here." The reality of that statement crushed me.

Cici continued, "Dawn, I don't want you in town till we know that guy is gone. He might remember seeing your van leave the parking lot. I don't want him following you."

"Agreed," I said. "Let's eat and discuss our options. Cici, give me those bags. Would you mind bringing that drawer into the kitchen so we can all eat at the table?" He looked in the drawer, then back to me. "It's an impromptu bed for Sophie."

Taking the drawer, he followed us to the kitchen, which was my favorite room. The cabin was built on a bluff above Broken Bow Lake. There was a bay window that overlooked the water and formed a nook for the table. The back wall held a set of French doors in the center, which framed a spectacular view of the lake and led out to a deck.

Angi cradled Sophie in her arms and slid into a chair while Cici placed the drawer next to her. He was a handsome man in his early forties. There was an air of confidence about him, a calmness that I hoped would put Angi at ease.

Cici settled at the table while I doled out the burgers and fries. I eased into a chair and realized I was famished. I hadn't had an appetite in months. I swallowed a mouthful of burger, wiped grease from my chin, then began. "We need to discuss some logistics. Angi, do you need anything for yourself or Sophie?"

"I… I'm going to need a few things in a couple of days. And I'll need to get a job soon."

I reached over and patted her arm. "Don't worry about a job right now."

Cici contemplated a moment, then spoke. "Angi, make a list of things you need, and I'll pick them up. Same goes for you, Dawn."

We demolished dinner, and I cleared the table. Angi and I made our lists and handed them to Cici. He tucked the lists into his coat pocket while I followed him to the front room.

"I'll be back in a couple of hours," he said.

I nodded and closed the front door behind him. Angi edged up behind me. Turning from the door, I said, "Come on, I'll show you your room."

The area was spacious with a large bathroom at the far end of it. The room was complete with a claw foot tub, walk-in shower, long vanity with double sinks, and a walk-in closet.

Angi's eyes went wide as she glanced around the bathroom. "Wow, this is nice. Uh, Miss Dawn, I still don't understand why you are helping us like this. I'm a complete stranger."

"Angi, I want you and Sophie kept safe. It's as simple as that."

Before she could ask any more questions, I showed her how to work the TV remote and left her to unpack. I poured myself a glass of wine and curled up on the loveseat with my Kindle. The logs shifted in the fireplace, sending sparks up the flue. The sounds of Angi settling into the other room comforted me. Soon, the lilting melody of a murmured lullaby and Sophie's baby sounds warmed me more than the fire.

At nine, the driveway alarm sounded. Cici's earlier warning made me nervous, so I grabbed my gun from the side pocket of the loveseat and went to the window. A vehicle rounded the bend, and Cici's truck came into view. Relief filled me as my pent-up breath escaped in a whoosh. Angi tensed in the doorway of her room, a stricken look on her face. Her concern was evident as her eyes fixed on the gun.

"It's okay, Angi. Cici's coming up the drive, and this," I held up the gun, "better safe than sorry. I know how to use it. In fact, back in the day, I was in the Army, and I qualified 'Expert' with an M-16."

She blinked and gave a slow nod.

I opened the door, gun in hand.

Cici eyed the gun with a raised eyebrow. "Hunting land sharks?" He chuckled.

"Don't tempt me, oh Great White One." I peered past his shoulder and was shocked by the sheer volume of items in the bed of his truck. "Good lord, man."

A sheepish grin tugged at his lips. "Well, you know how my little sister is. I figured Angi could use a few things for the baby, you know—all the baby paraphernalia. Diane was holding onto all this because she planned to have a garage sale. She was excited to get it out of her garage. If you'll get the groceries out of the cab, I'll carry this gear in."

I grabbed my coat and brought in the groceries. Angi helped unpack the bags, then we made our way to the front room. Laughter erupted in me as I observed the chaos that used to be my peaceful living room.

Cici snapped his head in my direction. "What?"

"I see that obsessiveness runs in your family."

"Well, you know Diane. When she's on a mission, she won't take no for an answer. And she said all these things are must-haves."

"Angi, we are not messing with all this stuff tonight. Oh look," I pointed, "there's a crib, a bassinet, and a playpen. We're in business now." Then it hit me, we hadn't discussed what Angi's plans were or how long she would stay. All the equipment Cici delivered indicated he thought she would stay awhile. I worried she would feel coerced. Angi did appear overwhelmed as her gaze moved around the room. I leaned in and nudged her shoulder. "Angi, we can talk about your plans tomorrow. Whatever you decide—whether you stay or go, it's your decision. Let's get some sleep now." I turned my attention to Cici. "Hey, I'll walk you out." When we got to his truck, I asked, "Did you get the tag number from the guy's vehicle? Can you call in a favor?"

"Already done, and it's bad. This guy, Jimmy Sutton, has had multiple protective orders filed against him, and he's been arrested for assault with a deadly weapon."

I shook my head. "You know if he shows up here—if he tries anything–I'll protect Angi and Sophie."

He stared at me for a moment. "That's what I'm afraid of. Dawn, I don't—"

I interrupted him to avoid a lecture. "Can you come out tomorrow evening and help me replace batteries in the security cameras?"

"Yes, and I'll bring Blane with me. We can get the crib put together and whatever else needs assembling."

"Thank you, Cici. I'll see you tomorrow, and I'll feed you guys, too."

I helped Angi settle herself and Sophie into the guest room. Doors locked and lights out, I climbed into bed. I laid awake. The tension was unbearable. It didn't matter if I shut my eyes or stared into the darkness. I continued to relive the horror of that morning over a year ago that struck without warning and changed everything forever. It was like a scene from a movie playing on an endless loop in my head. I tried to suppress the memories of Mike and Gracie's bodies. And the blood—I could smell it. The flashback, no doubt, was brought on by my worry for Angi and Sophie. *Not again—never again!*

Shaking, I struggled to breathe. I got out of bed and padded to the kitchen. Perhaps some chamomile tea would relax me. *Maybe I'll read some by the fireplace.* As I waited for the microwave to finish, I glimpsed the first flash of lightning out the window that faced the woods. Oh, how I loved a good rain. The lightning lit up the sky, forming a backdrop to the bare trees of the woods and conjured up impressions of the Headless Horseman.

"What is wrong with me?"

Tea in hand, I made it to the sofa as the first drops of rain splattered. I sipped my tea, then grabbed my legal pad and wrote.

> *I sit on the loveseat and listen to the hint*
> *of rain. I hear it lightly at first in the fireplace,*
> *then the windows, and the roof. It starts*
> *tentatively like (like what?) a musician, teasing*

out the notes to a new song, then picks up tempo with confidence as the melody reveals itself.

It's late and as I listen to the rain and contemplate reading... just a few pages, I'm slowly engulfed in the warmth of gratitude, ~~Like a blanket It's as though~~ as if a lover tenderly wrapped a blanket around my shoulders. I am grateful that at the end of a long day I can find joy in the simple pleasure of listening to the rain. I am blessed.

Relaxed, I put down the pad, got into bed, and fell into a deep sleep.

3.

Morning Medicine
The Healing Force of Secrets Shared

The next morning, I breached the surface of wakefulness in slow motion. *The mattress feels softer. My head is burrowed deeper in the pillow. How can this be? It's the same bed, the same pillow. Wait a minute. Am I relaxed?* I hadn't spent the night fighting with my demons. I slept.

As I wrestled my way out of bed, I caught my reflection in the mirror over the bureau. *Woah buddy! Is that me?* I was wearing yesterday's sweats. The ponytail was a ratted mess, and for the first time in months, I noticed how gaunt my face appeared. Even though I had slept well, it would take more than one night to erase the dark circles shadowing my eyes and clear the pallor of my complexion. I sniffed my armpits. *Maybe these sweats are from the day before yesterday. A shower is in order.*

***

I stood by the microwave awaiting the "ping" that signaled my oatmeal was done. The Keurig was brewing coffee when I sensed someone watching me. My intuition told me the person was someone who meant no harm. The feeling was a pleasant pressure, like a warm hug—a friend.

18

Not turning from the microwave, I spoke. "Good morning, Angi."

Angi asked, "How did you know I was here?"

I turned and smiled at her. *This is not the time to explain the nuances of my empathic gift.* "Oh, I uh, saw your reflection in the microwave door. Angi, I start most days with a workout, have a light breakfast, then grab a second cup of coffee at Cici's so I can people watch. But I'll be skipping Cici's today. What would you like for breakfast? I have oatmeal, some cold cereals, or bacon and eggs. Pick your poison."

"Oatmeal sounds good, Miss Dawn, but I can make it."

"Today you're my guest, tomorrow you're on your own." Nodding towards the kitchen table, I continued. "Look what I found in that pile of stuff Cici brought over." A bouncy seat sat on the table. "Why don't you strap Sophie into the bouncy seat, and I'll bring this oatmeal over for you." I smiled and felt my features softening. "I'd like for us to talk this morning so we can get to know each other better." I set the oatmeal on the table. "Do you want coffee?"

Angi smiled. "Oh, yes, please." She gazed at a sated Sophie, whose eyelids drooped as she drifted into a contented slumber.

I set the mug in front of her, then made more cereal and coffee for myself. Returning to the table, I sat across from her. Not letting the silence draw out, I jumped right in. "So, tell me about Jimmy Sutton."

Angi's eyes darted to mine. She looked frightened. Anger boiled within me at the sight of her fear. I could feel her distress. I knew that panic. Angi's emotions buffeted my empathic sensitivity and took me back to my own nightmare experiences—*I will have to shield myself from her emotions*. I took a couple of deep breaths and calmed myself.

"How… How do you know his name?" she asked.

"Cici told me." Feeling her discomfort, I continued. "Perhaps I should go first—Cici was an MP in the Army. After he got out, he settled in Tulsa. He worked for the Tulsa Police Department for several years. Tired of police work and Tulsa, he moved to Chance and bought the café. He still has friends on the force, so he got the tag number off Jimmy's truck and called a buddy at the station."

Angi studied me. "So, you and Cici…?"

I laughed. "Gawd no. We are just friends. I'm old enough to be his mother."

Looking puzzled, Angi asked, "How old is Cici?"

"He's fortyish."

Her eyes rounded when she looked at me. Transformed from yesterday's unkempt appearance, today my long hair shined and I wore yoga pants and a spandex top. "So, you're like—sixty?"

I laughed. "I'm sixty-five. You see now why I didn't want you calling me ma'am?" I glanced at the lake, then back at Angi. "I met Cici about eight years ago in Tulsa, back when he was a cop. He pulled me over for speeding and noticed the veteran status on my driver's license. We got to talking, and he didn't give me a ticket. I was active in the veteran community back then, and I hooked him up with some related organizations. We kept running into each other at events and became friends. I introduced him to my husband, and they hit it off. Cici invited us down here for a Fourth of July lake party hosted by his sister who lived here. My husband and I fell in love with the lake, the people, and the entire area. We decided to build this cabin—our weekend and holiday retreat. A few years later Cici moved here, and we were elated when he did."

Angi thought for a moment, then asked, "What about the other guy at the café?"

I couldn't help but smile. "That would be Blane, Mister Charming… the guy who flattened Jimmy's tire. He's Cici's younger brother. He's been out of the Army for about a year. He was stationed in Afghanistan and needed some down time to decompress and re-enter civilian life. So Cici put him to work at the café 'til he can figure out what he wants to do. Okay, now it's your turn, Angi. Tell me about Jimmy."

Angi focused her attention on the coffee cup in her hands, then raised her eyes to meet mine. "There's not much to tell. Not about Jimmy anyway." She lowered her eyes again, and her shoulders slumped. "Last year, when I was a senior in high school, I worked at a diner in Tulsa. My mom has issues, and I don't even know who my dad is. Mom doesn't work. She's on disability and is very needy. She spends most of her money on cigarettes and beer, so I worked after school and weekends. I got to eat free at the diner the days I worked.

"Anyway, there was this guy, Nick, who came into the diner every Friday. He was a salesman, and his route brought him through Tulsa. He was older, but he treated me nice. He was good-looking, polite, and funny. After a couple of weeks, he asked me out.

"He was always surprising me with gifts. Then he started getting a room at a hotel and staying the weekends." She raised her eyes and implored me. "You have to understand, no one had ever been that nice to me. Anyway, I got pregnant." Angi looked at Sophie, took a tiny foot in her hand, and rubbed her thumb across the pad of it. A hint of a smile played at her lips. She wiped her eyes and looked at me. "When I told Nick I was pregnant, he got mad. He… he told me to 'get rid of it.'" Angi hugged herself and looked away as she remembered. She winced, her head jerked, and she shuddered. Angi rocked her body and sobbed.

The force of her fear and despair hit me like an Oklahoma tornado and catapulted me out of my chair. I had her in my arms before I was conscious of moving. I held her tight and stroked her hair.

"Oh, Miss Dawn, he tried to make me lose my baby. He slammed my head into a wall. He threw me on the ground and kicked me. My stomach hurt so bad. I was so scared."

"Shh, I've got you, Angi." I continued to cradle her. Minutes passed, and she stilled in my arms. The sobs quieted, and she took a shaky breath. I took the chair across the table to give her a little space.

She continued her story. "He threw money at me and yelled at me to get an abortion. I… I just couldn't do that. I didn't know Nick was married. He didn't wear a wedding ring, and he never told me he was, at least, not until I told him I was pregnant.

"I never saw him again after that. He stopped coming to the diner. That was in December of my senior year. I was able to finish the school year and graduate. Sophie wasn't born until August first. I started working full time at the diner after graduation, and I moved in with one of the other servers. I couldn't continue to live with my mom. I didn't think I could take care of her and the baby. Plus, I didn't want my baby around her.

"Jimmy was friends with my roommate's boyfriend, so he was around all the time. He would stare at me. The way he looked at me gave me the creeps. Jimmy knew I was pregnant, but it didn't matter. He kept asking me out. I told him I didn't want to date anyone. A couple of days ago, he insisted I go out to dinner with him. He told me having dinner wasn't a date. He said he knew I hadn't been anywhere since Sophie was born, and he thought I might want to get out of the house for a bit. When we got back from dinner, it was time to feed Sophie, so I asked him to leave. He tried to kiss me, and I pushed him away. He went berserk and hit me. He said I was a tease and told me I was his. He said it wasn't over, and he'd be back." Angi started shaking. "Miss Dawn, I couldn't go through that again. Not after Nick beat me, and not after the way I grew up. I saw my mom knocked around by different men. When the fighting would start, I would sneak next door and hide in the neighbor's doghouse." I winced but said nothing. "After Jimmy hit me, he left, but I knew he'd come back. So, after feeding Sophie, I packed what I could, went to the bus station, and ended up here. You know the rest."

"Angi, how do you think Jimmy found you?"

"Process of elimination? He knew I didn't have a car. I left a note for my friend telling her I wouldn't be back, but I didn't tell her where I was going. I waited a while for the bus to

Chance. If he asked around at the station, I'm sure someone would have remembered me. There was no one else there with a baby."

She looked down at the table again, no longer able to meet my eyes. I took her hand. "Angi, look at me, please. You have been taken advantage of and victimized, but I won't call you a victim because you are a survivor. You are intelligent, brave, fierce, and loving. You just need a little help, that's all."

She looked at me in disbelief. "How can you say I'm brave? I ran." She shook her head, then buried her face in her hands.

"That's how I know you're smart. When you pushed Jimmy away, you stood up to a bully. You ran to save your baby and yourself. You protected your baby. Nothing is more important than that. Running isn't a weakness, Angi. Starting over takes a lot of strength, so don't sell yourself short. Do you have a plan?"

"My only plan was to get away from Jimmy. I looked at a map on the bus station wall, and Chance stood out to me. You'll probably think this is stupid, but I felt like… the map spoke to me. Like maybe I had a chance here, you know?"

"Yes, I do know. May I make a suggestion?" Angi nodded. "I'm retired, and the truth of the matter is I'm lonesome. I would love for you and Sophie to stay here with me until we get the Jimmy situation under control. After that, we can regroup and see where to go from there. Are you okay with that?"

Angi looked confused. "You're lonesome? But your husband—"

"He's not around, and that's a story for another time. What do you say, will you stay here with me until the Jimmy situation is rectified?"

"Are you sure, Miss Dawn? Aren't you worried that I might be a mooch? Are you sure you want us to stay?"

"I'm positive. You'd be doing me a favor."

Relief radiated from her. She sat straighter in her chair, and her chin rose. "Yes, I'd like that very much." She looked down at our clasped hands. I was surprised to see I was still holding her hand. I gave it a squeeze before letting go.

Holding Angi's hand felt so good, and cradling little Sophie yesterday had been magical. It occurred to me that I had not been touched in months. I wondered if Angi had been touched in a loving way—ever.

"Angi, there's something you need to know about me."

A look of concern crossed her face. "What?"

I smiled and confessed. "I'm a hugger. I'm a touchy-feely kind of person. I just can't help it. When I'm talking to people, I may touch them on the arm or take their hand like I did with you just now. And when I leave a gathering, saying goodbye takes forever, because I have to hug everyone—twice. So, if hugs make you uncomfortable, please tell me, and I will try to curb hugging you."

That shy smile was back. "I like hugs." She looked down at the table. "My mom wasn't a touchy-feely person at all. In fact, I don't think she even likes me." Her eyes glistened.

I felt her loss as well as my own and I was done-in. For the second time, I embraced her in a gentle hug. "Alrighty then, lots of touchy-feely it is. Come on, there's something I want to show you. You're not going to believe this," I said.

4.

A Safe Place
A Hidey Hole—Who Does That?

Angi and I stood together to the right of the fireplace. "What do you think of my bookcase?"

"I like it," she said. "I love to read, and I've been checking out your books."

"It's more than a bookcase. Run your fingers down the inner-left side and feel for a button. Let me know when you find it."

Angi started at the top and ran her hand down to waist height. "Found it."

"Okay. Press the button, then stand back, because the bookcase will swing toward you."

Angi's eyes got big. She pressed the button, and the cabinet swung open without making a sound. She looked through the doorway into a bathroom. A trap door stood open. "This is way cool."

I chuckled. "I know. I've loved secret stuff like this since I was a kid. Through that trapdoor, at the bottom of the stairs, is a safe room that doubles as a storm shelter. Without knowing what Jimmy's intentions are—well, I thought it would be wise for you to know how to access the safe room. Why don't you put Sophie in her bassinet, then follow me down the stairs? We will be done in no time."

I showed her the light switch on the wall just above the handrail and flipped it on to illuminate the decent-sized room below. The space looked more like a basement than a safe room because it was so large. Mounted on the wall in front of us was a large screen monitor in split-screen mode showing a freeze-frame of all the security camera inputs. There was a large desk that ran the width of the wall with a computer terminal on it as well as a landline phone.

"When any of the cameras are activated, a live feed will show up on the monitor. I also will receive an alert on my cell phone. I can watch live footage or replay a clip anytime from my phone and the terminal."

Angi turned in a slow circle and surveyed the space that was set up like an apartment. "Miss Dawn, I think you're prepared for everything."

"Not everything, but close." I smiled. "I need to explain how a couple of things work in case you ever need to use this as a safe room. Oh, I almost forgot. See that door on the wall to the side of the monitor? It's an exit door that leads through a short tunnel to the storage shed under the deck." Angi peered into the tunnel and shivered. "Come back upstairs. I want to show you how to shut the trap door. I know it's a lot to take in." I led Angi back up to the bathroom. We went over the intricacies of opening, closing, and locking the doors, and how to use the manual applications if the power failed.

Angi shook her head as a smile played across her face. "I feel like I'm in a spy movie."

"It's a little over the top, but my husband and I had fun planning it."

"Does the trap door open every time the bookcase is opened?"

"That's the last thing I was going to show you. If you pull on the bookcase instead of pushing the button, the bookcase opens without activating the trap door. That's how the bathroom is accessed if you just need a bathroom."

"I'm going to have to practice pushing all the buttons a couple of times and fiddle with the manual switches so the sequence is natural. I don't want to have to think about what I'm doing if I need to use it," Angi said.

"See, you are a smart girl."

Once Angi was comfortable with all the aspects of accessing the safe room, we moved to the living room and continued talking while we organized the menagerie of baby items. Angi filled me in on the details of her childhood. She told me about growing up on the *North Side* of Tulsa which was not an affluent area of town and was known for gang activity.

We left the playpen, swing, and bassinet in strategic spots of the front room, so they were out of the way but easy to access, and we stashed the crib parts in Angi's bedroom.

"Miss Dawn, if you have a Philips and flat-head screwdrivers, and a set of Allen wrenches, I'll put this crib together."

I was a little surprised. "So you know your way around tools, do you?"

She grinned. "Since I had to do everything around the house, I took all the shop and mechanic classes I could in school, and I've watched a lot of YouTube videos."

"You are my kind of gal. But here's the deal. Cici and Blane are coming over this evening to help, and they'll be disappointed if the crib is already put together. I don't doubt your abilities, but sometimes it's a kindness to let people help. Doing so gives them a sense of fulfillment and makes them feel good."

"Miss Dawn, how do you know so much?"

I laughed. "Well, besides being old, I learned that particular lesson from a Ropes course. And before you ask what that is, I'll explain. A Ropes course is designed to teach teamwork. One of the exercises consisted of a log elevated about four feet off the ground. About thirty individuals in the exercise group took turns walking across the log, one at a time. The rest of the participants were on the ground, providing support. Everyone held their hands up in case the person walking across lost their balance, they could reach for a helping hand. I walked first. I didn't want any help. I wanted to do it myself.

"I had always been fierce in my independence because, from a young age, I, like you, couldn't rely on the people that should have taken care of me.

"I lost my balance and grabbed a hand. Instead of being grateful for the assistance, I was resentful that I needed help. Then I was on the ground as a helper. All the rest of the group took their turns going across the log. At the end of the exercise, the instructor asked how we felt going across the log, to need help and receive it. Some were grateful, others were not. Then he asked us how we felt to be on the ground offering support, assisting when needed, and saving people from falling. I loved helping. In fact, everyone enjoyed helping.

"Angi, that was one of the most powerful and life-changing lessons I have ever learned. The reason I hated asking for help was because it made me feel weak and inadequate. I also didn't want to impose on people. But that experience taught me that most people enjoy helping; it is empowering to assist someone to reach their potential. We didn't see the recipient as weak; we saw them as someone who simply needed a hand.

"That exercise also taught me that I, too, could accept help when needed. Accepting help took nothing away from me or my independence. In fact, it could make me stronger."

Angi looked thoughtful while we continued our task of sorting the baby items. Once we finished, I started putting dinner together. While Angi tended to a fussy Sophie, I was surprised at the sense of joy and purpose the sounds fostered in me. After nursing, Sophie settled, and Angi curled up on the sofa with a book. The day passed in pleasant coexistence with Angi and I, more content and comfortable than either of us had been for some time.

***

The driveway alarm sounded a little before five. I grabbed my gun. Standing by the front window, I glanced back at Angi. "Have you ever shot a gun?"

"Does a BB gun count?"

I grinned. "Sort of. Did you like it?"

Angi's forehead wrinkled as she thought about it. "Yes, shooting was fun when I hit something."

"If you want, Cici, Blane, or I can teach you how to shoot. We get together from time to time for target practice."

"Yes, I'd love that."

Cici's truck rounded the bend with Blane's SUV right behind. I put the gun away. It was mid-September, and the warm fall day was cooling off, so I grabbed my jacket. "Cici and Blane are going to help me change the batteries in the cameras. Would you mind pulling the lasagna out of the oven if the timer goes off before I'm back?"

"Sure."

Stepping out the front door, I was grazed by brisk cool air and the fragrance of autumn—that mixture of damp earth and fallen leaves served up with an explosion of vibrant colors.

Blane parked so close to Cici's driver's side door that Cici couldn't get out. Blane shot out his door and walked around to the front of his SUV. Grinning, he gave me a wink.

Cici tapped his horn. "Hey, move your truck over."

Blane laughed. "Nope."

Cici slid across the bench seat and exited on the passenger side, mumbling, "You little piss-ant, you did that on purpose."

Blane shrugged. "I owed you one."

Cici grunted, then grabbed a tool belt and extension ladder out of the bed of his truck. "Refresh my memory, Dawn, where are all your cameras?"

I pointed out the cameras. Blane steadied the ladder, and Cici changed the batteries. We rushed to finish. Cici stowed the ladder in his truck bed, and the men body-checked each other going up the steps, jockeying to be first through the door.

"Boys!" I snapped in my best Army Sergeant voice. Their bodies stiffened and heads swiveled in my direction. "Ladies first," I said, then I plowed my way through them. A stunned look passed between them.

When we entered the cabin, we were greeted by a tantalizing array of scents that encircled us like the arms of an old friend. Cici's eyes closed, and with a deep inhalation, his lips crooked into a smile. "Is that your homemade lasagna I smell?"

"Yep. You two wash up and meet us in the kitchen."

When I walked into the kitchen, I was pleased and surprised. A cork lay beside an open bottle of my favorite red wine. The combined scents of butter, garlic, and yeast slipped from the oven. The lasagna rested on the counter, the table had been set, a salad sat in the center, and from the smell of it, a loaf of garlic bread was heating.

"Wow. Thank you, Angi."

With a slight duck of her head, she said, "I wanted to help. I hope you don't mind. Would you like a glass of wine?"

"That would be perfect."

Angi and I sat on the side of the table with the best view. The fellas sat across from us with their backs to the waterscape. From my vantage point, I admired a panorama of the lake at sunset. The hues of the evening sky combined as if an artist had dragged a paintbrush through colors on a palette. Mirrored in the lake, the pigments intensified. The display was breathtaking. I got up and turned out the lights.

"Dawn!" Cici protested.

Blane snorted. "I don't know why you waste your breath, Cici. You know she's obsessive and can't help herself."

With a quizzical expression, Angi glanced around the table.

Blane saw her confusion and explained. "It's like this, Angi," he pointed his butter knife at me for emphasis, "Dawn is an artsy, fartsy, free spirit, new-age kind of gal. And when she sees a beautiful sunset, she turns out the lights so she can see the colors better. She's been shutting off the lights for years."

I rolled my eyes. "Angi, don't let them ruin the experience for you. Just look at all that beauty out there."

Angi took a deep breath, and a sigh escaped. "Wow." I sensed a kindred spirit. Angi looked at Blane, then back at me. "Artsy, fartsy, free spirit, new age? Free spirit I get—"

Cici groaned. "Can we turn the lights back on?"

I turned the lights on. "Blane calls me 'Artsy Fartsy' because I paint and write. Free spirit…. Well, I just am. And I assume 'New Age' is because I practice yoga."

Getting his ornery on, Blane winked at Angi. "And she's argumentative, too."

"Blane Rossi. I. Am. Not. Argumentative."

"See?" he crowed.

Angi glanced around the table, and a subtle grin crossed her face. I concluded that she had never experienced camaraderie like this. My maternal instincts kicked into high gear. I was all in for whatever it took to rescue Angi and Sophie. I turned to her and ignored the man-boys. "I'll have to take you out to the shop tomorrow and show you around. My studio, office, and a gym of sorts are housed there. The building has heat and air, so you can bring Sophie, and if you want, do some yoga or whatever kind of exercise you like."

Angi's expression reflected her amazement over another revelation of the world in which I lived. When dinner was finished, I suggested Angi show Blane where she wanted the crib set up.

"Cici, you mind keeping me company while I clean the kitchen?" I wanted to talk to him about Jimmy.

Blane and Angi headed off to the bedroom. As soon as I heard the rattle of the crib parts, I told Cici what I knew. "The good news is that Jimmy is not Sophie's father, and Angi wasn't in a relationship with him. He is best friends with the boyfriend of her former roommate. The bad news is they weren't in a relationship, which means that SOB is crazy if he can get that possessive over someone he never dated." I related the details she told me that morning.

Cici shook his head. "This is Sunday. I imagine he'll have to get back to work, so he'll be scarce by tonight. His car registration showed a Tulsa address. Is he still living in Tulsa?"

"I think so. That's where Angi was living before she caught the bus to Chance. She grew up in a trailer park. After she graduated, she moved into an apartment in midtown Tulsa with her friend. Jimmy works construction for a national outfit, so he travels some. Maybe we'll get lucky, and he'll get sent out of town."

"We can hope. With Chance being a three-and-a-half-hour drive from Tulsa, it won't be convenient for Jimmy to harass her… but not impossible."

***

In her room, Angi could hear the clatter of dishes and the low buzz of conversation coming from Dawn and Cici in the kitchen. Blane inspected the parts of the crib as if evaluating what tools he needed. This was the first opportunity for Angi to study him without him being aware of her scrutiny.

His dark hair was cut short, but not too short. Shiny curls gave him a boyish look even though she guessed he was in his mid-twenties. She estimated he was over six feet tall. His rolled-up shirt sleeves exposed toned forearms attached to large, capable-looking hands. He moved with fluid athleticism, and the overall effect verged on beautiful.

Angi shied from the attraction. *So not my type, way out of my league. And besides, a man is the last thing I need.*

Blane turned and almost caught her studying him. "I'm going to grab the tools out of my car. I'll have this put together in no time."

As Blane worked on the crib, Angi admired the open toolbox on the floor several feet from where he worked. She bent over and took the hex key set out of the toolbox. Blane turned to scan his toolbox, and Angi handed him the hex key set. His eyebrows drew together as he studied her briefly and took the tools. "That's what I needed."

"I know," she stated with authority.

Next, she took out the flathead screwdriver and handed it to him a few minutes later when he needed it. Then she walked to the opposite side of the crib from him and steadied the panel just as he began to speak. "Angi, would you… " Blane looked up and saw her steadying the panel just like he was going to ask her to do. He flashed her a grin, his eyes, the color of blue sea glass, crinkled at the corners. "You could have assembled this crib yourself, couldn't you?"

Her face flushed, and she gave a little shrug. "Maybe, but it's nice to have help. I'm not used to having help." She felt even more embarrassed then.

Blane's eyes met hers. There was still bruising around her eye. Her hair was that odd combination of natural blond with darker brown mixed in. It crowned her head in a messy bun. Long strands had escaped and brushed the sides of her face. She wore no makeup but radiated a simple beauty that even the black eye couldn't disguise.

"Would you teach me to shoot?" she asked. There was no trace of her earlier discomfort.

Blane cocked his head to the side. "Whoa, where did that come from?"

"Dawn asked me if I knew how to shoot. She said you all could teach me. I'd like to learn."

"Sure, how about next Saturday? There is a clearing in the woods on Dawn's property where we have targets set up. I'll bet Dawn will watch Sophie for you. Does Saturday work?"

Angi smiled and tried to suppress her excitement. "Saturday would be great."

"Alrighty then, it's a date."

Her smile vanished, replaced by a stricken look.

"Not that kind of date, Angi. Just a scheduling date. I don't date—at all."

"Are you gay?" The words were out of her mouth before she could stop them.

Blane's eyes rounded in shock just before he threw back his head and laughed—the first good laugh he'd had in months.

He wiped his eyes and shook his head. "Hardly, Darlin'. I like women just fine. It's a commitment I have issues with. Don't get me wrong, I have my fair share of hookups, but I wouldn't classify them as dates."

Angi's face bypassed pink and lit-up bright red. "I am so sorry. I don't know why I said that. It just popped out."

"Don't worry about it. That's the best laugh I've had in a while. It felt good."

5.
Surprises
Revelations

The following morning, Angi was up before me. I found her relaxing by the fireplace and rocking Sophie. I stroked the top of Sophie's head as I walked past. "You want to see the shop this morning?"

"Yes." She left the rocker and followed me into the kitchen.

"Let's grab breakfast first. I need some coffee."

I turned toward the countertop and was surprised to see a K cup already in the Keurig, my mug in place, a spoon resting on a napkin, and a protein bar beside it. My heart expanded, and my eyes stung.

"Thank you, Angi." I gestured toward the display. "That was so thoughtful."

A modest smile appeared, and she ducked her head for an instant before raising her eyes to mine. "I like helping."

I wrapped my arm around her shoulders and gave her a squeeze. "Good. You can assist me with several projects I have been putting off."

After eating, we bundled up Sophie and ourselves. Stepping onto the front porch, which ran the width of the cabin, we descended the steps.

Angi peered across the drive. "I hadn't even noticed the shop until now."

"In all fairness, you haven't been outside except for when we arrived, and you were a little preoccupied at the time."

We crossed a thirty-five-foot expanse of yard and driveway to the shop. The structure was situated parallel to the cabin, facing the side of it. The earth brown color of the shop allowed the building to blend into the woods.

The road we drove in on forked. One branch formed a circle-drive in front of the cabin. The other led to parking areas in front of and beside the shop. Angi studied the two overhead doors in the center of the building while I opened the front door.

"Angi, I want to show you my studio first."

We passed the bathroom by the back wall as I led her up the staircase to the loft. A faint scent of linseed oil and turpentine infused the atmosphere of the studio. The sun's rays shot through multiple skylights, filling the space with natural light and highlighting small dust particles. Angi walked to the center of the room, raised her face to a skylight, and closed her eyes. Sophie nuzzled her neck, and a Mona Lisa smile shaped Angi's lips. Again, I was struck by a sense of familiarity. Was it the smile? Her stance? Something niggled at the back of my mind, but I just couldn't grasp it—a déjà vu moment.

Angi moved to the easel and tall stool that stood in the back corner between two windows. She contemplated the view of the woods behind the shop, then turned her gaze to the lake through the adjacent window. A desk sat in the opposite corner.

"What an awesome studio," Angi said.

I glanced around as if I were seeing the studio for the first time. "Yes, it is. Now that I'm up here, I realize how much I've missed my art. I haven't painted in a year or more." A sudden longing filled me, not just for painting, but for all I had lost. The yearning threatened to overwhelm me. "Come on, Angi, I'll show you the rest of the shop."

Downstairs on the ground floor again, we moved toward the opposite end of the shop. "I like to keep the center area cleared out in case of bad weather so we can pull a couple of vehicles inside if needed." As we neared a partition, I said, "Check out the other side of the wall." A sense of melancholy bathed me as bittersweet memories surfaced.

Angi's mouth formed an "O" as she looked at an entertainment area that resided in the corner of the shop below the loft. Mounted on the partition that separated the entertainment area from the front end of the shop was a large, flat-screen TV. She sat in one of the four theater seats opposite the TV and caressed the leather. She then stood and strolled along the bar, trailing her fingers across the top, which extended the length of the wall to the partition. She bent to open the door to a mini fridge beneath the bar. Liquor and glasses were shelved above the counter. A small sink nestled in the bar top, and a microwave oven completed the setup. Scanning the entire entertainment area, all Angi could say was, "Wow."

I laughed. "We used to entertain a lot. On game days, this was the best place for people to get rowdy. I also use the big screen for my exercise DVDs. The mount swivels." I pointed to the opposite side of the building. "Over there is the workout area. The blue box has yoga mats, smaller weights, and exercise balls. Cici and Blane use the larger mats and the free weights for martial arts and general workouts."

Angi, sounding wistful, shared, "I'd like to exercise, but it's hard for me to keep any weight on while nursing."

I chuckled. "We'll put some meat on you, don't you worry. Feel free to use anything out here. You don't have to ask. I'm going to do my workout now, then I'll check in with Cici and see if Jimmy is still hanging around town."

"Okay. I'm going back to the house." She paused in the doorway and looked around. "I still can't believe everything that you are doing for me. Thank you."

Her gratitude assured me I was doing the right thing. Snuggling Sophie, she crossed the driveway and yard to the cabin.

***

The clatter of dishes sounded in the background. "Last Chance Café. Cici speaking."

"Hey, it's me," I said.

"Hey, back. Before I forget, Diane wants to have a birthday party for Sophie."

"She does?"

"Yes, Little Sis is dying to meet Angi and Sophie. Sophie will be two months old on October first, which is this Saturday. Little Sis figures that will give her a good excuse for a party and an introduction. Since Blane is going to give Angi her first shooting lesson Saturday, Diane said she can get everything ready while they're in the woods and make it a surprise party."

"How many people are we talking about, Cici?"

"Diane doesn't want to overwhelm Angi. She thought Steve and little Katie, you, me, and Blane. We'll save the rest of the clan until Angi gets more settled. Diane said to tell you that she'll bring a cake and decorations."

My brain shot into party planning mode. "I like it, Cici. We'll keep the party simple. I've got a pork shoulder in the freezer. I can make pulled pork sandwiches, coleslaw, baked beans, chips, and dip."

"That's my girl. It's good to have you back, Dawn." A gentle tone crept into Cici's voice, and I could hear the smile in his words.

I blinked back the moisture and whispered, "It's good to be back. I can't explain it, Cici. Having Angi and Sophie here—things are different. I haven't struggled to get out of bed the past couple of mornings. I feel like my head is above water. It's as if someone has thrown me a lifeline."

"Have you told Angi about—"

"I'm not ready yet. Talking about that day would be like ripping the scab off a wound. I don't want to think about the horror, let alone talk about it." Changing the subject, I asked him, "What about Jimmy, is he still in town?"

"It appears he has left, but I'd like you to wait another day before you come into town."

"Not a problem."

***

Blane watched Cici disconnect the call. He stood with his hip cocked to the side balancing a bus stray of dirty dishes. "Was that Dawn?"

Cici nodded, a pensive expression playing across his face.

Blane shifted the tub to the counter. "She's… different. Better."

Again, Cici nodded. "I've been worried about her. I didn't know if we'd ever see the old Dawn again. But just now, when I told her that Diane wanted to have a party for Angi, she was all in, talking about food and organizing the party."

"Yeah." Blane tilted his head. "And last night she was spunky, elbowing us out of the way when we came into the house. She was all chatty at dinner, too."

Cici nodded, and Blane picked up the tray of dishes and went back to work.

6.

The Gun Range
Exhale and Squeeze

During the next five days, Angi and I fell into an easy routine. I did my morning workouts, but instead of going to the café for people watching, I enjoyed a second cup of coffee with Angi. We visited like old friends, as if we'd known each other forever. We just *got* each other despite our age difference. Our deep connection so soon was unusual, but we both needed it.

Sitting at the kitchen table, steam rose from my coffee, beckoning me to inhale the warm scent of the hazelnut creamer. I sipped and savored the moment. The kitchen filled with warmth, and sunlight danced on the lake, issuing the promise of a glorious day for the birthday party.

Setting my cup down, I called out to Angi. "I'm going to town to pick up a few things. What time will Blane be here for your shooting lesson?"

Angi skittered into the kitchen with Sophie on her hip. Her nervous energy buzzed and pelted me with minute jabs.

"Blane said he'd be here around eleven. How cold is it outside? I'm not sure my jacket will be warm enough."

Angi was smaller than me, a couple of inches shorter, and weighed maybe fifteen pounds less. She did need to gain a few pounds.

"I have plenty of outdoor gear that will fit you. The coat may be a little loose but will keep you warm."

Angi grimaced. "I need to get a job. It's not right for me to sit around and let you provide everything."

"Well, first, you haven't just been sitting around. I appreciate all the help you have given me. Second, you gave birth two months ago. Also, I trust you are not going to take advantage of me or the situation. I have a feeling something may come along in a couple of weeks. And besides, I have money I haven't spent yet. We'll talk about you working later. I need to run to town now, so I can be back in time to watch Sophie for you."

***

The air had a fresh scent and chilled me. I shut the van door and wrapped my hands around the sunbaked steering wheel. The short drive to town was invigorating. As I got out of the van and made my way into Doc's grocery store, I felt a momentary sensation of pinpricks. The sensation, although fleeting, was long enough to trigger my empath gift. Someone, not a friend, watched me for just an instant. Using my gifts, I reached out to see if I could feel anything else. I didn't. *It might be nothing.... Got to tell Cici about this, though.* I would have stopped by the café, but he didn't work weekends. I imagined Cici was helping Diane get things ready for the party today.

***

The van door glided open. I loaded groceries into the middle row of seats. *There! There it is again.* That time, the feeling lingered. A sensation, like a thousand needles, pricked my skin. The hair on the nape of my neck rose. *This is not good.* I didn't look around. I didn't want whoever watched me to know that I was aware of their presence, that I could feel them watching me. A perceived weakness could sometimes be a good defense, giving an individual an element of surprise. I acted unaware.

Inside the relative safety of the van and behind tinted windows, I scanned the parking lot and around the street. I didn't see anyone watching me, but that didn't mean they weren't there. Maybe they were hiding. I kept checking the rearview mirror, but

I didn't see Jimmy or anyone else. The feeling faded as I drove away.

When I arrived home, Blane's SUV was already parked by the shop. I wasn't late; he was early. *Hmm, I think Mr. Charming may be looking forward to the target practice session.* When I walked into the house, I was gobsmacked. Blane sat in the rocker with a cloth over his shoulder, burping Sophie.

"You can close your mouth, Dawn. Don't look so surprised. You know how many little kids there are in my family. I have burped many a baby at our gatherings."

I just nodded and kept staring. "Where's Angi?"

"She's getting ready. Oh, Diane wants you to call her as soon as we leave."

I still couldn't get over Blane holding Sophie. He looked like a pro. There was no awkwardness, and Sophie burrowed into him. Angi walked in from her room, and I saw a softening of her features–a yearning as she looked at Blane holding Sophie. No longer patting Sophie's back, he moved his hand in a circular motion to calm her while he talked to me.

I held my arms out. "Blane, Angi appears to be ready. Give me that baby." He handed Sophie to me as if he were reluctant. "You all take your time and be sure to police the brass."

Blane gave me a two-fingered salute. "Yeah, Sarge."

"Don't get lippy with me, buster."

We both chuckled. Blane and Angi donned their jackets and left for the range.

***

Angi followed Blane to a foot trail beside the shop. Trees stood like sentinels along both sides of the path. Bare branches were raised, as if in supplication, creating a canopy of spiny fingers. Leaves crunched underfoot as Blane and Angi hiked the trail for half a mile. A Blue Jay sounded a warning as they entered a clearing. Angi's eyes widened at the stark beauty of the autumn scene. She sucked in a deep breath, and her posture relaxed.

Blane spoke for the first time since they had started on the trail. "I've always liked the walk out here; the woods calm me."

Angi looked up at the cloudless sky. She spoke in a soft, reverent tone. "I know what you mean."

He grinned. "It won't stay calm for long, not when the shooting starts."

Blane led Angi to an elevated, rectangular platform. Across from it, on the backside of the clearing, was a berm about three feet tall. Behind that, a steep hill. Several metal targets were set up in front of the berm. Plywood boards, placed at strategic intervals, stood ready for paper targets to be mounted.

Blane laid the gun cases he had been carrying on the table located behind the platform. He opened them both and glanced at Angi. "How much do you know about guns?"

"Absolutely nothing."

"Alrighty, we'll start with basic safety first. Then I'll go over the proper way to grip a gun, then sight alignment. We'll do some dry fire, then we'll shoot some live rounds."

"What's dry fire?"

"That's when there is no ammunition in the gun, and you practice aiming and squeezing the trigger."

Blane took the smaller gun out of its case. "This is a Lady Smith, a thirty-eight-caliber revolver made by Smith and Wesson. Because of the design, it's a good concealed-carry gun for a woman. The hammerless design eliminates the chance of snagging on items in your purse. The smaller grip is easier for a petite hand to hold, and the barrel is short, making it easier to conceal, but also less accurate. The gun is called a revolver because this thing here," he pointed, "is a cylinder with five chambers. Each chamber holds a bullet, and it indexes, or revolves, each time you pull the trigger. I like revolvers for novices because revolvers seldom jam. This other gun is a semi-automatic pistol, and as you can see, there is no revolving cylinder."

Blane worked with Angi, allowing her to dry fire and get used to the action of the Lady Smith. Then he stapled a silhouette target to a board about twenty feet away and returned to hand her the loaded Lady Smith with the cylinder open. "Okay, always keep the gun pointed down range. Go ahead and close the cylinder. You have your earplugs in?" Angi nodded. "Sight in on the chest and fire all five rounds."

Angi's armpits prickled with sweat, her heart pounded, and her breaths were short and shallow. She tried to remember everything he told her; there were a lot of details. Sighting in on the target, she fired all five rounds. "Darn it. I missed the target three times."

Blane chuckled. "At this distance, with that short barrel, I'm surprised you hit it twice. If you don't mind me standing behind you, I'll help you sight. I can show you what I told you about earlier. Instructions are easier to understand if you see the objects while they are being explained."

She nodded her confirmation while she reloaded.

Blane continued. "One of the things I noticed is that the two times you did hit the target, your shots were about three inches apart, one below the other, which tells me you were breathing while you fired. Also, the bottom hit was to the right, which indicates the trigger was pulled instead of squeezed. When the trigger is pulled the barrel is pulled, too. This time, after you aim, ease your breath out. At the bottom of the exhale, hold your breath, and squeeze the trigger. Take your time. If you need to breathe, go ahead, but don't fire till you exhale."

Angi nodded, and as she raised the gun to aim, Blane stepped behind her. His rock-solid chest pressed against her back, and his arms wrapped around her as he placed his hands over hers to steady her. When the skin of his hand touched hers, a sensation like an electric current ran into her hands and up her arms. His tall frame engulfed her, but instead of feeling intimidated, she felt safe. His natural scent mingled with the outdoor woodsy smell creating a heady mixture. Her stomach clinched, and her skin felt hot where he had touched her. *Focus, Angi, focus.*

"Okay," Blane said. "I want you to focus on the front sight and put it right in the middle of the notch of the rear sight. Align the top of the front sight with the top of the rear sight. You got that?"

"Yes."

"Now, with the sight aligned like that, point the gun at the center of where you want to hit. The front sight will be in focus. The rear sight and the target will be out of focus—kind of fuzzy looking… See that?"

"Uh huh." Angi licked her lips and took a deep breath, which pressed her closer to him. Her exhale was immediate.

Blane cleared his throat. "Take a breath, let it out, then squeeze the trigger."

Angi took another breath and released it, then squeezed the trigger twice. She stopped, took another breath, let it out, and squeezed the trigger three more times. Blane hesitated, then stepped away. "Nicely done, trainee."

Angi focused on the target. Even from that distance, she saw she hit the target all five times and the shots formed a tight grouping. Slapping the gun down on the railing, she threw her arms up and proceeded to do a happy dance, then shouted a resounding, "Yes!"

A huge grin broke across Blane's face. "Can I assume you like shooting?" he asked.

Angi was so caught up in the moment, she hadn't realized she was doing her signature happy dance. Her hand flew to her mouth as she turned to look at Blane. Her face burned red in the process. She tried to regain her composure and look serious, but one look at Blane and they both burst into laughter.

"What was that?" he exclaimed.

"That, Mr. Instructor, was my happy dance. Oh my gosh. Shooting is so much fun. I can't believe I hit the target all five times, and right where I was trying to hit."

Angi shot the Lady Smith a few more times, then Blane introduced her to his 9mm Glock. When they finished shooting, picking up the brass shell casings, and hiking back to the cabin, the time was close to 2 p.m.

7.

The Party
A Novel Celebration

I stood with my guests as anticipation and excitement mounted. The front door opened, and when Blane and Angi entered, they were greeted with an enthusiastic, "Surprise!" Angi's eyes widened, and her jaw dropped. She scanned the room, and her forehead wrinkled when she saw the birthday balloons and decorations. Everyone, including Sophie, wore a party hat.

Clutching the elastic chin strap of a party hat in her fist, Diane's little girl ran to Angi and raised the hat aloft. She then blasted a party horn and said, "Hi. I'm Katie. Mommy said to give you a hat."

Diane, who looked like Cici—except in a pretty, voluptuous way—strolled across the room and extended her hand. "Hi, Angi. I'm Diane, Cici and Blane's sister. Katie is my five-year-old, and that handsome fella over there is my husband, Steve."

Angi offered her hand in slow motion. "Uh.... Hi. Whose birthday is it?"

Diane grinned. "It's Sophie's. It's October first, which makes today her two-month birthday."

I laughed at the look on Angi's face. "You'll have to excuse Diane's exuberance. She is Chance's one-woman welcome wagon, and she loves babies. In fact, she runs a daycare out of her home. She's probably evaluating you to see if she can turn you into a future client. Okay everybody, let's move this party into the kitchen. Lunch is ready."

The kitchen table was covered with a bright, decorated tablecloth. A beautiful layered cake adorned the center of it. A six-foot-long folding table was set up perpendicular to the kitchen table with a matching tablecloth. Folding chairs surrounded it. The counters were loaded with all the lunch fixings.

Angi blinked in quick succession. "It is so awesome that you went to all this trouble for Sophie. I've never had a birthday party."

Blane stood behind Angi, and I caught a glimpse of his face at Angi's admission. His eyebrows drew together, and his lips pressed into a firm line. *Hmm…*

I put my arm around Angi's shoulders. "You've never had a birthday party?"

"No, but that's okay. It just makes this party for Sophie extra special."

Everyone filled their plates and jockeyed for seats around the tables. With deft precision, Diane held Sophie, ate one-handed, and peppered Angi with questions. Sophie smiled as if she knew she was the guest of honor.

After lunch and cake, Angi took Sophie to the bedroom to feed her. Diane and I cleared the tables and brought out the gifts.

Angi stopped midstep on her way back into the kitchen. Her eyebrows raised, and her mouth fell open. "There are presents, too?"

Blane let loose with his trademark snort. "Angi, it's not much of a birthday party without gifts."

"Angi," I instructed, "sit at the long table with the gifts. You get to open them for Sofie."

Angi beamed; the look of anticipation mixed with excitement was unmistakable. "I don't know where to start." Her gaze swept the multitude of gift bags and wrapped packages.

"Just grab one and let 'er rip," I said, pushing a large, gift-wrapped box toward her. She read the card, looked up at

Blane, and blushed. She ran her palms over the top surface, her fingers skimmed the texture of the pink foil paper, and curled around the edges where she found the taped seams and began to ease the tape back, trying not to tear the paper.

Diane shook her head. "Please, tell me you're not one of those people that takes an eternity to unwrap gifts, never tearing the paper."

Angi looked at Diane and, in a hushed tone, said, "It's just so beautiful. How am I supposed to do it?"

Diane reached over, grasped a corner, and said, "You let 'er rip like this." Then she proceeded to tear off a long swatch of the paper. "Now you do it."

Angi pinched another loose corner of paper and glanced around the room as everyone nodded their encouragement. She inhaled, ripped, and the room erupted with applause. A huge grin lit up her face. The unicorn mobile that was revealed elicited a squeal from her. She shot Blane an adoring look and announced, "I love unicorns. This is so perfect."

Blane's chest puffed up, and he stood a little straighter. "It plays 'Unicorn's Dream,' and that light pink bag with the hot pink hearts goes with it."

Angi grabbed the pink bag next and pulled out a beautiful stuffed unicorn. Pressing the toy to her cheek, she closed her eyes, and the sweetest smile appeared as she whispered, "I wanted a unicorn room when I was a little girl."

I moved some more bags toward her. "Well, it's a darn good thing. Wait till you open the rest of these."

Next, she unwrapped unicorn sheets and blankets for the crib from me. Cici contributed matching unicorn pajamas for Sofie and Angi. Diane and Steve gave a unicorn nightlight and large wall hanging. Katie rushed forward and pressed a bedtime story book about unicorns into Angi's hands.

Angi looked up at everyone, her eyes bright. "I don't know what to say. Besides the day Sofie was born, this is the best day of my life. Thank you all so much. You have no idea how much this means to me."

She turned to Sofie, who watched from the bouncy seat on the table, and tickled her cheek with the stuffed unicorn. Sofie smiled and let out a coo, waving her arms and kicking her feet.

Blane lifted a single eyebrow and rested a hand on his hip. "Looks like Sofie likes my gifts the best."

Diane rolled her eyes at her little brother. "It's not a competition, Blane."

Cici eyed Blane. "Speaking of competition, how did our girl do at the range?"

Blane gave Cici a side-eye look. "That wasn't a competition either. Hang on a sec, and I'll let you be the judge." He found his jacket and retrieved the targets Angi had shot. He unfolded them and held them up for everyone to see.

"Dang!" Cici looked at Angi. "Remind me to never tick you off when you have a gun in your hand."

Angi colored. "Blane is a good teacher."

***

As Blane drove home from the party, he flashed back to hearing Angi say she had never had a birthday party. He got angry all over again. Coming from a large, close-knit family, hardly a month went by without a birthday party. Perhaps he had taken his big, obnoxious family, who were always in his business, for granted. What must life have been like for Angi, growing up without that? He couldn't get Angi off his mind. He wondered what she looked like with her hair down. Holding Sophie had been special. The way she snuggled up to him— damn, holding a kid had never affected him like that before. He wondered how it would feel to hold Angi. *Whoa, buster. Slow down. She's too young for you, and she's not even your type. Who am I kidding? All women are my type.*

Blane was a player. Always had been. More so since the military—since Gina. He feared getting close, commitment, more loss. What if he couldn't keep it together? He was still a mess.

***

I surveyed my almost empty cabin. Everyone had left the party but Cici.

Angi slumped as if her energy evaporated. "Miss Dawn, I'm going to feed Sophie and take a nap. Thank you so much for the party."

"I'd like to take all the credit, but the party was Diane's idea. I just jumped on board quickly."

Cici reached for his jacket on the back of a chair. I placed my hand over his. "Stay and have a glass of wine with me by the fire. I need to talk to you."

"Sure. You know me, I'm not one to turn down a glass of wine with a pretty lady."

I chuckled. "You're as bad as Blane. I need to find you both a woman, and let me be specific, separate women."

Cici cut his eyes to me. "And let me be specific, Dawn, neither one of us needs any help in that department. Perhaps we should find an eligible bachelor for you."

I leveled my gaze at him. "Uh, no. Absolutely not. Once you've had the best, you just can't settle for less, and Mike was the best of the best."

Changing the subject, Cici asked, "What did you want to talk to me about?"

I handed him a glass of wine and poured one for myself. Moving to the living room, Cici took the couch facing the fireplace. I settled on the loveseat and took a sip of wine.

"I sensed Jimmy was in town today," I said. "When I got out of the van to go into Doc's, I felt pinpricks on my skin. Just for an instant, so I wasn't sure. When I came back outside, a sensation like a thousand needles pricked me all over. Whoever watched didn't follow me. The sensation diminished the further I got from town."

Cici was one of the few people who knew that I had… gifts. "Damn it. I was hoping he'd stay away. Keep alert, Dawn. There's not much we can do until he shows himself or makes a move."

"I know. I just wanted you to know."

Frown lines appeared between his eyebrows. "I'm glad Blane took Angi shooting today."

"Me too. Blane seemed to enjoy himself today… a lot."

"I noticed. Pretty Boy does appear smitten."

I nodded. "Yeah, but I don't think he realizes it yet. Either that or he's in denial."

Cici took a sip of his wine and smirked. "He's in denial. He's trying to convince himself that he's not attracted, but I guarantee you, he's hooked. I can't wait to see how this plays out. It's going to be hard on him because Angi will need convincing. He's not accustomed to a woman like her, one that can tell him no."

"It sounds like you have firsthand experience—"

"Let's just say, it's part of the Rossi charm."

I laughed. "Charm, is it? Sounds more like over-confidence, perhaps conceit?"

Cici gave me his best roguish grin. "Perhaps."

"Speaking of Blane," he said, "that security job he applied for came through. I'm going to have to replace him at the café."

"I've got the perfect candidate for you. Angi was just telling me yesterday that she wanted to get a job. I know she's an experienced server."

Cici considered it. "Yeah, but what about Jimmy?"

"What better place for her to be than with you if he decides to show up and cause trouble?"

"You've got a point. Will you tell Angi that I'd like her to stop by the café to talk about the job?"

8.

The Attraction of Fractured Souls
Engines and Hearts Race

Monday morning over coffee, I broached the subject of work with Angi. "You mentioned that you wanted to get a job. I told you I thought something might come along."

"Yes."

"Well, Blane got that security job he wanted, so Cici wants to talk to you about working at the café."

"I'd love to work at the café. I just need to figure out what to do with Sophie. Didn't you say Diane has a daycare?"

"She does. But what do you think about me taking care of Sophie for the rest of October, then letting Diane take over? I'd have Sophie all to myself. You'd be doing me a favor. And with me watching her, you would have an opportunity to settle in and get used to working before you add the stress of taking Sophie to daycare. Plus, you could get to know Diane better. Don't get me wrong, Diane is great, but I know her, and you don't."

"That sounds perfect. I'll talk to Cici today. Can you take me to town? I'll need to get a bicycle."

"No, you won't. I have an extra car, and you are welcome to drive it. You'd be doing me a favor. Driving the car will keep the battery charged. I'll take you to town today because the extra car isn't drivable yet. It's under a tarp outside the far end of the shop."

Angi smirked. "I don't know, Miss Dawn. More favors so soon? I just did you a favor when I accepted your invitation to

56

stay with you, and now you want me to let you watch Sophie and drive your spare car?"

"I know. I'm kind of needy that way. I see more requests for favors in your future."

***

Angi and I arrived at Cici's in between the breakfast and lunch rush. As we entered the café, Blane looked up in surprise. He finished bussing a table and strolled towards us with his arms outstretched.

"Give me that little angel. I'll hold her while you get settled in the booth."

Angi smiled and handed Sophie to him. "I'm here to talk to Cici. I understand you got some good news."

Blane cut his eyes to Cici. "Who's been blabbing my personal business around town—Cici."

Cici shrugged. "Cool your jets, Junior. I mentioned your new job to Dawn because I needed to find a replacement for you."

"I'm irreplaceable, Senior. And I do mean *Senior*."

A bark of laughter escaped Cici. "We can settle this on the mats, at Dawn's, little man."

Before Blane could respond, Sophie cooed and swung her dimpled fist, hitting his chin. He smoothed Sophie's fingers open with his thumb and kissed her palm. "Hey there, slugger."

Angi's gaze lingered on Blane when she saw him kiss Sophie's palm.

Cici motioned Angi to follow him to his office. Scooting a chair up to the booth, Blane eased onto it and crossed an ankle over the opposite knee, creating a nest where he laid Sophie.

Watching Blane's gentle interactions with Sophie generated a sense of warmth and nostalgia in me, which led to my request. "I need a favor, Blane. Would you stop by sometime this week and go over Mike's car to make sure it's drivable? I thought I'd let Angi use it. It's just sitting there serving no purpose."

"Are you ready for that?"

Blane's concern touched me. "I am. It's hard to explain, but since Angi and Sophie came into my life… well, everything is just easier. I have them to focus on. I'm finding purpose again."

Blane nodded and grinned. "Alright, sugar, I'll stop by after work tonight and check The Beast out."

The Beast was a 2009, 4-wheel drive Range Rover. That automobile was Mike's baby, which he lovingly called Roxie. I had covered and moved the vehicle out of sight. I was unable to bear the constant reminder of Mike's vitality, adventurous nature, and now—his absence. But at the same time, I couldn't part with the vehicle. I looked forward to seeing Angi drive it. The Range Rover would be a safe, dependable vehicle for her and Sophie.

***

Angi opened the door to a grinning Blane around three that afternoon.

"Hey, Darlin', you want to help me with Roxie?" Blane asked. "That way, I can show you everything you'll need to know about her?"

She couldn't help but notice his blue eyes with the slightest hint of green…. And that sexy grin, and the way he had his hip cocked. Her stomach did a little flutter thing, which aggravated her. Several thoughts ran through her mind before she could respond. *So not my type. How can he flirt with me like that? Does he think I'm just some hookup?*

"Roxie? Who's Roxie?"

Blane chuckled. "Roxie is a what, not a who. It's the beast of a vehicle that we're going to make sure is road-ready for you to drive."

***

Angi and Blane worked together to get the tarp off Roxie. They started at the front bumper. Angi struggled with the first fastener on her side. Swiping an errant strand of hair from her face, she glanced up to see Blane almost done with his side. Frowning, she asked, "How did you do that so fast?"

"Easy, Darlin', it's like undressing a woman." He gave Angi a wink as he rounded the back of the car and continued the fluid movements from the opposite end.

"You are such a guy," she responded. But her mouth went dry, her heartbeat raced, and she tingled all over. *How can one guy be so hot?*

A few minutes later, Blane pulled his SUV around to jump-start Roxie. "Angi, go open one of the overhead doors in the shop, and I'll pull Roxie in to work on her."

Not trusting herself to speak—her mouth still dry—she nodded and left to open the door. Inside the shop, Blane turned the car off, popped the hood, and clipped a charger to the battery. Angi opened a cabinet and saw a shop-vac. Pulling it out, she vacuumed the interior while Blane tinkered under the hood. When Angi finished, she stood beside Blane and looked at the engine. She could feel the heat of his body. A subtle scent emanated from him, which had an unsettling effect on her. She took a step to the side, away from him.

"This is a nice car," she said. "It didn't need vacuuming. I mean, the interior was dusty, but other than that, the inside was immaculate. Everything under the hood looks pristine, too."

Blane nodded. "Roxie was Mike's baby. He always kept her spotless. I'm glad Dawn is taking her out of storage."

"Who is Mike?"

Blane snapped his head in Angi's direction. "Hasn't Dawn told you about Mike?"

"No."

"Mike was Dawn's husband."

"I've asked about her husband a couple of times, but she always changes the subject. And what do you mean, was her husband? Are they divorced?"

"I'm sorry, Angi, it's not my story to tell. You need to ask Dawn to tell you. Getting Roxie out and letting you drive her tells me she may be ready to talk about him now."

Angi went back to the cabin while Blane finished with Roxie.

***

Nestled on the loveseat, I watched Blane saunter into the cabin. His eyes settled on Angi, who relaxed in the rocker by the fire with a dish towel draped over her shoulder. Angi's eyes rounded, and she blushed crimson. She sprang from the chair, leaving it rocking in her wake, and rushed to her room without a word.

Blane's eyebrows knitted together. "What was that about?"

"Angi is still a little self-conscious about breastfeeding." His neck and face flushed. "What's the matter, Blane? Getting a little warm in here?"

Angling away from me, he cut his eyes back. "You did that on purpose."

I giggled with delight. "Yes, yes, I did. So, tell me, what kind of shape was The Beast in?"

Blane moved to the fireplace. Poking at the embers, he asked, "Why do you always call her The Beast when Mike always called her Roxie?"

I smiled at the memory of a heated discussion I'd had with Mike about Roxie's name. I shrugged and chuckled. "I suppose I was jealous. *Roxie* was a much sexier name than Dawn. I thought maybe he had named her after an old flame. Mike laughed at me, saying he named her Roxie because she reminded him of me—tough, dependable, in for the long haul, and beautiful. Then he told me to look the name up and see what it meant."

"So, what does Roxie mean?"

Tenderness filled me with the remembrance of that day. "In Persian and Greek, the name means star, bright, dawn."

Blane grinned. "That Mike. He always was a charmer. Well, the grand dame got all her fluids topped off, belts checked, tire pressure checked, and oil changed. Angi vacuumed her out, and I've had the battery charger on her for an hour and a half. I thought I'd take her for a spin first, then have Angi drive her. What do you think?"

"Sounds great, and Blane, thank you for doing this. It's time for Roxie to see the light of day."

***

Angi got behind the wheel as Blane opened the passenger door and yelled, "Shotgun!" She rolled her eyes and turned the key. A grin spread across her face as she gunned the engine. "Man, would you listen to that? Three-hundred-five horsepower, 4.4-liter, V-8 engine."

Blane's mouth dropped open, and his eyes bulged. "You know cars?"

Angi shrugged. "I took a few mechanic classes in school. When I was growing up, my mom was pretty helpless." Angi's demeanor changed. Her mouth formed a tight line, and her eyebrows drew together as she mumbled, "I will never be helpless."

Blane studied Angi for a moment, then showed her the controls for the wipers, lights, and seats.

Angi adjusted the mirrors and drove to the intersection of the highway. She and Blane lowered their windows. A cool breeze fanned her hair. Her heartbeat increased. She felt exhilarated and empowered. Cutting her eyes toward Blane, she gave him an ornery grin, looked both ways, and floored the gas pedal as she pulled onto the highway.

"Shit!" Blane clamped the window frame with one hand and grabbed the bill of his ball cap with the other, yanking it backwards on his head to keep the wind from blowing the cap off.

Angi's face glowed. There was a charge in the air, a mixture of her excitement over driving Roxie and hope for her future. For the first time in her life, she had a sense of family, security, and confidence.

At that moment, Blane couldn't take his eyes off her. An expression of longing mixed with what appeared to be melancholy swept over his features. Angi gifted him with a radiant smile, an infectious giggle, and in an instant, his demeanor changed. "Where are you taking me, Danica Patrick? You drive like a bat out of hell."

Angi let off the gas and eyed him playfully. "You squeal like a girl."

"Whatever. Hey, let's run Roxie through the car wash."

***

Angi pulled into an open bay of the vintage car wash. The sprayer wand rested in a metal tube. Blane went to the change machine to get quarters. As he fought with the machine to take a five-dollar bill, a leggy brunette with big hair, low-cut shirt, and miles of cleavage, sidled up to him. She stuck her hands in the back pockets of her painted-on jeans, thrusting her cleavage in his face. She propped one booted foot on a cinder block, which allowed the opposite hip to jut out.

Angi couldn't hear the conversation, but the woman's body language spoke volumes.

Blane nodded a greeting and stepped back, creating distance from the woman. She took a step to close the gap. Laying a manicured hand on his arm, she faced Angi and raised her chin to peer down her nose in a dismissive gesture.

A jolt of jealousy hit Angi. Yanking the wand out of the holder, she glared at the woman and crossed her arms. And in that instant, Blane inserted quarters into the carwash controller and all hell broke loose.

The wand, held in Angi's hand, lay along her crossed arm and was aimed directly at Blane. A pressurized stream of water hit his shoulder and ricocheted onto the leggy brunette, drenching her face and hair. Angi hadn't realized Blane was turning the water on. Shocked but not sorry, Angi's head rocked back as she belted out a solid laugh.

"You did that on purpose!" the drenched woman screeched.

Blane's eyes went wide, his mouth formed a large circle, then morphed into a leer as he turned to face Angi. Ignoring the brunette, he ran at Angi and grabbed the wand from her. Angi screamed and ran to the other side of The Beast. Blane followed and nailed her with a stream of water. The brunette continued to throw a full-on hissy fit. As they broke into gales of laughter, the leggy interloper stomped away.

***

Riding back to Dawn's in the passenger seat, Blane studied the now-drenched Angi. She resembled a participant in a wet T-shirt contest. He was struck by how her wet hair, jeans, and T-shirt, which clung to her petite frame, made her look sexier than the busty brunette ever would.

Angi moved strands of wet hair out of her face. Glancing at Blane, she asked, "So how do you know Daisy?"

Blane's brow furrowed. "Daisy?"

"Yeah, the Daisy Duke wannabe from the car wash."

"Oh, that's Jessie. She's nobody. I, uh, just… know her from… around."

"Un huh. Sure."

Angi's smile made him squirm. Blane began to sweat. He was in trouble all right.

9.

The Horror Recounted
Purging the Torment and Unburdening the Heart

That evening after dinner, Blane left, and Sophie slept. Embers glowed in the fireplace as Angi and I settled under soft blankets on the sofa, drinking chamomile tea. After a short pause in conversation, a puzzled expression crossed Angi's face.

"Miss Dawn, I'd like to ask you something, but if it's too personal, you don't have to tell me."

"Go ahead."

"Blane mentioned that Roxie was Mike's car, and when I asked him who Mike was, he told me he was your husband. But he wouldn't tell me anything else. He said it wasn't his story to tell and that I should ask you. So… will you tell me about Mike?"

I took a shuddering breath, and my chest constricted, as if the jaws of an industrial vise held me in its grip. My eyes burned. For a moment, I remained silent, contemplating the depth and magnitude of the information I'd been asked to reveal. "I'll try, Angi, but it's… difficult for me. I've been trying to forget for over a year, but that hasn't been working. So, maybe it's time to talk about it. Just a minute. I'll be right back."

***

Standing in the closet in my bedroom, I looked at the multitude of photo albums that chronicled my life with Mike and Gracie. I selected two albums and plodded back to the living room, where I laid them on the coffee table, then poured myself a glass of wine. Tipping the glass, the liquid ambrosia rolled over my tongue and down my throat, but did little to calm my nerves. "Angi, this may take a while. I need to start at the beginning and work my way up to the finale."

Angi reached out, took my hand, and gave it a squeeze. "That's okay, I've got plenty of time." She released my hand and took a sip of her tea.

Wanting to put off the torment of *that day* as long as possible, I opened the first album. "This was my baby girl, Gracie. I was so excited when I found out I was pregnant because, being older, I didn't know if I could get pregnant. I was thirty-seven. Her biological father was a poor excuse for a husband and even worse as a father. We divorced when Gracie was five. He dropped out of her life soon after." I turned each page and narrated the scenes of the entire album, reliving magical moments.

Angi took the photo album from me and turned back to the first page. "Miss Dawn, is it just me, or does your Gracie look like my Sophie?" She pointed to a few of the pictures of Gracie when she was about the same age as Sophie.

"Oh my, how did I not notice that? When I think of Gracie, I remember her as an adult. But you're right, they look like they could be sisters. How strange is that?"

We scrutinized Gracie's pictures a while longer, then I pulled out the other album. "These are Mike's and my wedding pictures and some photos of the three of us. Mike couldn't have kids, but he loved Gracie like she was his, and so she was. And Gracie loved him back. Fiercely. She was a daddy's girl. Those two were inseparable."

We continued to browse through the pictures of my early life with Mike and Gracie. That walk down memory lane was cathartic for me. The memories cleansed the negativity from me and filled me with the joy of my family's love. "This last picture of Gracie was taken a year and a half ago. This is how I remember her." Warmth spread through me as I gazed at my lovely daughter. Gracie sat on a porch wearing jeans, a Henley shirt, and hiking boots. Her arm was thrown around a sturdy dog whose large, square head pressed against Gracie's shoulder, and its eyes gazed up at her, a smile evident on the dog's face.

Angi studied the photograph. "Gracie is beautiful, and so is the dog. What kind of dog is it?"

"She's an American Boxer, and her name is Maisy. She belongs to Gracie's ex-boyfriend, Wayne, but she and Gracie had a special bond." My heart hammered at the thought of Wayne, and a coldness coursed through my veins, obliterating all signs of the previous warmth. "Wayne loves that dog more than anything else in this world, even more than he loved Gracie. I had reservations about Wayne when I first met him. I don't know why; I just felt a bad vibe. I found out later that Wayne had a troubled childhood, which followed him into adulthood. Anyway, I figured he must be okay because of the way he loved that dog, and Maisy loved him. I was wrong. His love for Maisy is his *only* redeeming quality." I closed the album after the last page and looked into Angi's eyes. My breath hitched, and my cheeks slicked with tears. I grabbed a tissue off the end table. I knew I would need it for the horrific journey. "Angi, they were taken from me over a year ago. Murdered."

"Oh, Miss Dawn." She took my hands in hers, and as she did, I felt an electrical jolt pass between us. Tears streamed down Angi's face, too. Then something odd happened. After she took my hands, my pain eased. I gave her hands a squeeze and let go so I could wipe my eyes. I took another sip of wine and a deep breath. Now that the journey had begun, I couldn't stop. Words tumbled out of me as if they were rocks in a landslide.

"Gracie's relationship with Wayne became abusive. He got into drugs and beat her. The last time was bad enough to put Gracie in the hospital. It was Maisy who saved her. Maisy went berserk, barking and jumping around... the commotion was enough to break through Wayne's rage, and he stopped. Being hospitalized was the straw that broke the camel's back. After months of abuse, Gracie broke up with him, pressed charges, and moved from Missouri back to Oklahoma. She filed a protective order, but living in a rural area, the protective order was useless. He wouldn't leave her alone. The harassment was constant.

"We convinced her to move home. Mike drove to Gracie's on that Friday evening. She lived about a half hour away in Kellyville. He was going to help her finish packing that night, spend the night, load up, and drive to our house the next day. I stayed home at our Liberty Mounds house. I readied her room and cleared a spot in the shop to store her furniture. Angi, she was only twenty-seven years old and so full of life. My God. She was so smart, so beautiful."

Clutching a tissue, I wiped my eyes and continued. "At about ten that night, I called to tell them goodnight. The call was wonderful. Mike put me on the speaker. Gracie was so happy and relieved to be moving home. We talked and laughed. We were all so excited.

"I awoke in a panic around three the next morning. I didn't know what woke me, but I had a sense of foreboding. After checking the locks of the doors and windows, I went back to bed. I couldn't sleep, so around five, I got up. I felt... empty." My eyes met Angi's, and I hesitated. Taking a deep breath, I continued. "I called to check on them. Mike didn't answer. So, I called Gracie's phone. Her phone went straight to voicemail. I wanted to believe they didn't hear their phones because they were sleeping, but Mike was a light sleeper, so I knew something was wrong. I felt it and left for Gracie's house immediately. When I arrived, the front door wasn't closed all the way."

A stillness settled over me as I re-lived that day. *I eased the door open, the hinge moaned, and a floorboard creaked. Every detail of the room came into sharp focus. Dread burned through me.*

I took another sip of wine to calm myself. "Mike was on the couch in the living room. When I reached him, I... I knew he was dead."

Angi gasped.

As I continued the narrative, I saw the scene projected like an old-fashioned movie playing out in black and white, frame by frame. I got up from the couch and paced, dreading what was coming next. I collapsed back onto the couch and continued in a monotone voice that wasn't more than a murmur. The horror of that day filled me. I hesitated, then continued. "I stumbled to Gracie's bedroom next." Trembling, I wiped my eyes. "She was…." My voice faltered and my head dropped. "It was…." I took a shuddering breath. My next words were a mere whisper. "I'll never forget the coppery smell of blood—the stench of death."

I wrapped my arms around myself. Shutting my eyes, I continued to tremble. I rocked and keened. Angi grabbed me and held me tight. An eventual awareness of her baby-scented warmth, her breath, her heartbeat, infused me. And again, my pain eased. My wailing quieted. I reached up and patted her shoulder. I filled my lungs and exhaled. "Thank you, Angi. I'm… better now. Or I will be." Grabbing a handful of tissues, I blotted my face.

Angi sat down. "Oh my God, how horrible, how… devastating. I am so sorry for what happened. I had no idea. Did they catch the murderer?"

"Yes, they did, but catching and proving are two different things, Angi. That son-of-a-bitch is in jail, but he hasn't been charged with their murders. Everyone knows Wayne did it, but they can't prove it, yet. They're holding him in Sapulpa on unrelated weapons charges while the detectives continue to search for evidence to tie him to the murders."

Feeling like a monster had been purged from my soul, a hesitant smile appeared. I felt lighter, cleansed. "Angi, you did me another favor. I've been running from this terror for over a year. It was past time for me to confront it and not let the terror rule me. I feel so much better having told you. I suspect suppressing the pain of that day also suppressed all the good memories and feelings. And now it's like I've opened a Pandora's box of emotions. I can feel everything again. The pain isn't gone, but perhaps it's tempered by the love and wonderful memories I'm in touch with once more. Thank you for that, Angi."

Angi smiled. She looked exhausted. "Is there anything I can do for you tonight?" she asked.

"You already have—your being here, listening, and holding me—those things were a tremendous help. Why don't you go on to bed?"

Angi lurched to her feet. "I haven't been this tired in a long time."

***

I laid in bed, deciding whether to read. My eyelids made the decision for me. I couldn't keep them open. As I turned out the bedside lamp and drifted away, a dream unfolded.

> *I sat at a small table, across from the bar, watching the regulars lined up around it, engaging each other in barroom chatter.*
>
> *It was open-mic night. The fella tuning up to sing cast a glance my way. A smile played on his lips—a hint of unspoken promises. His eyes lingered on my face, as if caressing my cheek. Our eyes met. He gave me a wink and began to play the guitar. His words followed in a beautiful song. He continued to hold my gaze, as if he sang just for me.*

He finished the song and made his way to my table.

"Is this seat taken, Beautiful?"

I slowly eased the empty chair back with the toe of my boot—an invitation. I gazed into his deep brown eyes. They had a soft sheen like velvet. He sat, then leaned his face near mine. He didn't touch me, but I could feel the heat of his skin so close to mine. He whispered a suggestion in my ear. His breath was tantalizingly warm.

I gently withdrew from him. My eyes focused on his lips as I told him, "Later."

We laughed. After almost twenty years, Mike still flirted with me.

10.
Best Day Ever
Secret Gifts

I awoke refreshed, happier than I had been in a long time. The dream about Mike was fresh in my mind. A smile greeted me in the mirror. I couldn't stop thinking about the dream and how much fun Mike and I always had on our date nights. I dressed for my workout and looked forward to the demanding activity for a change. I was up earlier than usual and hadn't heard Angi stir yet.

***

Workout over and breakfast finished, I sipped my coffee. Angi shuffled into the kitchen. She had dark circles under her eyes.

"Sit down, Angi, you look beat. I'll make you a cup of coffee."

"I am beat, Miss Dawn, but I don't know why. Oh, by the way, I had a dream about you last night."

"You did? Was it a good dream?"

Angi smiled and nodded. "Yes, it was. You were in a bar sitting by yourself, and there was a man tuning a guitar, and then he sang a song. You were flirting with each other. After he sang, he walked over to your table, and you pushed a chair out for him to sit down. He leaned over and whispered something to you. You said something back to him, and you both started laughing. I enjoyed watching you two flirt."

72

I almost spilled coffee on her as I set the cup in front of her. I couldn't believe what I was hearing. Then it hit me. "Well, that explains a lot."

"Explains what?"

I contemplated whether to discuss empathic abilities now or later. I had put too many things off this past year, so now was the time.

"Angi, I want to talk to you about something, and I want you to keep an open mind, okay?"

"Sure."

"Have you ever felt like you picked up on other people's emotions? Do people seek you out, confide in you? Do you sometimes feel others' pain, maybe get uncomfortable in crowds?"

Angi's eyes went wide. "How... how do you know all that?"

"I'll explain. Do you know what an empath is? Do you know that *you* are an empath?"

Angi moved her head from side to side. "No. What's an empath?"

"An empath is a person who senses and feels other people's emotions as if those emotions were their own. There are different degrees or strengths, but honey, I think you are a very strong empath. And the reason I know about empaths is because I'm one. All the females on my mother's side have *gifts*.

"I've met a few empaths outside of my relatives, but none as strong as you. You shared my dream last night. I had that exact dream. In addition to that, when I told you about Mike and Gracie's murders, you shared my pain. All empaths can feel other's pain, but you took some of my pain and gave me relief. That is not something all empaths can do. That's why you are so exhausted today. I should have realized what was happening last night, but I was so caught up in my grief, I didn't put it all together.

"Did you notice that when you touched me, a sensation like an electric current ran between us? When you touched and hugged me, my pain lessened. You took some of my pain, and I took some of your energy. I'm sorry about that. I didn't protect you. Had I known, I would have shielded you from me. I'll have to teach you how to do that."

Angi looked stunned. Although empathic ability was natural to me, hearing about empaths could be startling for someone who didn't know about such things, especially if they were told they were one.

"I'm sorry. I see I've overwhelmed you. You must think I'm crazy. You can read about empathic abilities online, and I have a few books. But right now, I'm going to fix your breakfast, then I'll explain how you can revive yourself."

Angi studied me. She took a sip of coffee, then asked, "You had the same dream last night? Who was the man?"

I nodded. "That man was my husband, Mike."

"I did feel the electric current when we touched, and I experienced *your* pain, as if the pain were mine, as if my heart were breaking. And I couldn't stop the tears."

"I know, Angi. I assume the emotions were so strong because we are both empaths. The day you walked into Cici's, I saw your fear, and I also felt your fear. After what happened to Mike and Gracie, I couldn't let that happen to another person. Not if I could stop the violence. That's why I helped you.

"After you finish breakfast, you need to get outside in nature. Take a walk in the woods or relax on the deck and enjoy the view of the lake. Nature will ground and revive you. I'll take care of Sophie today. After your nature walk, I'd like you to take the day off. Drive into town if you want… just take a day for yourself. You need time for yourself anyway, but after last night, you need to recharge."

"I'll take you up on that, but I don't want to go to town. I want to take a walk in the woods, then wrap up in a blanket on the deck and drink a cup of hot chocolate with marshmallows. Then I want to soak in that clawfoot tub, wash my hair and blow it out, and paint my toenails. You know, just spend the day pampering myself."

"I think that's a perfect idea, and I'll help spoil you."

After a quick breakfast, Angi took off for the woods. I grabbed the phone and called Diane. "I need a favor, and it's an emergency. A sweet, fun, emergency, not a bad emergency."

"Oh, thank God, you scared the bejeebers out of me when you said emergency. What do you need?"

I told Diane what I wanted to do, and of course, Diane was all in. "We'll get this thing pulled together. She won't know what hit her."

A short while later, I heard Diane pull up. I ran outside and helped carry the bags in. Diane scanned the living room and blasted a whispered question. "Where is Angi?"

"She's outside, and it's a darn good thing, because you can't whisper for shit. She's on the deck drinking hot cocoa. I made the homemade kind. There's enough for another mug, but we better get a move on."

In Angi's bathroom, Diane pulled out a satiny pajama set and matching kimono robe from one of the bags and flung them at me. "Quick, hang those up on the back of the door while I raise these shades."

The tub sat in an alcove of the bathroom that had a window overlooking the lake.

Diane continued to empty the shopping bags. "I also picked up one of those round brush blow dryer doodads, a straightener, and all the shampoo, conditioner, and styling gel one girl could possibly need for long hair. Do you have something for music?"

I nodded. "I have a Bluetooth speaker, and I've got a playlist ready to go."

Diane eyed me with a look of distrust. "It's not Frank Sinatra and Lawrence Welk, is it?"

I gave her *the look*. "I haven't totally lost my cool factor. She'll like it."

Diane pulled out a zippered bag. "I got a nail kit like you asked. Look at this polish. I figure with her coloring, this shade will look great on her."

We continued to work fast, staging candles, bath bombs, and such. We were winding down and gathering empty bags and wrappers when Angi walked in.

"Miss Dawn, what's all this?"

Diane's head whipped around, "Busted!"

I shrugged my shoulders in response. "You said you wanted a spa day."

Angi bounced on the balls of her feet, all signs of exhaustion replaced by excitement. "It's an honest-to-goodness spa day!" She rushed in and hugged both of us. "This is the best day ever."

***

Three hours later, I peeked out the doorway of my room when the doorbell rang. Angi emerged from her room, her long blond hair shimmered all the way to her waist in soft, loose curls. Her nails had been painted pale pink. The pajamas and robe were a perfect fit. She glanced around the living room as she moved towards the door. I ducked out of sight, then popped my head out when Angi opened the door to Blane. He flashed a roguish smile and announced, "Special delivery." He pulled a dozen pink roses from behind his back.

She clutched the robe together and took the flowers with her free hand. "I… I…" Her head swiveled from side to side, as if looking for an escape route.

Blane winked. "Don't worry, darlin', I'm not staying. Diane asked me to drop these off." He leaned over and placed a benign kiss on the top of her head, as if he were kissing a toddler. "Later," he said, then turned and walked back to his SUV. Angi stood in the doorway as she watched him stroll away. If I were a betting woman, I'd lay odds that she was following the cadence of his firm hips.

She eased the door shut, then leaned against it. Her eyes closed, and an angelic smile graced her face.

I grabbed my cellphone and texted Diane. "Mission accomplished." She texted back an assortment of emojis: smiley faces, little cupids, and hearts with arrows through them.

That was the most matchmaking fun I'd ever had. I walked out of my room while Angi was still leaning against the door. "Who was that, Angi?"

Her eyes popped open in surprise. "Oh, uh, just Blane. He said Diane asked him to drop these flowers by. I can't believe everything you and Diane did for me today. Even Blane, helping Diane like that."

"I'm glad you enjoyed it. Every gal needs a day like that now and again."

11.

Taking Care of Business
He Should Have Broken the Guy's Wrist

Blane started the security job the first week of October. He stayed in Tulsa while he trained. Once his training was completed, he would be based out of Chance and commute to his assignments. He said he couldn't give us details other than he was part of a security team and would stay on the move.

By mid-November, Angi had settled into working at the café. She started at the Last Chance when Blane left, and she loved it. Cici said business picked up after she started. The truckers spread the word about the pretty server at Cici's. Blane had a couple more weeks of training left. I relinquished Sophie to Diane's care and returned to my morning routine of coffee at the café. Sitting in my favorite booth, which welcomed me like an old friend, I indulged in a little people-watching, which was where I relaxed that morning.

I heard the bell before I saw the man walk in. There wasn't a hair out of place; his eyebrows appeared to have been waxed into perfect contours. Although handsome, he appeared too slick, and he reminded me of a used car salesman. Leading with his chest, he strutted to a booth, resembling a banty rooster.

78

Angi had her back to him, and I noticed he eyed her in a suggestive way; his eyes lingered and probed.

Angi finished serving the truckers at the booth behind the stranger. Sensing him, she turned to take his order. He flashed her an overconfident smile. "Well, well, well. Angi. How have you been, Sweetheart?"

Angi tensed, her eyes narrowed, and there was a sharp intake of air. She exhaled, then slowly inhaled. Taking a deep breath, she appeared to calm down. She had gained a lot of confidence over the past few months, and it showed. She met his gaze and in a bored tone, she said, "Hello, Nick. Would you like some coffee?"

My eyebrows raised. Nick…. So this was the man who had fathered Sophie.

His gaze roved over her like he was groping her with his eyes. He made my skin crawl. "Yeah, I'd like some coffee, among other things."

She ignored the innuendo. "I'll bring you a menu."

She returned and set a cup, saucer, and menu on the table.

I heard the bell over the door jingle again, but didn't look away. I didn't like this creep, and I kept my eyes on him.

As she started to pour the coffee, Nick reached out, ran his hand up the back of her thigh, and rested his palm on her backside. In one fluid motion, Angi's arm drifted sideways, and the steaming coffee found its way onto his lap.

"You bitch!" He jerked spastically and raised a hand as if to strike her.

The truckers at the adjoining booth moved to intervene, but were too slow. In a blurred movement, I saw a muscular hand

and forearm piston forward to grab the wrist of the offending hand. A thumb was applied to a pressure point on Nick's wrist, and his arm was wrenched away from Angi.

Angi looked over her shoulder to see Blane standing behind her. He did not ease up on the pressure he applied to Nick's wrist. In fact, he looked like he wanted to break it. Nick glowered at Blane.

Blane scowled back. "Keep your hands to yourself, Asshole." He let go of Nick's wrist. Nick rubbed it and glared at Blane, who narrowed his eyes and said, "It's time for you to leave."

By this time, the four truckers from the next booth had moved behind Blane in a show of solidarity and glared at Nick.

Nick raised his hands in surrender. "Chill, I was just saying hi to an old friend. I'll leave, okay?"

Cici opened the front door and stood watch.

Nick exited the booth and sauntered toward the door. Anger and arrogance radiated from him. When he reached the yawning doorway, Cici raised an eyebrow. "Don't come back."

Angi gave an involuntary shiver. "How could I have ever thought he was nice?"

Blane's eyes widened and eyebrows raised. "You know that asshole?"

Her face turned red, and she couldn't meet Blane's eyes. She nodded her head and whispered, "Yes," as a tear streaked down her face.

Cici scowled at Blane and pointed to the ceiling. Then to Angi he said, "The rush is over. Why don't you take a break?"

Blane put his arm around her shoulder. "You know I live above the café, but you've never seen my place. Come on, I'll show you my apartment."

***

Blane dropped his arm from around her shoulder and took her hand. He led her to the stairs. Anger ignited in him. He couldn't stand to see Angi cry. He hadn't seen her in weeks. As much as he had tried to put her out of his mind, she was all he could think about—her and Sophie. He hadn't even had a hookup. No one else interested him.

At the top of the stairs, Angi walked through the doorway into a cute, efficiency apartment. Blane led her to the small table in the kitchenette. "Have a seat. You want some water?"

Angi nodded, and Blane grabbed a bottle from the refrigerator and handed it to her. She still hadn't made eye contact with him.

"Hey, Angi, look at me." When their eyes met, he gave a little chuckle. "You wield a wicked coffee pot." She smiled and looked down again. "Darlin', we all have pasts. I'm in no position to judge you or anyone else. I was just surprised that you knew that guy. So, if you want to tell me about him, I'd like to hear about how you know that jerk."

"Dawn hasn't told you?"

"No. Why would Dawn tell me your business? That's not the way we operate."

"I thought maybe she told you. Nick is Sophie's biological father. He doesn't know about her because when I told him I was pregnant, he told me to 'get rid of it.' He also waited until then to tell me he was married. I haven't seen him since that day, and I don't want him to find out about Sophie. He had his chance, and he wanted to get rid of her. He doesn't deserve her."

Blane's eyes narrowed, and one corner of his mouth pulled down. "I should have broken his wrist. I tell you what, I doubt he'll ever find out about Sophie, but if for some reason he sees you with Sofie and asks, you tell him she's mine. Understand?"

Surprised, Angi said, "I couldn't do that. What would people say? What would your… hookups say?"

Blane cringed at the memory of the conversation they'd had about his fear of commitment while putting the crib together.

"Angi, I'm not interested in random hookups anymore. I'm getting my life together. I want something better. Something more meaningful.

"When I got out of the Army and came home, I was a mess. I still am, but I'm getting it together. Being by myself in Tulsa these past weeks has given me a lot of time to think. I figured out the way I've been living isn't the way I want to continue living." He reached out and took her hand. "I'd like for us to get to know each other better. I want to know about your childhood, your parents. I don't know, just you."

Angi eased her hand free. "Blane, I… I don't know what to say, I mean, you're a player. Can you just turn that off? And I have Sophie to think about. And… I just don't know."

Blane smiled. "Relax, Angi, I just want us to get to know each other better. I want to be your friend–yours and Sophie's. We can take our time and just see where our friendship goes. No pressure. And if that jerk asks about Sophie, you tell him she's mine. Okay?"

She nodded her head. "Thank you. I, uh, better get back to work." She made a hasty retreat to the safety of the café, muttering under her breath, "He is so not my type. Way too pretty. I'd always be competing with other women like ole Daisy Duke at the carwash."

12.
A Sperm Donor Versus a Good Man
The Manipulator is Unmasked

Later that evening at dinner with Angi, I thought about what a jerk Nick was. "So, Nick is the sperm donor that made Sophie possible? I won't call him her father because he is in no way her father."

Angi's face colored. "How could I have been so stupid? How could I have ever thought he was nice?"

"Angi, he is a masterful manipulator. An expert con artist. He showed you what he wanted you to see. Besides that, you were young and inexperienced. You had nothing to go by. You saw his true self today, and the day he beat you. What are you going to do if he finds out about Sophie?"

Angi looked up from her plate and ran her hand over Sophie's head. "Blane said if Nick asks about Sophie, that I should say she's Blane's. I asked him what people, as in his hook-ups, would say? He said he didn't care, and that he wanted more than just hookups, that he wanted to get to know me and Sophie better."

Whoa, that got my attention. "Blane said all that?"

Angi smiled."I know, right?"

"Well, what do you think?"

Angi sighed." I think he's out of my league, and I have major trust issues. I always have, but since Nick—"

"I understand. I do. One thing I know for sure, Blane is a good man. He is dealing with some challenges of his own. His experiences in Afghanistan nearly broke him. If Cici hadn't stepped in, I don't know what would have become of Blane. Even if you don't want a romantic relationship with him, you can't have too many friends. It couldn't hurt to get to know him. And, by the way, you're in a league of your own. Maybe you're out of his league. You ever think of that?"

She rolled her eyes. "Yeah, right. What happened to him in Afghanistan?"

"I don't know the full account, but Blane will tell you himself when he's ready."

"He is nice. He's also fun to be with, and he's good with Sophie."

I gave her a sly smile. "He's kind of easy on the eyes, too."

"Miss Dawn!"

I grinned. "What? I know a good-looking man when I see one, even if he is too young for me."

13.

The Watcher
A Menacing Presence

The following morning, I heard the driveway alarm at seven. I looked out the window and saw Blane and Cici parked out front. Greeting them from the doorway, I asked, "What are you two up to this Saturday morning?"

Cici mounted the steps two at a time. "Well, for starters, I thought I'd mooch a cup of coffee off you, then, me and the Italian stallion here, thought we'd go a few rounds."

Blane snorted. "As if you'll last a couple of rounds."

"Careful, junior, don't make me pull out my can of whoop-ass."

I looked back and forth between them. "Oh, one of those kinds of mornings. Come on in. Angi and I were just having our coffee."

Angi must have heard the exchange because she was pulling out coffee mugs when we entered the kitchen. Sophie was in her bouncy seat on the table, and the lake glimmered in the morning light.

Blane sat down by Sophie and started tickling one of her feet, which caused her to kick both feet and swing her arms. "That's my slugger."

Angi looked over her shoulder at him and her face softened. Blane was oblivious to Angi at that moment because Sophie captivated him.

86

As we drank our coffee, Cici cleared his throat. "Oh, Diane wanted me to invite you both to our Thanksgiving festivities. Just a small gathering. No more than twenty or twenty-five people, thirty-five tops. We're trying to get Dad to come this year."

That surprised me. "Your dad? I've never met your dad."

"Well, when Mom passed, Dad kind of went off the deep end. After the funeral, he took a promotion which kept him traveling all the time. He turned the promotion down in the past because he didn't want to be away from Mom and us kids. But after she died, he was lost. Being around all of us without her was just too painful for him.

"It's been five years, and I think he's coming to terms with everything. Besides that, he's thinking about retiring. He wants to check out Chance, see if he wants to retire here."

I was quick to accept the invitation. "Count me in. I wouldn't miss a Rossi gathering unless I was sick or dying. You should go, Angi. It's an event not to be missed. Cici and Blane have three other siblings. You already know Diane. There are two additional brothers, several cousins, and a lot of in-laws, which means there's a lot of noise, the best food you've ever eaten, and lots of love. You can ride with me if you want." I looked at Cici. "It's at Diane's, right?"

"Yes, and she asked me to tell you that she has a hankering for your spinach dip and your pineapple upside-down cake."

I glanced at my calendar. "That's the Thursday after this upcoming Thursday. I'll make the cake, the dip, and I'll bring chips."

Blane piped up. "Angi, why don't you ride with me? That way, I can run interference with our clan, because they're going to mob you when you walk in. They're always challenged when it comes to respecting personal space, and with you being new, everyone will want to meet you." He gave her a little wink.

"I, uh…" Angi stammered.

Blane didn't let up. "I'll help you with Sophie. Dawn's going to be busy bringing the food in." He leaned over and kissed the top of Sophie's head.

I gave him *the look.* "You know, Blane, you could help me carry in the food."

Cici chuckled. "How about I pick you up, Dawn. I can help load and unload."

"That's more like it. Since I won't have to drive, tell Diane I'll bring some wine, too," I said with a grin.

***

The following Saturday, I ventured to town to pick up everything I needed for the Thanksgiving party. Bernard, the owner of the liquor store, walked me to my van carrying the case of wine I just bought. An easy smile and relaxed gait hinted at his affable nature.

As I slid open the passenger side door, the sensation began. Mild pinpricks all over my body. "Bernard, you see anybody new in town today? Maybe a skinny, young guy driving a dirty white pickup?"

He tilted his head and rubbed his smooth chin. "Would this skinny kid be the one that followed Miss Angi here?"

"How do you know about that? Never mind, this is Chance. Of course, you know."

Bernard raised his shoulder in a lazy shrug. His mocha skin glistened from the direct sunlight. "You gals have the beauty shop grapevine, and we men have the liquor store pipeline."

"You know you're being sexist, right? I mean, I'm a woman, and I was just in the liquor store."

"Yep, and you and I didn't gossip, did we?"

"Okay, point taken. Have you seen him?"

"No. I wasn't looking, though, but I will. You want me to text you if I see him?"

"Yes, please. I've just got a feeling he's here."

When I got in the van, I checked to make sure my gun was in the console before I drove to Doc's Market.

By the time I got out of the van in the market parking lot, there were no more needle-prick sensations. However, when I emerged from the store forty-five minutes later with my basket of groceries, I felt stinging again. As I put the groceries in my van, the hair on the back of my neck and arms rose. There were so many pinprick sensations that my skin should have been hot, like it was on fire, but although the sensation was intense, it was dulled and muffled. *How strange.*

In the van, I called Cici. "Jimmy is in town. My skin is on fire, sort of, and the hairs on my neck and arms are standing at attention."

"Do you see him?"

"No, but I can feel him. He's close."

"Okay. I'm loading up. Go ahead and pull out of the parking lot. Maybe stop for gas to give me a little time to get there. If you just sit in the parking lot, he'll know something is up. I'll follow you at a distance to see if he pursues you. If he does, I'll let you know so you can drive past your road."

I stopped for gas, and when I got a quarter mile from my turnoff, Cici called. "It's all clear; no one followed you."

"Thank you, Cici. Sorry I interrupted your Saturday."

"Not a problem. I'll see you Thursday if not before then."

***

Jimmy smiled as he put the monocular telescope in the glove box of his friend's Jeep. From his vantage point in the parking lot across from Doc's Market, he had a perfect view of the highway, northbound and southbound. He had watched the woman in the van as she turned north, stopped for gas, and then turned back onto the highway headed south. He was able to follow her with the scope until she turned off the highway.

He didn't know if she was connected to Angi, but he remembered seeing that van leave the parking lot the day he followed Angi here. He saw the woman once before too, but Angi wasn't with her. Still, someone must have helped Angi that day.

The couple of times Jimmy came back were always on the weekends. He didn't see Angi, but his gut told him she was here. He would keep watching, and if this woman knew anything, he'd make her talk.

***

Angi rose from the couch as I entered the cabin. "Can you give me a hand carrying the groceries?" I asked. "Then we need to talk."

"Sure. Is everything okay?"

"Yes, but it's about Jimmy. I think he's in town today."

"No." Angi's eyes widened, and her hand flew to her mouth.

I gave her a reassuring hug. "Everything is going to be okay."

After putting the groceries away, we sat in the kitchen having hot tea while we discussed Jimmy.

"Where did you see Jimmy, Miss Dawn?"

"I didn't see him, I felt him. Do you remember when I told you about empaths? I mentioned that my female relatives have gifts." Angi nodded. "One of my abilities allows me to sense if someone is watching me. Remember that first morning when you were watching me from the doorway, and I told you I knew you were there because I had seen your reflection in the microwave? Well, I didn't see your reflection. I sensed you. The sensation was pleasant, like lips being pressed to my skin, so I knew someone who meant no harm was watching me. If someone has negative intent towards me, I feel pinpricks on my skin. Today, the pinprick sensation felt different, muffled but there."

"How do you know the person watching you was Jimmy?"

"Because everybody loves me, Angi. I mean, what's not to love?" Angi laughed. "I'm serious, I haven't made anyone mad. I had the sensation a few weeks ago, and that time was on a Saturday, too. I assume he comes down here during the weekends to look for you when he's not working. It has to be him. I just wanted you to know because you need to stay vigilant."

"Okay, I will, but the thought of him coming here is creeping me out."

"I know. I'm glad you're not working weekends. Will you do me a favor and stay out of town on the weekends unless you're with Blane, Cici, or me?"

"Yes, ma'am."

14.

No Way!
A Blast from the Past

Thursday arrived without incident, and the driveway alarm announced the approach of Blane and Cici.

Blane got to the door first. "Good afternoon, ladies. You ready to get this party started?"

"Yes, we are," I said. "Angi's stuff is there by the door, and mine is in the kitchen."

The fellas loaded everything, and we left for Diane's. The drive took less than ten minutes. Diane opened the door wide and greeted me like a long-lost relative she hadn't seen in months, instead of a few short days. Cici and I made our way to the kitchen with the wine and food. We decided to arrive before the other partygoers so Angi wouldn't have to walk into a house full of strangers. She could meet them as they arrived.

Diane assured me there was nothing I needed to help with, so I poured both of us a glass of wine and kept her company in the kitchen while she finished up.

Through the doorway to the living room, I viewed Blane holding Sophie. I waved to Diane in a flame-fanning motion. "Diane. Quick. Come here and look at this. Doesn't that look natural? Doesn't Blane look content?"

Diane peeked around the door, and her face split into a grin. "Oh man, he's a goner. Look at him making goo-goo eyes."

"The question is, who's he making goo-goo eyes at, Sophie or Angi?"

"Looks like both to me. Has he taken her out yet?"

"No, they're taking their time, getting to know each other."

Diane smirked. "You mean Angi is taking her time. Blane doesn't take his time."

I heard the squeak of the back door behind us, and Diane squealed. "Daddy!" She ran towards a tall, well-built man.

The waves of his golden-brown hair, streaked with silver threads, caught in the light. He wrapped his arms around her. "Sweet D. I've missed you."

"Daddy, I want you to meet a friend of mine."

As he released her, our eyes met. I knew those eyes. That strong jaw. The feel of those lips. Recognition flared in his eyes, and I was transported back more than forty years, to a going-away party for a handsome young soldier leaving the next day for his new duty station. Soft lips had probed mine. Sweet words brushed my skin. Limbs entwined with mine then encircled me in a passionate embrace. Strong yet gentle hands had explored my body.

I boomeranged back to the present. All the oxygen appeared to have been sucked from the room. A small current of air escaped my mouth, and with it a whisper of a sound. "Rossi?"

Standing immobile, he looked as stunned as I felt. "Johnson?"

Diane looked back and forth between us. "You two know each other?"

Too overwhelmed to speak, I nodded. My heart raced. My stomach lurched. Tony Rossi was the one that got away. His memory haunted me for years. The events of that night shouldn't have happened. I was dating someone else. Our coupling wasn't planned; it just happened, and then he was gone.

Tony smiled at me, and without taking his eyes off mine, he answered Diane. "Yes, we met in the Army. We were both stationed at Fort Gordon for our Advanced Individual Training. I started the course before Dawn did, so I finished, was assigned a duty station, and left before she completed the course." His smile broadened, and a dimple appeared. "I've thought about you often over the years. Wondered what became of you. Did you marry Jim?"

I felt the heat creeping up my neck, suffusing my face. Diane's keen eyes didn't miss a thing. She issued a shrewd smile with one eyebrow raised in silent communication. This would be discussed later.

I told myself to get a grip, then flashed my best *friend* smile, not my come-hither smile. Who knew if I even had a come-hither smile in my arsenal? "Tony, it's good to see you. Although, you are the last person I expected to see today. I never realized that this Rossi crew was yours. Weren't you from Chicago? How did you end up in Oklahoma? And no, Jim and I didn't get married. He was already married."

A look of surprise crossed Tony's face at my last remark. "My first duty station was Fort Sill. I met my wife, Beth, in Oklahoma City when a few of us drove over for the weekend. There's just something about Oklahoma women—"

He let the sentence dangle in mid-air. *I'll be darned, he winked at me.*

Diane saw him wink. She slapped a hand over her mouth and spun to face the counter. I saw her shoulders pogo up and down, and I knew she was trying not to laugh aloud. She cleared her throat and regained her composure. "Daddy, would you like a glass of wine?"

"That would be perfect."

I decided to make a hasty retreat. "I'm going to take the dip and chips to the living room, Diane. Tony, it's good to see you." I grabbed the snacks from the counter and beelined for the coffee table in the living room. The front door opened, and Cici's brother, Dell, and his wife appeared. Their three sons tumbled in carrying trays and bags.

With the chips and dips deposited on the table, I suggested to Dell's wife, "Hey, let me help carry some of that." She handed me a pecan pie. "I'll take this to the laundry room with the other desserts." She nodded and headed to the kitchen.

94

I dropped the pie off on the washer and went back to the living room. The door opened again, revealing that Cici's brother, Jamey, his wife, and their daughter and son, had arrived. The volume ratcheted up, and the front door yawned open as the mob continued to arrive. Everyone seemed ready to give thanks and enjoy each other's company.

Angi sat at the end of the couch holding Sophie. Blane stood beside her, making introductions. She looked relaxed. Sophie was wide-eyed, taking it all in.

I heard a hoop and a holler from the kitchen. Tony's attendance must have been kept a surprise. I looked around the house at all the faces of the people I had come to know and love. Although there was no shared DNA, this was my family. The scene reminded me how blessed I was—another deposit in my emotional bank account.

***

I pushed back from the dining table. Crowded with the banquet remains, the table was ringed by several other adults. More people were gathered in the kitchen. Shouts echoed from a rowdy group huddled in the living room, a football game in command. Giggles floated in from the den where children sat in tater fashion around a low-slung table.

I leaned back and rubbed my stomach. "I am stuffed."

Diane grinned. "You know you have to take some of this food. I do not want to eat leftovers for a week."

The day had been full of the four F's—food, friendship, football, and fun. Lighthearted teasing, the telling of old stories, and love… so much love. My eyes teared as I reflected on my intimate family and the happy times we had shared. I felt a hint of sorrow, but the heartache was diluted by the love that filled Diane's home and cloaked me in its soft embrace.

Tony had taken the seat beside mine. "I can't believe you've been hanging out with my kids for eight years and I didn't know it."

"Not all of them. I've known Cici for eight years, but I didn't hang out with the rest of the clan till about five years ago, when they started coming down here for holiday gatherings. I've got to tell you, Tony, you and Beth did a marvelous job of raising your kids. They're all great, and, well, they're my chosen family."

He gave me a hesitant smile. A shadow of emotions crossed his face. "Beth was responsible for that. She was the best mom."

His pain and loneliness washed over me, but I didn't block it. I wanted to know what he was feeling. I placed my hand on his forearm. "I never met Beth, but I know she was a lovely woman and wonderful mother. I mean… look at her legacy all around us. You're a lucky man, Tony Rossi."

"Yes, I am. When Beth died, I didn't deal with her death very well. I abandoned my children and grandchildren. That was five years ago, which explains why I didn't know about you. It's time for me to make amends. I need to know my grandchildren—be a grandfather. I've decided to retire, and I'm thinking about moving to Chance. Three of my five kids live here, and the others aren't that far away. I'm staying with Diane and Steve through the weekend. I want to look around, get a feel for the town."

I gave his arm a squeeze before removing my hand. "This town is a rare gem. I think you'll like living here."

Angi walked up, stifling a yawn. "Miss Dawn, Blane's going to take Sophie and me home. You want to ride with us and save Cici a trip?"

Diane, who sat directly across from me, spoke. "You all don't worry about your pans or the leftovers. My sisters-in-law will help me clean up, and I'll get your stuff to you tomorrow."

I grinned at Diane. "Sold. I'm beat." I pivoted my head and spotted Cici on the couch. His socked feet were propped on the coffee table, his head laid back against the cushions with his eyes closed. "Cici, did you hear that? You're off the hook. I'm riding home with Blane and Angi."

He opened one eye and squinted at me. "Thank God. I don't think I'll be able to move for at least an hour."

I smiled at Tony. "I'll see you around."

He flashed his dimple at me. "Yes, you will."

Blane, Angi, and I said our goodbyes and headed to Blane's SUV. We were all quiet on the ride home. After unlocking the front door, I said my goodnights and went straight to my room.

Before washing my face, I gazed at my reflection, evaluating it. I wanted to see what Tony saw when he looked at me tonight. *Not too bad if you're into dull, natural, and mundane.* I hadn't worn makeup since the deaths of Mike and Gracie. The first six months, makeup was pointless because I cried endlessly. Then I just didn't care. I pushed myself to exercise every day. Some might say I was obsessive about it, but I hadn't been obsessive about my appearance—sleeping in my clothes, leaving my hair in an unkempt ponytail. That would have to change.

15.

Old Business
Moving Forward with Purpose

The following morning, I woke before the alarm sounded and powered through my workout. I passed on making breakfast and opted for a protein bar with coffee after I showered.

The urge to primp ignited. Instead of my usual sweats or jeans and T-shirt, I pulled on a pair of black leggings and a soft, teal blue turtleneck sweater. *A turtleneck to hide a turkey neck.* I applied a sheer layer of foundation, a little blush, eyebrow pencil, eyeliner, and mascara, and finished with neutral lipstick. A blow dryer tamed my errant waves into submission, and big silver hoop earrings completed my revitalized look. I stood back from the mirror and scanned the outcome. *Much better.*

With an elbow perched on the kitchen table, I leaned my face onto my fist and looked out over the lake. A fish jumped, and I watched the light refracting off the ripples in the water. I heard the scuff of Angi's house slippers as she approached. She rounded the corner of the table. "Good morning, Miss Da—" She faltered and stood there dumbstruck staring at me.

I took a sip of coffee. "What?"

"You're… beautiful."

Embarrassed by her reaction, I wondered how bad I had looked the past several months. "I, uh, well, I just figured it was time to start paying more attention to my, uh… grooming."

The driveway alarm sounded so I made my way to the front window and watched Diane's car bank around the curve. I slipped into my gardening clogs and strode out the door. She bounced out of the car with her *morning person* exuberance. Diane took one look at me, and said, "Wow, you look amazing. Well, except for the clogs. You need to lose those bad boys."

"They were by the front door; I just put them on so I could help you carry stuff in. Speaking of which, hurry up, it's cold out here."

She handed me a large paper bag. "That's your leftovers. Go on in. I'll bring the rest."

I made Diane a cup of coffee. A smirk spread across her face. "Okay, Dawn, spill it. What went down between you and my dad at Fort Gordon?"

I knew this was coming, but still, I wasn't prepared for Diane's question.

"What?" I asked. "No preamble? No good morning? You're just going for the jugular first thing? What makes you think anything *went down* between your father and me?"

"You just answered my question with a question. You're stalling."

Angi's head swiveled between Diane and me. "You knew Mr. Rossi when you were in the Army?"

Diane now leered at me before addressing Angi. "If you ask me, Angi, I'd say her *knowing Dad* was a bit more than just *knowing* him, unless you meant that in the biblical sense. Look at her. She's blushing like a schoolgirl."

The heat had inched up my neck to my face and seared the tops of my ears. Both Diane and Angi continued to study me. "Would you stop it? We never dated." *Technically, that was true.*

Diane's head bobbed up and down like an apple in a barrel of water. "I don't recall asking if you dated. You know a whole lot can happen without a *date* ever occurring." Diane bulldozed ahead. "Angi, you should have seen the two of them yesterday. I was going to introduce Daddy to Dawn, but before I could, their eyes locked, and Dawn whispered, 'Rossi?' Then her complexion morphed into the color of a sunburned co-ed on spring break. Dad said 'Johnson?' Then they started talking about being stationed at Ft. Gordon together. And at some point, Daddy winked at her! By the way, where did the name Johnson come from?"

"My daddy. Johnson is my maiden name."

Angi hadn't said a word, but she didn't need to. Her gleeful grin said it all.

Diane continued. "And look how nice she looks today? Makeup, hair, something besides jeans—oh yeah, something went down."

"Would you stop? Can't a gal get tired of looking stale, and just foofoo a little without you making a federal case out of it? I did this for myself. I don't even have any plans to see your father today."

Diane's eyebrows reached for her hairline. "Methinks you doth protest too much, and the day is young. Oh… should I call you Mom?"

My lips pressed into a firm line. "You're pushing it. Am I gonna have to whip your ass?"

Diane slapped her thigh and guffawed. She laughed so hard she grabbed a Kleenex to swipe across her eyes. "I'm sorry, Mom—Dawn! I just couldn't resist."

"Whatever," I mumbled.

Diane's phone chirped. "Hi." She listened, then cut her eyes to me. "Well, as a matter of fact, I'm at her house right now." Another pause, then, "Okay." She offered the phone to me. "It's for you." With a big grin, she said, "Yep, the day is young."

I took the phone. "Hello?"

"Hi. It's Tony. I was wondering if you'd have lunch with me at Cici's. Then, show me around Chance. I'd like to catch up… find out what you've been up to since Fort Gordon."

I turned my back to Diane's scrutiny and continued my conversation. "That sounds good. Why don't I just meet you at Cici's at one? The rush will be over, and I won't feel guilty about hogging a booth." Tony agreed. We ended the call, and I handed the phone back to Diane.

"It's not a date," I said. "I'm meeting him at Cici's. We're just going to have lunch, catch up, and then I'm going to show him around Chance."

"Right," Diane said, her head moving like a bobble-head on a car dash.

"Can we talk about something else, please?"

Diane grinned even larger and shifted her focus to Angi. "How are things with you and my little brother? He was smitten with you yesterday."

Angi's eyes rounded. She took a gulp of coffee and eased out of her chair. "Uh, look at the time. I've got to get ready for work. I'll see you later." She dashed to the safety of her bedroom.

Diane called after her. "I can take Sophie with me and save you the trip this morning. Dad is watching Katie for me, and I'll head back home after I finish my coffee."

I shook my head. "I know you're a morning person, and you've always been an instigator. But stirring the pot this early in the morning—really?"

Diane gave a casual shrug. "Sometimes, I just can't help myself."

When Diane and Angi left, I nursed the last of my coffee and wondered what to do with the rest of the morning. I hadn't drawn or painted in months. It was time.

***

The cabin door clicked shut behind me as I trekked across to the shop. In the loft, music and light intertwined in a rhythmic dance that soothed me as I scrolled through the pictures on my phone. I saw a darling one of Sophie from her two-month birthday party. She was sound asleep in the bouncy seat, her hair a series of cowlicks protruding at odd intervals. I printed it, grabbed a sheet of watercolor paper, and sketched.

I set my pencil down and studied my drawing with a critical eye. "Hmm, not bad, but I am out of practice."

It was a good time for a break. I forgot how much I enjoyed listening to music while drawing and painting, and how that combination always transported me to my happy place. Feeling lighter and more like the old me, I grabbed my keys in anticipation of… what? I was unsure. Perhaps a new chapter in my life, whatever that may consist of.

Outside, I breathed in the fresh, fall air, the scent redolent of cherished childhood memories. The stark limbs of the trees swayed, as if moving to the rhythm of a stringed quartet. A hawk floated overhead and pierced the serenity with its call, adding to my own private concert of nature. I was at peace yet filled with excitement at the same time.

***

Tony lounged in my booth.

"You're in my spot," I said.

His mouth quirked up on one side, dimpling his cheek. "Well, hello to you, too. I know this is your spot. Cici told me. It does have the best vantage point in the place for looking at the front door. Now that you're here, it's all yours. I warmed up the seat for you." He gave me a quick wink.

My entire body gave an involuntary response as my pulse quickened. Tony moved to the opposite side of the table, his back to the door, and I took my now warm spot. "I hope you're hungry, Tony. I plan to eat like a lumberjack."

"I respect a woman that's not embarrassed to eat like she means it."

Cici walked up to take our order. "Where's Angi?" I asked.

"She's on her lunch break, and if I'm not mistaken, she's upstairs with Blane."

"Ooh," I crooned.

"So, what are you two having?"

We placed our order, and Cici left.

Feeling sheepish, I peeked at Tony. "I owe you an app—"

"Dawn, I'm sorry—"

We stopped and regarded each other. Tony took the lead. "I'd say ladies first, but I've been waiting years to tell you I'm sorry."

Disappointment flirted with my heart. "Sorry for the night we spent together?"

He shook his head, a bad-boy smile surfacing. "No. I'm unrepentant about that. I wanted to apologize for not trying to contact you afterward. I thought I was doing the right thing by walking away. You thought that no one knew about you and Jim. We understood why you kept your relationship a secret—fraternization rules since he was an instructor. But everyone knew. I'd had a crush on you since the day on the parade field, months before that night. Do you remember that day?"

I nodded as the memory surfaced. *We marched in formation around the parade field, practicing for an upcoming ceremony. The company broke ranks and headed towards the shade of trees at the edge of the field. I sat near Tony. His long legs stretched out in front of him, crossed at the ankles. His elbows and forearms were on the grass behind him, propping his torso. The sunlight glinted off the waves of his hair. We chatted about our hometowns and inconsequential things.*

He had caught my eye, but I was in a relationship, so we just kept the encounter friendly. *Oh yes, I remember that day.*

He continued. "I knew the events of that night shouldn't have happened, but I was incapable of stopping them from happening. Incapable is inaccurate. I just didn't want to stop."

I chuckled. "Neither did I."

"Because I cared for you, I thought I should leave you alone. I was leaving, you were with Jim, and I didn't want to complicate things for you, so I just left. I heard you had an engagement ring a couple of days later, so I figured I'd done the right thing. Last night, when you told me he was already married? I felt like such a fool."

I gave a sardonic chuckle. "No more than I did when I found out."

Cici arrived with our food, and we paused our conversation. Eating like a lumberjack precluded having a decent conversation. Besides that, I was nervous about my own forthcoming apology.

As we left Cici's, I jangled my keys. "Why don't you let me drive since I know Chance?" Tony nodded his response, and we got into my van. I drove to my favorite spot at the lake. Although the location was less spectacular at this time of year, without the lush foliage of spring and summer, there was still a simple beauty to the view.

We sat at a picnic table facing the lake, which reflected the surrounding cliffs. A steep incline rose behind us, covered in bare trees. I pointed across the lake. "See that bluff over there with the cabin and deck?" He looked at the bluff and nodded. "That's my place."

"Does the staircase leading down to the beach and dock belong to you, too?" he asked.

"It does, but the dock doesn't."

I got up and walked to the other side of the table so I could look him in the eyes. "Tony, I owe you an apology, too. That night, I should have stopped us. I could have, but the truth is, I didn't want to either. My regret is the way I acted the following day. I avoided you. I didn't tell you goodbye. I was so confused and embarrassed. I didn't understand how I could be in a relationship with Jim and still be with you that night. You were leaving, and I figured that night was just a fling for you. I felt so guilty."

Tony reached out across the table and took my hand. I felt a current flow from his hand to mine. I registered his emotions, a tangle of them—remorse, friendship, empathy, joy, and the smallest bud of something else.

His dimple punctuated the smile that had etched across his face. "Well, I suppose we're both guilty. You know, we were young. Although we could have made better decisions concerning that night, I feel no remorse. So, what do you say we put that event behind us and move forward? I see no reason to let that night cause any awkwardness between us now. What do you think?"

I gave his hand a squeeze before releasing it and stood up. "Deal. You ready to see some more sites?"

His eyes drank me in. "I'm enjoying the one in front of me. I like what you've done with your hair today."

I felt the burn surging up my neck and face. "It is a different look than the bun last night. Come on, you need to see the wineries."

"There are wineries in Chance?"

"A couple of them and a sports bar. The next town over has a movie theater and a couple of fine dining restaurants, as well as a hospital."

I drove to both wineries which were closed for the holiday. Then I showed him some available lakefront properties and townhomes. There was no awkwardness between us. I enjoyed being with him.

We arrived at the diner before four. When I got out of the van, I felt a prickling on my skin. My perception of the sensation was somewhat different than usual. Like last time, the discomfort was muffled. There were a lot of pinpricks, but instead of a searing hotness, there was a buffer between the pricks and my skin. The pain wasn't as intense as normal for that many pricks. That was odd. I had experienced that diminished feeling only once before—when I left Doc's.

***

Jimmy hunched over the steering wheel of the jeep and peered through the small telescope at the woman. He watched her get out of the van. She paused as if contemplating something. An older man walked around the van from the passenger side, and they entered the café from the back door. An hour had passed since he saw Angi through the front window. He continued to watch the parking lot to see which car Angi drove.

***

Angi and Cici were cleaning the café for the next day's business. I hurried in and announced, "We need to have a group discussion." Cici quirked an eyebrow at me. "Jimmy is close," I said. "I just felt him. Is Blane upstairs?" Cici nodded. "Angi, would you get him, please?"

Tony raised an eyebrow but didn't say anything. We moved to a table and waited for everyone to gather. "This isn't how I planned to tell you some personal… quirks about myself, but these are extenuating circumstances." Tony gave me his full attention. "Please keep an open mind. You can verify with Cici and Blane what I'm about to tell you. They've seen first-hand what I'm about to share. Are you familiar with the term empath?"

"Yes, I've read about it," Tony said.

"Good, maybe this won't be so difficult after all. You see, I'm an emotional empath as well as an intuitive empath. I feel other people's emotions unless I shield myself, and I sometimes have heightened intuition. Why I'm telling you this now is so you'll understand why I want to talk to the group. An abusive man hit Angi and followed her to Chance a couple of months ago. I'm sure he's in town because I can feel it when I'm being watched. In the parking lot, just now, I was being watched."

I heard Blane and Angi descend the stairs. Cici put his broom away and joined us at the table. Tony masked his expression; I saw no indication of how he felt about what I had told him. I lowered my shields and tapped into his emotions. I felt a little confusion, an openness, and a desire to know more. No negativity. I was relieved.

Blane sat down. "What's up?"

I looked around the table. "Jimmy is in town. I was being watched when we got out of the van a few minutes ago. I don't want Angi leaving here by herself today."

I focused on Angi. "I can take you to pick up Sophie. We can pick up The Beast later when we know Jimmy isn't around."

Blane interjected. "We were going to Steve and Diane's for board games tonight anyway. I'll drive Angi over and bring her and Sophie home later."

"Good."

Tony asked, "Have the police been notified?"

I emitted a wry chuckle. "We can't notify the police of my feelings. They'd just think I was a nutjob. No one has seen him since the day he followed Angi to town, but I have felt his presence a couple of other times."

Tony's head tilted. His brow bunched. "I'd like to know more about your abilities. May I come over this evening? I'll bring dinner."

"Well, that's an offer I can't refuse. How about six?"

Tony gave a quick nod.

Blane and Angi stood, said their goodbyes, and left out the back door.

***

Jimmy watched the back door open and saw Angi. A predatory smirk shadowed his feral features. Then he noticed the tall guy following behind her. "Damn it!" When she got into the passenger seat of the SUV, Jimmy contemplated his options. Follow her—she probably wasn't going home since she was with the dude—or check out the old lady. He had seen where the old gal had turned off the highway. He could scout around, see if he could find her house. *I think it's time to introduce myself to the old girl. Yeah, time to meet and greet.*

16.

A Dangerous Man and a Capable Woman
The Aftermath

I parked in front of the cabin, exited the van, and was near the steps before registering the burning pain on my skin. Then I remembered my gun was in the center console of the van. I darted back to the passenger door and scrambled for the handle. A rustling noise sounded behind me. A sharp pain seared my shoulder as my right arm was wrenched backward. I clutched the door handle with my left hand, a vise-like grip of desperation. I glanced over my shoulder. Jimmy's lips curled back in a sneer.

"Let go, Bitch. You're coming in the house with me and we're gonna have us a little talk about Angi."

The rage started to build in the pit of my stomach. It worked its way up, firing my central nervous system. My senses vibrated—taut piano wire. I didn't experience a blind rage. My fury was cold. Dark. Calculating. I had lost two loved ones to a violent man. I wouldn't lose more.

I strengthened my resolve and my grip on the door handle. He leaned away from me. His entire weight strained to wrench me free. I released the handle and lunged at him. The combination of my forward momentum and his backward trajectory launched us into the air. His collarbone connected with the porch rail. I heard a snap. His head cracked against the support post. The air reverberated with the recoil of the sound.

We fell to the ground. Jimmy was beneath me. I lay on my back across his body. I tasted his sour odor and sensed an excruciating pain in his right collarbone. His left arm whipped around my neck in a headlock. I was pinned to his chest. He increased the pressure around my throat. I couldn't breathe. I struggled to break his hold but failed. My vision began to blur. I felt myself slipping away. Desperate, I fisted my right hand, pistoned it backward over my shoulder, and hammered his broken collarbone. He grunted. I continued to pummel the injury. He screamed in pain. His hold loosened. I gasped a breath and rolled off him. As I rose to my elbows and knees, he grabbed a handful of my hair and jerked me back against his side. I pounded my fist into his cock with the intent of driving his gonads up through his chest. He shot into a fetal position, still clutching strands of hair yanked from my scalp. Reacting to the threat, adrenaline surged through me. I felt no pain. Pushing to my feet, my body filled with an overwhelming sense of strength and energy. I kicked him in the kidney, then crashed my boot into the back of his skull repeatedly. He lay motionless. I ran to the van. My hands trembled as I tried to open the passenger door. My thumb grazed the button on the door handle, locking the door. Leaves rustled behind me. In a frenzied attempt, I pushed the button again. The door unlocked. I retrieved the gun and darted a glance behind me. Jimmy was still huddled on the ground. His leg twitched, but nothing more.

I pulled my phone from my coat pocket and called Cici. "I need help. Jimmy is unconscious. Call the sheriff. My gun is pointed at him. I don't need any distractions."

"What? Dawn! Are you okay? Where are you?" Cici asked.

"I'm okay. In front of my cabin. Call the sheriff and get out here. Call an ambulance, too." I pocketed the phone and stayed hyper-focused on Jimmy. The minutes crawled by. A low moan and a sigh parted Jimmy's lips as consciousness returned. "Don't try anything, Jimmy. I'll shoot you if I have to."

His eyes snapped open, and a groan followed. Rolling to his back, his gaze focused on me. I felt fire on my skin. I could feel—him. He was alert but playing opossum. His pain and rage were slamming into me in waves.

In a swift movement, his left hand jerked toward his waistband and snatched the butt of a gun. I exhaled and squeezed the trigger of my revolver. Jimmy's head jerked. His gun-hand flailed outward, fell to the ground, and opened, releasing the weapon.

I approached him with caution and kicked the pistol out of his hand—away from his reach. Then I backed away. I heard a car coming up my drive. In the distance, the wail of an ambulance pulsed.

Cici pulled up, jumped from his truck, and charged towards me. He wrapped me in a bear hug and looked over my head at Jimmy's body. "Is he alive?"

I started shaking. "I… I don't know. He was going to shoot me. I warned him. I told him I'd shoot. He went for his gun anyway. After I shot him, I kicked the gun out of his reach. I couldn't bring myself to touch him."

Part of me wanted him to live. I didn't want to be a killer. The protector in me, the dormant soldier, felt otherwise. If he lived, he'd never leave Angi alone.

A cacophony of sirens echoed up the drive. The lights of the ambulance strobed through the trees. The sheriff's car was close behind.

Cici walked me to his truck. "Why don't you sit in the truck where it's warmer?"

I watched from the passenger seat as a gurney was pulled from the ambulance.

An EMT, already at Jimmy's side, laid his fingers across Jimmy's neck. "We have a pulse!"

I watched as they lifted Jimmy onto the gurney and wheeled him towards the ambulance.

The driver's side door of the truck opened, and Tony climbed in. He took my hand and placed it between both of his. "Cici called me. I'm here for you, Dawn, for whatever you need."

I heard his words and felt his sincerity. Not trusting myself to speak, I nodded in acknowledgment.

The sheriff and one of his deputies walked over. "Dawn, I need to take a statement," Sheriff Calvin Hobbs said.

Cici intercepted Calvin. "Before you take Dawn's statement, why don't we go take a look at the camera footage?"

"What camera footage are you talking about?"

"There are two cameras with different angles of the front porch area and four more cameras around the property. There is also a security monitoring station in Dawn's safe room."

Calvin motioned to his deputy and pointed to where Jimmy had lain. "Deputy, outline around where the body was, that area where the leaves and dead grass have been depressed. Secure the area, then get some pictures." He turned to face me and placed a weathered hand on my shoulder. "You, stay put."

Cici motioned for Calvin to follow him. They disappeared through the front door.

***

Cici pressed the button to open the bookcase and trap door.

The sheriff huffed out a grunt. "This is quite a setup."

Cici nodded. "Wait till you see the safe room." Cici led Calvin downstairs and took a seat at the computer station. He changed the mode on the monitor from split screen to full screen and selected the footage from the doorbell camera first. He backed the digital display until the time stamp was an hour before the shooting. Then, he fast-forwarded until he saw a person at the edge of a frame, stopped, rewound, and then started at regular speed to catch the movement. Jimmy walked into the frame from the north like he came in through the woods. "The timestamp indicates he got here at 4:10 pm, Sheriff."

Jimmy moved in and out of view as he stepped onto the porch, looked into the window, and walked around before going back down the steps and out of range of the camera.

Cici fast-forwarded until Dawn's van appeared, then reversed the display a few seconds and played at regular speed again. The time stamp indicated it was 4:40 pm. They watched the van pull up, and Dawn got out. She walked to the steps, hesitated, then rushed to the passenger door of the van.

Jimmy came back into the frame. He grabbed Dawn's arm from behind. Dawn turned and saw him. Both men gasped at the look of controlled fury that radiated from her.

Cici switched to slow motion, and they watched the scene unfold until Dawn and Jimmy fell from view of the doorbell camera. "She called me, Calvin. She asked me to call you and get an ambulance."

Cici entered more commands on the computer. "Dawn got to my café before four and left just past 4:30. Jimmy was here before Dawn—waiting for her, or more likely, Angi."

Calvin cut his eyes to Cici. "You want to give me the rest of the story, like who Angi is, and why Jimmy would be waiting for either of them?"

Cici pointed to the monitor. "Let's finish looking at the camera footage, then I'll fill you in."

Cici rewound the footage from the camera located in the tree across from the front porch. He knew the timestamp to look for and went right to it.

They watched everything again, but from the vantage point of the tree, which enabled them to see Jimmy and Dawn after they fell. Switching to slow motion, Cici and the Sheriff watched the fight play out. From this camera angle, they saw the sequence of events right up to the impact of the bullet as it entered Jimmy's skull.

The Sheriff shook his head, then looked at Cici. "Damn! That is one woman I never want to tangle with."

Cici nodded in agreement. "She is a capable woman, Sheriff."

The sheriff tapped his fingers on the tabletop. "Looks like a clear case of self-defense to me. I'll still need to take her statement though. Can you burn me copies of the footage from both cameras?"

"I'll do that while you take her statement. Can you bring her inside for her statement?"

"I will. I think I'll let her tell me who Angi is and what this is all about."

Cici contemplated his next statement. "Calvin, didn't you collaborate with a psychic on a missing persons case once?"

Calvin shifted and frowned. "Yeah. Why do you ask?"

"So, do you agree that some people have abilities that defy explanation?"

Calvin's lips tugged down at the corners. "Let's say I'm open to the possibility. I'll ask you again—why do you ask?"

"Dawn has a few abilities that may defy understanding. I know first-hand. She's not a psychic per se, but she… knows things. She doesn't tell many people because most people aren't open to the possibilities. I'm telling you in case she mentions her abilities to you. I want you to know that I will vouch for her. They're real."

"Okay." Calvin nodded and headed for the stairs.

***

I sat at the kitchen table, my cold hands wrapped around a mug of chamomile tea.

Calvin took a sip of coffee as he studied me. "I'd like to record our conversation, so I can focus on what you're saying without being distracted."

"Okay."

"I want you to tell me what happened today, and I want the background on this, too. Cici indicated that there is some history with you and this—" He glanced at a pocket-sized notebook. "Jimmy fella. And is there also someone named Angi involved?"

I nodded and started with the day that Angi walked into the café with her black eye, then sneaking her out the bathroom window. I recounted her story of the events that drove her to flee Tulsa. Then I told him about coming home today—Jimmy grabbing me and everything that led to me shooting him. I left out everything concerning my gifts. I didn't want my credibility questioned.

When I finished, Calvin nodded his head. His forearm rested against the edge of the table, where he tapped an ink pen on its surface and appeared to study me for a few seconds. Stopping the recording, he cleared his throat and fidgeted. "Why did you hesitate at the steps and go back to the van?"

"Uh, I just got a funny feeling, and then I remembered that I had left my gun in the van."

He took a deep breath and appeared to consider his next words. "Cici said that you have some abilities that I may not understand. I want you to know that I have worked with a psychic, and although I didn't understand how she did what she did, she got results. I believe in her abilities. I've turned off the recorder, and I want you to know that what you choose to tell me now is off the record. Okay?"

"Thank you."

"I want you to tell me how your abilities influenced these events."

"I don't have any real superpowers or anything. Sometimes I just know things when there is no reason for me to know. Most people don't understand. People fear what they don't understand."

He nodded at me, encouraging me by not saying anything. An expectant look settled over his features as he waited.

I lowered my shields, my senses telescoping to touch his emotions. "Okay, common sense tells me that you are inquisitive about what I can do, but for me, my senses go beyond that. Right now, I can feel your curiosity, and I can sense your openness. If I didn't, I wouldn't go any further with my explanation."

"Go on."

"I'm an empath, and I can feel other people's emotions. Sometimes I just know things before they happen, and I can feel when people are watching me. On rare occasions, the gift is useful, but for the most part, it's not. For example, I'll have an

114

urge to find my phone. It may be in the other room, and when I pick the phone up, a text will come in, or the phone will ring. Before I look at the screen, I'll know who is calling.

"I share a bond with some people, and I can feel when they need or want to talk to me. I just get an urge that I can't ignore, so I'll call them, and they'll say, 'I've been thinking about you,' and I'll say, 'I know. I've been trying to ignore you for a half hour. What do you want?' Or I'll think about someone I haven't seen in years and, out of the blue, they'll call me.

"When people are watching me—if it's a friend or someone who means me no harm—I feel a soft pressure, like marshmallows pressing against my skin, or a soft kiss... pleasant.

"If someone wants to hurt me or has negative thoughts towards me, I feel pinpricks on my skin. The worse the intention, the more intense the sensation—it can feel like my skin is on fire.

"As for how my abilities influenced these events—the day Angi came into the café and saw Jimmy in the parking lot, I felt her fear. I could also feel the love for her child, her honesty, sincerity, and her utter desperation. That's why I helped her, why I invited her to stay with me.

"I sensed Jimmy watching me on three separate occasions before today, although I never saw him. Today, I felt him watch me when Tony and I got out of my van in the parking lot behind Cici's, but not when I left.

"Just as I got to the steps of my porch, my skin started burning. I knew he was watching me. From the way my skin burned, I knew his intentions were bad. Then I remembered my gun was in the van. That's what prompted me to go to the van.

"When he came to, he groaned. I could feel his anger and pain. I knew he was alert, although he acted like he wasn't. When he went for his gun, I knew he intended to kill me. That's what I sensed, but I can't prove that to you."

Calvin flashed a reassuring smile and nodded. "Well, you don't need to prove anything to me or anyone else. The camera footage and Cici corroborate your story without any mention of special abilities. On the camera footage, it's evident that you made a call while Jimmy was unconscious. Cici told me what you said to him when you called."

We were interrupted by the sound of footfalls hammering across the floor from the front room, then Angi yelling, "Dawn! Where are you?" She burst into the kitchen, her face ashen, and she grabbed my shoulders, examining my face and body. "Oh my God. I'm so sorry. This is all my fault. I brought that crazy man into your life."

My shields were still down, and her emotions overwhelmed me. I cradled her in my arms. "Shh, shh, shh, it's okay, sweetheart. I'm fine. I'm better than fine, and I am so glad you and Sophie weren't here when it happened."

Pulling back from her, I smoothed the hair out of her eyes and cupped her face in my hands. Her luminous eyes searched mine, then they opened wide, and a startled, "Oh," whispered across her lips. A large smile transformed her worried expression. "Wow!"

Confusion engulfed me. "Wow what? What are you talking about?"

She continued to smile at me. "You don't even know you're doing it, do you?"

I saw the sheriff watching, looking back and forth between us.

I shook my head. "Doing what, Angi, what are you talking about?"

She put her hands over mine, and her eyes grew larger as she murmured, "Wow. It's like what you told me about the other day. Like what you said I could do. You know, when you said I took your pain? Just now, when you touched my face, I felt a soft vibration, and then calm poured into me, then love and joy. Oh, wow. I've never felt anything like this before."

We both laughed. Calvin shook his head in wonder as he watched. The moment was interrupted by the ringing of his phone.

"I've got to take this. I'll be right back. Angi, I'll need to talk to you."

***

Cici, Tony, and Blane entered the kitchen. Blane carried Sophie. Cici was first to speak. "We saw Calvin go outside to take a call, so we snuck in. What's going on with him? Has he finished taking your statement?"

"Yes, but he wants to talk to Angi next."

Blane handed Sophie to Angi, then wrapped me in a tight hug. "You scared us. All we heard was that there had been a shooting at your place, so we raced over. Cici told us what happened."

His shoulder muffled my reply as he continued to crush me to his chest. "I'm not hurt, but I shot Jimmy. He had a pulse when they loaded him in the ambulance. The two cameras out front caught everything. You can watch the footage if you want. I don't want to see it. I can't."

Calvin walked into the kitchen. A grimace shadowed his face. "Jimmy didn't make it. He died in the emergency room. That doesn't change anything, Dawn. It's clear that you shot him in self-defense. Now, all you yahoos need to clear out of the kitchen. I need to get a statement from Angi."

Angi handed Sophie to me. Swaddled against me, her baby scent and the warmth of her small body comforted me. The fellas and I moved to the living room.

Blane paced. His hand jingled change in his pocket. "I want to see the footage, Cici. I need to see it."

Tony took my hand. "Do you need me to stay with you, Dawn?"

"No, I'm fine. I have Miss Sophie here to keep me company. Go on with Cici and Blane."

I sat in the rocker, the lilting notes of a forgotten lullaby surfaced. Accompanied by the receding footsteps of the men, I sang to Sophie as I had sung to Gracie many years ago. Numb to the fact that I had killed a man, the reality of Jimmy's death was impossible for me to grasp. The detachment insulated me from the eventual revulsion I knew I would feel. I prayed for the strength to deal with the consequences of my actions. Rocking Sophie, I embraced her innocence and relished the reprieve.

The rest of the evening was out of focus. After giving her statement, Angi baked some frozen pizzas and made a salad. Cici, Blane, and Tony ate with us.

The sheriff had the footage from the cameras, and the forensic team had finished gathering evidence. Cici was allowed to hose down the bloody area where Jimmy had lain. He left soon after. The sour odor of Jimmy lingered on me. Imagined or not, I had to wash him off of me, so I showered and put on pajamas.

Angi put Sophie to bed. She and Blane watched a movie in her room.

Blane was more freaked out about the events than anyone else. He was scared for me, but I imagined the events triggered thoughts of his own traumatic losses. Perhaps he struggled with the possibility of what could have happened to Angi had she been there.

Tony built a nice fire, and I poured us both a glass of wine. We sat side by side on the couch, gazing at the fire, sipping wine, sharing a comfortable silence. I felt something land on my hand. Looking down, I saw a tear glistening. Then the dam broke. My heart ached for the loss of life. No matter how dangerous Jimmy was, I had taken his life. The full impact of what I had done hit me. A sob erupted from my throat.

Tony took the wine glass from me and set it with his on the table. Then he pulled me into a gentle embrace and just held me, comforting me while I wept.

At some point, we reclined on the couch, him on his back, me beside him with my head on his chest. In a languid motion, his hand caressed my head.

He didn't kiss or talk to me; he just let me cry. He comforted and reassured me with his steadfast presence. That was the last thing I remembered until the next morning.

17.

Life Goes On
A Walk with God, a Burden Lifted

I breached the surface of wakefulness in a lazy assent, aware of scents and sounds that I became unaccustomed to over the past year. Something poked my cheek. *Is that a button?* Then the steady rhythm of a heartbeat played against my cheek. A soft inhale and exhale of breath skimmed across my hair. Tony's scent assailed me. I was wrapped in a cocoon of fragile emotions. *Oh, I could get used to this.*

My deep inhale was greeted by a whisper from Tony. "Good morning."

I smiled against Tony's chest. "Good morning yourself, and thank you for staying with me."

He chuckled. "I didn't have a choice. You fell asleep on me, and that's the last thing I remember because I must have fallen asleep right after you."

"I need a favor."

"What?"

"Please keep your eyes closed and indulge a gal while she tries to maintain her vanity. I know my entire face is swollen and puffy. I'm going to retreat to my bathroom to wash my face, then

I'll make us some coffee. Do you know how to access the guest bathroom?"

"That I do. Cici showed me all about the bookcase on our way to the safe room last night."

***

My scalp throbbed. Running my fingers through my hair I found a few small scabs where the hair was yanked out. My right shoulder was stiff, and my entire body ached, but all things considered, I was in good shape. I washed the tears off my face, changed into my yoga outfit, and put my hair in a ponytail before making my way to the kitchen.

Tony was already seated at the table with a mug of coffee in hand. "I hope you don't mind me helping myself."

"Are you kidding? I love a self-sufficient man. What would you like for breakfast?"

"I'd take a bowl of Raisin Bran if you've got it."

"Independent and easy."

He shot me a smirk. "I'm not easy—but I can be had."

I felt my color rising again. "I see now where your sons get their flirtatious natures." Without turning, I asked, "How long have you been standing there, Angi?"

She giggled. "Oh, not long."

"Long enough," I muttered as I grabbed the milk out of the refrigerator and set the carton on the table. I noticed Angi tried not to smile or look at me. Her attempt failed. I joined them at the table with my protein bar and coffee.

Angi spoke. "You got here at the crack of dawn, Tony."

My jaw dropped, "Angi!"

Her head snapped towards me. "What?" Then she giggled. "I didn't mean it *that* way. I meant dawn with a little *d.*"

I rolled my eyes. "We fell asleep on the couch, and nothing happened. Honest, Mom."

She cackled. "I know. Blane and I saw you two fast asleep last night when he left, but I couldn't resist teasing you."

Tony laughed and enjoyed my discomfort way too much.

I narrowed my eyes at him. "What are you laughing about?"

He held up his hands in surrender. "I'm surrounded by two lovely ladies. It's a beautiful day outside, and I'm enjoying my breakfast. That makes me happy. I smile when I'm happy."

I looked from one to the other. "Whatever."

He placed his hand on mine. "I've got to head back to Tulsa tomorrow. Why don't you let me take you to dinner tonight? Didn't you say there are a couple of fine dining restaurants in the next town over?

"Yes."

"Great. I'll pick you up at six."

"I didn't say I'd go."

A crease formed between his eyebrows. He looked at Angi. "Did I imagine it, or did she say yes?"

Before Angi could answer, I did. "I said yes to your question about the restaurants."

"I see. Making me work for it, huh? Okay. Dawn, will you do me the honor of accompanying me to dinner tonight?"

I tapped my fingers on the table while I contemplated his invitation. A lesser man might have gotten frustrated, but he still grinned at me, unfazed. "Yes, I'll join you for dinner this evening, and six will be just fine."

He took his bowl and mug to the sink, and on his way back, he leaned over and kissed the top of my head. "I'll see you tonight, heartbreaker." Then he left.

I watched his backside all the way to the front door before I realized what I was doing. I turned back around in my chair to see Angi grinning at me. "Oh, Miss Dawn, I think you're smitten."

"Me? Me! What about you, young lady? How was your movie last night?"

"Hey, my guy went home."

We both started laughing. "Okay, well, after I take some ibuprofen, I'm going to the shop to do yoga and hopefully work off some of this stiffness, then I'm going for a walk. I'll take my phone in case you need me."

As I descended the stairs on my way to the shop, the crime scene tape fluttered and caught my eye. Instantly nauseous, I swallowed back the bile and studied the area where Jimmy laid after I shot him. My heart rate quickened, my breathing became shallow, and guilt consumed me.

Raising my face to the sky, I closed my eyes and offered up a silent prayer. *Lord, forgive me for taking a life.* In that moment, I experienced an astounding awareness. I felt as if a supreme presence surrounded me in infinite love. In my mind, I heard the words, "You saved lives." And my guilt... my burden... lifted.

I zipped my coat and decided to walk first. I wanted to remain in his presence—bask in the comfort of his forgiveness and the joy of his love.

As I entered the woods, I was entranced by the glory of my surroundings. The air was brisk, smelling fresh and clean. Billowy clouds filled the sky, some backlit by the sunlight and others shadowed, giving them depth and texture. Birds flitted around me and called to one another. Eventually, I found myself in the clearing where we fired our weapons, honing our skills. I thought of all the times I had practiced with Cici and Blane and contemplated my motivation. I wondered if I was led there that morning as a further sign of forgiveness… a reminder that at one time, I was a warrior. Not in the sense that I went to war, but I was a soldier. I was committed to the responsibility. I took an oath to protect and defend, and I trained to do just that. My oath was genuine.

There were incidents of terrorist activity that impacted me. I contemplated the times I was sent to look for bombs, remembering the bombs that detonated in the building where I worked. I flashed back to Jimmy grabbing me. To Angi with a black eye. To Mike and Gracie lying dead. I re-lived Jimmy reaching for his gun. As if walking under a waterfall, the truth cascaded over me. I was still a warrior who protected and defended. Jimmy would have killed me, or worse, he could have hurt or killed Angi and Sophie.

I didn't take joy from killing Jimmy, but I could put his death into perspective and live with it. At peace—guilt replaced by gratitude—I made my way back to the shop to indulge in my morning routine and speculate on what the evening might reveal.

18.

A Rekindling
Let's Get This Party Started

I lingered in the shower, washing my hair and using the body scrub I seldom took time for. I did all the feminine things that are a prerequisite for a first date. Wrapped in my fluffy bathrobe, I enjoyed a salad for lunch—*got to save those calories so I can splurge tonight.*

By the time six o'clock rolled around, I was coiffed, polished, and perfumed. My quintessential little black dress hugged my curves and showed off my legs. Black heels completed the look. My hair was loose and flowing. For the first time in a long time, I was excited about an evening out, not just going through the motions.

When I walked into the living room, Angi's jaw dropped. "Miss Dawn. Wow."

"Well, I didn't want Tony to forget about me after he gets back to Tulsa."

"Fat chance. If he hasn't forgotten you after forty years, he's not going to forget you—ever. Especially after he sees you tonight."

The driveway alarm sounded, and Angi, my co-conspirator, hissed. "Quick, go to the kitchen. I'll answer the door so you can make an entrance."

Bless her heart, she had me rushing for the kitchen in high heels. "I hope I don't fall and break a hip. That would put a damper on the evening."

I stayed out of sight around the corner of the kitchen doorway. A knock sounded at the front door, then Angi called out to me. "Miss Dawn, Tony is here."

I ran my hands down my dress to smooth imaginary wrinkles, then strode into the living room—the master of my heels. My breath hitched in my throat. *Oh my, he looks delicious.* We stood at opposite ends of the room admiring each other while Angi looked back and forth between us, a huge grin on her face. I snapped out of my reverie. "Hello, Tony. Let me grab my coat, and we can get going."

Tony helped me into my coat, and Angi gave us a little finger wave as we left.

The ride to Jake's Place in Skeeter took fifteen minutes. Jake had been a chef in New York but got tired of the big life. He moved back home to open Jake's Place. The name belied the culinary art and expertise within. The menu changed frequently. Seafood was flown in daily. Beef, lamb, fish, poultry, fruits, and vegetables were sourced locally. It was a mystery to some that he could make a living in the small, backwoods town. He was supported not only by people from surrounding communities but A-listers from all over came as well. He was just that good. The prices were indicative of that, too.

Tony opened my door.

"You sure know how to impress a girl. How did you know about Jake's Place?"

"After Googling fine dining near Chance, I asked Cici about it. He said I couldn't go wrong with Jake's Place."

We were right on time for our reservation. The food, wine, and ambiance were excellent. The company, even better.

I gazed at Tony by candlelight. His eyes shined, the lines of his face, and hopefully mine, were softened by the diffused light. The conversation was easy; there was a nice cadence to it. There was no pretension, and he wasn't afraid to make fun of himself. Tony was comfortable in his own skin, which put me at ease. Matured, he was so much like the young man I remembered, though better, more polished, just—more.

I couldn't remember the last time I had been so comfortable in someone's company. Tonight was a welcomed diversion from the past twenty-four hours. We steered clear of the "Jimmy" topic. In fact, we avoided all sensitive topics, like our former spouses. No need to bring them along on our first date after all.

We neared the last few sips of wine. Tony raised an eyebrow. "We need to either order dessert or leave. What's it to be?"

"Dessert, of course."

We stayed another hour, lingering over coffee, enjoying the intimacy of the surroundings and our shared past. I kept my shields up because if I experienced his feelings before he was ready to share them with me, that would be unfair and cheating. So, the evening rolled out like a dropped ball of yarn, and I enjoyed the mystery of a developing relationship.

We waited for the check. Tony held my hand on top of the table. "Rumor has it, you like to dance."

I chuckled. "There are no secrets in Chance."

"Would you like to go dancing? There's live music at the casino tonight."

"There is, and I'd love to."

***

We pulled up to valet parking at the casino. "You're going to valet park?" I asked.

Tony tilted his head to peer down at my shoes. "I didn't think you'd want to walk far in those heels. Thought I'd save your feet for dancing."

Oh, he's good.

We grabbed a table near the dance floor and we each ordered a glass of wine. The songs were hard rock. I leaned into him. "I've heard this band before. They play a wide variety of music. Something more danceable will play soon." I could smell his cologne and felt the warmth emanating from his skin, although we weren't touching. The combination was seductive.

I glanced at a large group of girls. It was obvious they were having a bachelorette party. One of the girls wore a tiara with the word "Bride" arched across the top in rhinestones. They sat in sedate silence; none of them danced, their mood subdued.

The band switched up the music, and Tony and I began to swing dance. He had a strong lead and was easy to follow. We moved into a waltz, then a two-step. "Okay, my feet need a break, Fred Astaire."

As we sipped our wine, my eyes wandered back to the bachelorette party. "Those girls need a lesson in how to party. Would you excuse me for a minute?" He nodded and watched me with a puzzled smile.

I approached the table and focused on the bride-to-be. The music pounded out a beat that made conversation difficult. "When are you getting married?" I shouted at her.

"Next Saturday." She yelled back.

"So, this is your last hoorah, right?"

Her head bounced up and down, and the band switched to "Brick House." I kicked off my heels and grabbed her hand. "Come on, girlfriend. Let's get this party started!"

I pulled her from her chair, motioning to the other girls to join us, and managed to get them all out onto the dance floor. The music engaged every one of them with its primal beat. We all danced, laughed, and created a commotion that grabbed the attention of several young men.

I caught a glance of Tony as I spun. His eyes followed me. I felt the heat of them.

After the song ended, I retrieved my shoes and scooted next to him. I was on a mission. "Tony, would you ask the girl with the tiara to dance? These young guys are intimidated by such a large group of girls, but if you ask her to dance, maybe it'll break the ice."

"Happy to oblige." He cut through the crowd to the guest of honor. With a slight bend at the waist, he offered his hand. Her eyes found mine. I nodded and gave her a thumbs up. She accepted Tony's hand and followed him to the dance floor. As they moved to the music, a wave of young men flooded the table of bachelorettes. The party had indeed started.

We lingered till almost midnight. I shared Tony with several of the bachelorettes. A skilled dancer, he was quite popular.

On our way back to Chance, Tony placed his hand on my thigh and gave it a squeeze. "I can't remember when I've had so much fun. Thank you."

"Thank you," I said. "The evening was lovely."

We arrived at my cabin. Angi had left the porch light burning—darn it. Tony opened my car door and walked me up the steps. He embraced me and lowered his lips to my ear. "I won't be back before Christmas. I'd like to see you then, and I'd like to call you while I'm away."

"Sure."

He skimmed his cheek along mine. The stubble of his whiskers tickled my skin and ignited a slow burn within me. Pulling away, he leaned down to place a kiss on my... nose? "Good night, Dawn." He turned and walked away. Over his shoulder, he said, "I'll call you." He slid into the driver's seat and gave me a wink. *Oh, he's such a tease!*

I walked inside, still feeling the heat. Angi poked her head out of her doorway, grinning. She had waited up. "Well? How was your date?"

"It was... it was incredible," I murmured.

Angi squealed and enveloped me in a hug. "I want to hear all about it."

"Okay, but first let me get into something comfortable. These shoes are killing me. How about we meet in the kitchen in ten?"

Angi nodded. I rendezvoused with my pajamas and washed my face before arriving in the kitchen. Angi set a plate of butter cookies on the table and a pot of apple cinnamon tea. Nibbling on cookies, she listened with rapt attention while I recounted the story of my evening with Tony. Starting with dinner, I told her about what we ate, the atmosphere, and the funny stories we told about ourselves. Then she went into a fit of giggles when I recounted getting all the girls dancing to "Brick House."

"So, what do you think, will you go out with him again?"

"Seriously, you have to ask? Of course, I will. But don't you dare tell a soul I said that. And would you look at the time? We better get to bed, girl. I haven't been up this late in ages." I hugged her and went to my room. I marveled at the bond she and I shared, how strong it was, and how fast the bond had formed. It was as if we were family, and in a sense, we were. I had always thought there was more to a family than mere blood.

***

The following morning, Sunday, I languished in my bed and did a full body stretch. The sunshine seeped around the corner of my drapes. My clock glared 9 a.m. *When was the last time I slept this late?*

A soft knock registered, and Angi poked her head in. "Are you up?"

"Yes, come on in," I said as I propped myself up in bed.

She carried a tray in and placed it across my lap, then turned to open the curtains. I laughed aloud. "Oh, thank you, it's my favorite breakfast." A protein bar and a mug of coffee covered the center of the tray, and a pink rosebud nestled in a bud vase toward the corner. I swallowed a sip of coffee—just the right amount of cream and sugar.

"This is so sweet of you, Angi. Thank you. Where did you get the rosebud?"

"It broke off. I found a dozen pink roses on the front porch this morning. I was hoping they were for me, but the card has your name on it. Don't get up, I'll bring them in."

She returned with a beautiful bouquet of pink roses in a gorgeous cut crystal vase and set them on my nightstand. I retrieved the card and read it aloud. "I couldn't find forget-me-nots, so these roses will have to do." The card was signed by Tony. I placed the card over my heart and sighed. Then Angi sighed. She stood, her head tilted back, a wistful smile on her face. "What?" I asked.

She giggled. "I was just enjoying your emotions."

"Stop that." I blushed. "I can see we're going to have to have a crash course in shielding and empath etiquette."

She laughed and left the room.

I figured Tony was driving back to Tulsa, and I didn't want to distract him with a call, so I sent him a text that he could read later.

Thank you for the beautiful roses. I look forward to visiting with you☺. Safe travels. Dawn.

Text sent, I got out of bed, put on my exercise clothes, and looked for Angi. I found her giving Sophie a bath. "What are your plans today?"

"Blane is picking Sophie and me up at noon. We're going to Skeeter for lunch, then to the indoor carnival. He leaves tomorrow for a week, so we may make an evening of it too. Dinner and a movie at his place. I'll be home by nine or so. I have to work tomorrow."

"Okay. If you need me, I'll be in the shop."

I did my workout first, then headed up to my studio. *I've got to start thinking about Christmas.* An idea formed for Angi's Christmas gift. *I'll finish the watercolor of Sophie and have it matted and framed. I can print the pictures.* I had been taking candid shots of Angi, Sophie, and all of the events since they had arrived—a documentary of sorts. *A camera, I'll get her a nice camera, too.*

I turned on my music and began to paint. I was lost in the music and the stroke of the brush. The sunlight warmed the loft, releasing the faint scent of turpentine and eraser crumbs. I thought of Tony, how he wasn't rushing me. How he left me wanting more than a kiss on the nose last night. A smile tugged at my lips. *That Tony is one smart man.* I was so lost in my own little world, I almost missed the sound of the door opening. Looking down from the loft, I saw Angi and Blane standing in the doorway.

130

"I brought your keys, Miss Dawn. I've locked the cabin. We're on our way to Skeeter now."

"Thank you, Angi. You three have fun. Do me a favor and lock the shop door on your way out. I'm working on a painting, so I'll be here for a while."

She placed my keys on the table just inside the door. They waved goodbye and locked up.

I had been disappointed to learn she and Sophie would be gone until that night, but I needed to be realistic. I couldn't expect her to keep me company all the time. The disappointment faded as I became engrossed in painting, planning for Christmas, and thinking of Tony.

I marveled at the healing I experienced the past several weeks and the unconscious shift in my focus, from what I considered a pitiful existence to one of a full life… one with people I cared about and who cared for me. It was a life full of purpose and fulfillment. Shaking my head, I reflected on my past, self-centered behavior. How I wallowed in my misery and wore it like a mantle, weighing me down. *It's time to shed the misery.*

***

Around five, pleased with the progress of my painting, I stopped for the day and headed to the cabin. After a soak in the tub, I donned my comfy jammies, lit the logs in the fireplace, and threw together a simple meal of summer sausage, cheese, olives, tomatoes, and crackers. Balancing the plate in one hand, I picked up a glass of red wine and settled on the sofa. Anticipating the ring, I set the plate and glass on the coffee table and reached for my phone. Without looking at the screen, I answered. "Hello, Tony."

"Hi. I got your text. I'm glad you liked the flowers."

The conversation was pleasant. I thought maybe our ease at the restaurant was a fluke, but we were indeed comfortable with each other. As the conversation drew to an end, Tony paused. "Dawn, I have a lot to transition in preparation for retirement, which will include quite a bit of travel. That's why I won't be back in Chance until Christmas. I'd like to stay connected with you."

"I'd like that, Tony." We said our goodbyes, and I contemplated how fate had brought us together again after all those years.

The wine, backlit by the fire, summoned me. I took a bite of cheese, a sip of wine, then grabbed my Kindle—it kept me company while I ate. A trace of wood smoke suffused the air, and the evening slipped away in contentment. The driveway announcer roused me just after nine. A few minutes later, Angi walked through the door with a sleeping Sophie.

"Where's Blane?" I asked.

"He dropped me off at Roxie, and I drove myself home." She sat in the rocker. Sophie continued to sleep.

"So, Angi, I hope you know we have some shopping to do."

"We do?"

"Yes, we've got to get this place ready for Christmas. I've never spent Christmas here. Mike and I always stayed home for Christmas, which means I have no decorations here. Zero. Zip. Nada. Should we get a live tree or an artificial one? And we'll need ornaments and lights."

Angi's eyes shined with excitement. "I've never had a Christmas tree."

"Angi McFarland, you can't be serious."

"I swear. I've never had a Christmas tree."

I thought for a moment. "That settles it. We'll get a real tree but not one that's been cut down. We'll get a live one that we can plant after Christmas. Do you feel like a road trip?" The ideas spilled from my brain directly out my mouth in a continuous flow. "Friday, when you get off work, we can drive to Tulsa and stay in a hotel on seventy-first street somewhere between Memorial and Mingo. We can have a shop till you drop day on Saturday and eat out. What do you think? You want to go?"

"That would be so much fun."

"Alrighty then. Get everything packed before Friday. I'll load the van while you're at work, and we can take off as soon as you get home."

It took me a while to fall asleep. The excitement of the impending shopping trip kept my brain alert, envisioning more things we could do and buy. In an attempt to divert my thoughts, I opened my Kindle and read. Sleep claimed me thirty minutes later.

19.

Fa La La La La!
Christmas Decorating Done Right

Tuesday through Thursday were much the same. Each day, I went about my morning routine, which included going to my studio to work on the painting for Angi. An idea had formed regarding a painting for Tony. Rooting through some old photos would be required.

My alarm woke me Friday morning. I usually didn't set it, but I wanted to ensure everything was completed, so we could leave on our Tulsa excursion as soon as Angi returned from work.

I met Angi in the kitchen. "How long have you been up?"

The excitement crashed off her like a tsunami. "I've been up long enough that I should be tired, but I'm not. I'm all packed and everything is sitting by the front door. If we're slow at the cafe, I know Cici will let me go early."

"Don't worry about the time, we have all weekend. I don't want you to stress. I want this to be a fun time for both of us."

"It will be. I've never had a Christmas tree." Eyes bright, she bounced with nervous energy. A few minutes later, Angi gathered Sophie and left me alone with my plans.

***

Angi arrived at the cabin around three. Cici had indeed let her go early.

"The van is packed and I'm ready to go. How about you and Sophie?"

Angi handed Sophie to me. "Let me just grab a few bottles for Sophie, and then we're ready."

We were on the road in no time. "I thought we'd stop in Okmulgee and grab a bite to eat there, then drive straight to the hotel. What do you think?"

"Sounds good to me. Where are we staying?"

"The Courtyard Marriott by Woodland Hills Mall. They have an indoor pool and a hot tub. Did you pack a swimsuit?"

Angi looked crestfallen. "No. I don't have one."

"No problemo. I packed an extra one just in case."

A mixture of emotions crossed her face. I could imagine what she thought her suit would look like.

On the road, Sophie was delighted with the sights that whizzed by the window. She entertained herself for about ten minutes before her head lulled to the side and her lashes brushed her cheeks. Angi and I sang along to Christmas music and enjoyed the scenic drive. We pulled into Okmulgee about five-thirty. "Do you like Mexican food?"

Angi shook her head. "No. I love Mexican food."

"Well, it's a good thing because we're stopping at El Tapatio. I've never eaten there, but they're rated four and a half stars out of five. How do you feel about driving the rest of the way to Tulsa after we eat? It's about an hour from here."

"No problem. I know where I am now."

"Good, because I want to try one of their margaritas. You can tell how good a Mexican restaurant is by the quality of their margaritas."

Suffice it to say, the margarita was excellent, and the meal was delicious. The smoky aroma of grilled veggies and fajitas clung to our hair and clothes when we left. Angi drove us straight to the hotel without incident. We arrived just before eight. Night had settled like a velvet throw. Soft white lights illuminated the off-white and salmon colors of the hotel exterior. Green neon lights circled the top of the building.

Angi parked in the portico so I could get us checked in. She leaned over the steering wheel and craned her neck upward to peer out the windshield at the hotel. "Oh, this is beautiful."

"Wait till you see the room. I kind of splurged. I got us a double king suite."

Her eyes grew larger. "You didn't."

"This is a special occasion, and I intend to celebrate. Besides, I have money I haven't spent yet."

I left Angi shaking her head and got us checked in. As we entered our room, Angi squealed. "Oh, it's so pretty. I've never stayed anywhere like this before."

That was the exact reaction I hoped for. I felt euphoric. My empath shields were down, and Angi's enchantment surrounded me. I floated on a cloud of elation and was overwhelmed by her wonder and our combined emotions.

Angi turned to me with a stunned expression. "What is that?"

"You mean that feeling of euphoria? Neither of us are blocking our emotions. It's not our individual joy we feel, but our combined emotions. This is the upside of being an empath."

"I've never felt anything like this. It could be kind of addicting."

"I have experienced something similar, but never with this intensity. I think it's because we're both empaths, and we have formed some kind of shared bond. Let's unpack, then visit the hot tub."

I threw a bikini on Angi's bed. A look of complete surprise crossed her face. "You wear bikinis?"

"I guess at my age I shouldn't, but age is just a number, right? I don't even want to know what type of bathing suit you thought I packed for you."

***

A warm mist hung in the air, a faint scent of chlorine tickled my nose, and tiny water bubbles popped as the hot liquid swirled around us. Sophie dozed in her baby carrier, and I relaxed and formulated a plan for the next day.

A half hour later, our plans were made, and the stiffness of the long car ride was eased by our soak. We collected Sophie and returned to our room. The message light blinked on the phone. After calling the front desk, I replaced the handset and looked at Angi while I tried to suppress a smile.

"What?"

"Someone has a delivery at the front desk, and when I say someone, I mean you."

"What?"

"I'll watch Sophie. You go get your delivery."

I may have mentioned to Tony how Angi had hoped the flowers left for me were for her. Knowing Tony, he probably mentioned that to Blane.

A few minutes later, the thud of a tennis shoe sounded against the door. When I opened it, I couldn't see Angi because of the profusion of flowers she held. Her disembodied voice filtered through the blooms. "Look!"

I rode the high of Angi's elation. "How can I not? That's all I can see. How beautiful."

She placed the arrangement on the coffee table. Her excitement buzzed with intensity.

"So, who are they from?" *As if I didn't know.*

A look of confusion crossed her face. "I don't know."

"Wasn't there a card?"

"A card?"

I walked over to inspect the flowers, and amidst the profusion of color and scent was a small white envelope nestled among the greenery. I pointed to it.

She eased the envelope from the green depths and slid the card out. As she read the card, her eyes brightened, her face softened, and a sweet smile lifted the corners of her mouth. A slurry of emotions emanated from her.

Oops, shields, Dawn—empath etiquette.

Angi looked at me. "They're from Blane." She read the card aloud to me. "'Missing my girls. Have fun shopping. I'll be home soon. Love, Blane.' He signed it with Love! He's never said that before."

"Can I drop my shields?"

"Absolutely."

We both laughed. I dropped my empath shields and was swept away by a torrent of elation. "That was a nice way to end the day," I said.

We were in bed by 10 p.m. with the lights out.

***

I was awakened by the vibration of my phone alarm at 7 a.m. In measured movements, I pulled on my jeans and dropped a turtleneck sweater over my head. Determined to let Angi sleep in, I slipped downstairs to retrieve a continental breakfast for both of us. Opening the door to our room, I was greeted by the aroma of fresh brewed coffee, and the lights were on.

I spread the breakfast out on the coffee table. Angi tucked Sophie into the corner of the couch and propped a bottle with a pillow for her, then joined me. Before long, we had completed our morning rituals.

***

We walked through the doors of Lowe's in Tulsa Hills and were blasted by a current of warm air and pine-scented spray mingled with the essence of sawdust. Christmas music played, and we were surrounded by frenzied activity in the lawn and garden department, where all the holiday decor and tree ornaments were staged. There were artificial trees, large snow globes, and inflatables galore.

"All I can say is, it's a good thing I drove the van," I exclaimed.

An hour later, wide-eyed Angi couldn't contain her excitement. "I can't believe all the stuff you're buying, and this is just the first store."

"Well darn it, you've never had a Christmas tree."

"Yeah, but most of this stuff isn't even for a tree."

I arched one eyebrow. "So, if you've never had a tree, I bet you've never had lawn ornaments either."

138

She shook her head, and a smile lit her face.

***

By the time five rolled around, we visited multiple stores and purchased every conceivable Christmas decoration I deemed necessary to initiate Angi into Christmas decorating done right. Being able to do this for her brought me more joy than I could have fathomed.

Angi and I loaded everything in the van, then buckled ourselves in. "What do you say we go back to the hotel so you can feed Sophie? We'll take a little breather, then go to dinner."

"Sounds good to me," Angi said.

"Angi, have you ever eaten at Fish Daddy's?"

"No, but I love seafood."

"Well, you're in for a treat then."

As soon as we walked in the door of Fish Daddy's, I spied an empty table in the bar area, and I saw my two favorite bartenders, Irene and Brandy. I hadn't seen them since Mike and Gracie's funerals. Mike and I came here almost every Friday night for years. Irene and Brandy always took care of us.

Irene was exotic-looking—Hispanic, with all the beauty inherent to that gene pool. Smooth brown skin, large doe eyes, and a personality that filled a room. She gave a scream of delight and rushed to me. Throwing her arms around me, she said, "It's about time you came to see me. And look at that beautiful baby." She held out her arms for Sophie. As if sucked into the vortex of Irene's charm, Sophie turned her head and leaned towards her. Angi handed Sophie over. We watched as Irene danced her around the tables of the regulars.

Brandy, who radiated a more subtle charm, placed menus on our table. "It's so good to see you, Dawn. Who have you brought with you?"

"This is my niece, Angi. We came to Tulsa to do some Christmas shopping. And you know I couldn't come to Tulsa without seeing my two favorite bartenders."

Irene continued to cavort with Sophie, so Brandy asked, "You want your usual limousine?"

"You better believe it. I haven't had one in about a year."

Angi asked, "What's a limousine?"

"It's the best frozen margarita ever, with sangria swirled through it. By the way, I hope you don't mind that I introduced you as my niece. That's how I feel about you."

Angi's eyes brightened, and her shy smile appeared. "I like that you called me your niece. It made me feel like you are my real aunt."

We had a delightful dinner. I paid the check and marveled at how much my life continued to flourish. My heart was full—until it wasn't.

"What's wrong, Angi?"

Her frantic energy pummeled me. She drew Sophie closer to her and looked past my shoulder. Her eyes rounded in fear. Then I heard his voice coming from behind me.

"Well, well, well. Angi. And a baby."

I turned to see Nick studying Angi and Sophie. I was about to tell him to move along when an attractive woman joined him.

She clutched Nick's arm to her breast in a possessive gesture. "Oh, Nicky, look at that precious baby." She spoke his name with intimate familiarity. And at that moment, I felt her longing as she gazed at Sophie, and then I felt her sense of loss and desperation.

Never let it be said that I would miss an opportunity for a payback. I glanced at the woman and Nick, then, flashing a pleasant smile, I zeroed in on Nick. "Hello, Nicky. How do you know my niece, and who might this enchanting woman be?"

Nick paled and mumbled, "I think our table's ready." Then he propelled the woman forward away from the bar area. I heard her ask him who we were.

Angi was dumbstruck. She looked at me in awe.

I gave her a wink. "And that, my dear, is how it's done."

"How what's done?"

"How you take out the trash without lifting a finger."

Her hand flew to her mouth to stifle a laugh, and her fear dissipated. "I'll bet that was his wife, and that's why he didn't say more."

"I'm counting on it." I chuckled. "Don't let him in your head, Angi. Don't give him any power over you. When you think about it, you have the ability to ruin his night and perhaps his life. Just imagine what you could tell her." My reasoning was working. As Angi considered the secrets she could wield, she felt empowered, and I felt her confidence return.

***

Back in our room, I informed Angi, "I'd like to go to the IHOP for breakfast tomorrow morning then head back to Chance because we need to stop and pick out a live tree. There's a Christmas tree farm on the way, and I know the guy that owns it. We can pick one out, and he'll deliver it."

Angi's hands fisted and moved in tandem with her feet as she did a happy dance punctuated by a one-armed fist pump. "Yes!"

As I lay in bed, waiting for sleep to claim me, I thought about the events of the past two days, and of how much fun I'd had. Thoughts of Mike and Gracie eased their way in like tendrils of smoke from a campfire. I wished they could meet Angi. They would both love her. I smiled as I drifted off to sleep.

In the depths of my sleep, I felt a presence. Then the side of the bed dipped down. I opened my eyes, and Mike sat on the edge of the bed. He placed his hand on my hip.

Gracie stood behind Mike, with her hand on his shoulder. They both smiled at me and looked over at Angi. Slowly, they nodded their heads, as if to tell me they approved of what I was doing. Gracie stepped around Mike and walked towards me. She bent down and gave me a hug. Mike patted my hip, and then my eyes truly opened.

I was alone in the darkness, except for the rhythmic breathing of Angi and Sophie. There was a feeling of love so intense that it took my breath away. A calmness enfolded me, and I slept.

I awoke to the sounds of Angi making coffee. "I know we're going to the IHOP, but I thought we could use a little jump start." She grinned and handed me a cup.

"Coffee in bed? You're spoiling me."

"I, uh, I had another dream last night."

I looked at her over the top of my coffee mug. "Don't tell me, let me see if I can tell you what you dreamed."

I proceeded to tell her my dream as her eyes got larger and larger.

"Yes!" she said. "That was the exact dream, except in my dream, they knew I was watching, and they looked over at me. They smiled, as if they were introducing themselves. I felt... I don't know, like I met them, and they liked me."

"Well, this is new territory for me. I've never shared dreams with anyone before, but I think it's pretty cool."

***

We arrived at the restaurant by eight-thirty and as we finished our breakfast, I lowered my empath shields to ask Angi a question. I wanted to feel her response as much as hear it.

"Is there anyone you'd like to see while we're in Tulsa? Your mother, perhaps?"

An immediate gust of emotions buffeted me like fast-moving winds of a rainstorm. Feelings of pain, desolation, and inadequacy rolled toward me—then, a glimmer of hope.

Angi's eyes searched mine. "I'd like to stop by my mom's. She's never seen Sophie, and she is my mother."

***

As we approached a series of dilapidated mobile homes, Angi placed her hand on my arm. "Stop between the pink and blue ones."

I nosed the van to the curb and kept the engine running. Angi's eyes darted around the two lots. Her breathing became rapid, and she gulped. "See that doghouse between the two trailers? That's where I used to hide. And that blue trailer, that's where I lived."

The skirting was missing, and the trailer listed to one side. The paint had faded to an oxidized wan-blue. Rust ran from the roof in intermittent streams. Window screens were either torn, missing, or leaned against the trailer at odd angles.

At that moment, the front door exploded open and crashed against the outside wall. A disheveled man stood on the top cinder block that substituted for stairs and leaned drunkenly against the doorframe as he endeavored to get a foot in a boot that was turned sideways. A cowboy hat sailed out the doorway to land on a desolate patch of yard, and an empty beer bottle soon followed. The man stumbled down the steps, grabbed his hat, and lurched towards his car.

An unkempt woman appeared in the doorway. A cigarette dangled from her mouth. "And don't come back!" she yelled as she gave him the one-finger salute, then turned back into her trailer, slamming the door.

Angi and I sat in stunned silence for a moment. Angi lowered her head, but not before I saw her eyes glisten and her nose turn red and start to run. I felt her embarrassment and shame. So, I did the only thing I could think of: I handed her a tissue, then eased away from the curb. "I hope you realize your mother and her actions do not define you. You are making a productive life for yourself and Sophie. She made her choices, and you get to make yours." Angi nodded and wiped her eyes. "Alrighty then, we're off to pick out a Christmas tree. And not just any old Christmas tree but the best Christmas tree ever."

A couple of miles down the road, I cranked on the radio. "Angi, you're in charge of tunes."

She sped through the stations and selected one. Before long, we both sang along as Sophie listened with an open-mouthed grin that allowed drool to string from chin to bib.

We arrived at *Shep's Christmas Trees* a couple of hours later, and as I pulled into the lot, I was flooded with memories of my childhood. My dad used to bring me here. Old Shep was gone, but his grandson, Jasper, ran the place now. I had known him since we were both kids.

When I stepped out of the van, Jasper leaned out of a small wooden shack that served as his office, a grin splitting his face. He loped towards me with an uneven gait and wrapped me in a hug.

"It's good to see ya, Dawn. Who's that perty little gal with ya?"

"Jasper, that's my niece, and she is too young for the likes of you."

He chuckled. "Well now, you know how us country boys are. You can't blame a man for tryin'."

"You're trying all right. Very trying."

Angi sidled up while we were still laughing. "Watch this one, Angi, he's a lecherous old man."

"Aw, I ain't lecherous. I just know a perty gal when I see one."

Angi bounced Sophie, blushed, and said, "Hi."

"Jasper, I want a live tree this year, one that I can plant after Christmas."

"Well, I can fix you up with a live tree sure enough, but don't go planting her right after Christmas. She won't survive the cold and the drying winds. You can put her in the garage and water her regular until early spring, then plant her."

"I was wondering about that. Hey, will you deliver the tree for me?"

I could see the wheels turning in his head, and I knew he'd angle for something.

"Well, I could be tempted to deliver a tree if the scent of a home-cooked meal was in the air."

"You're on, and instead of just a home-cooked meal, how about a meal and a party? Say, next Friday evening, six o'clock?"

"Now you're talking."

Jasper guided us down row after row of trees. After what felt like an eternity, I spied the perfect one. As I pointed at the spruce, Jasper's Old English Sheepdog hiked his leg and peed on it.

144

Jasper chuckled. "It appears Rags is in agreement with ya."

Angi gave a thumbs-up sign, so Jasper tagged the tree and jotted a note in a spiral pad.

Back on the road, Angi cleared her throat. "What party were you talking about with Jasper?"

"Sweetheart, you don't just decorate a tree when you've never had one before. You have a party and decorate—everything. We'll invite Cici, Blane, Tony—although Tony won't be able to come—Diane, Steve, and Katie. I'll fix dinner, make fudge, apple cider, and cookies. Oh, and eggnog."

It was happening again. Our empath shields weren't in place, and our combined energy billowed like a cloud, heightening our delight.

Up ahead, I saw a Dairy Queen. I made a command decision and whipped the van into the parking lot. "I need a dip cone. And not one of those candy-ass little ones either. I'm getting a large one."

Angi gaped at me. "I've never seen you eat junk food. I mean, the closest I've seen you come is a burger and fries from Cici's."

"Go big or go home. We're still celebrating."

Angi laughed. "Then I want a large one, too."

After relaxing over our cones, we drove the rest of the way to the cabin without stopping.

***

After dinner, I curled up on the couch and texted Tony. I knew he was in New York, but I told him about the party anyway. I figured it was always nice to be invited to an event, even if a person couldn't go. And, as I suspected, he didn't think he'd be able to come but appreciated being included. We texted a few minutes more, then I texted 'Good night.' I was ready to soak in my tub and sleep in my own bed.

20.

The Debatable Inflatables

How Many Lawn Ornaments Does One Woman Need?

On Monday, I called Cici and Diane to invite them to Friday's festivities. I let Angi invite Blane. Cici agreed to come over Tuesday evening and help me with the yard ornaments.

The painting for Angi was finished. I ordered a camera and photo album for her off Amazon. Then I took out one of my finds from the Dollar Tree store—plain, red and green Christmas stockings. I got out my glue gun, bedazzle kit, and glitter, and went to work.

***

Stew simmered in the crockpot. I expected Cici to arrive shortly and hoped Blane would show up, too.

At four, I heard the driveway announcer, and Cici pulled up soon after. I stepped outside to see him surveying the myriad boxes of decorations on the front porch. He cocked an eyebrow at me as he crossed his arms over his chest.

"Dawn Patterson, what have you gotten me into? I thought you had just a few things to assemble, and I'd be able to

146

knock it out tonight. This does not look like a one and done kinda deal."

"It's not as bad as it looks. A lot of those boxes have inflatable things. I mean, how hard can it be to put up inflatables? There is a large manger scene for the front porch and—"

"Dawn, how many inflatables?"

"Oh, well, let me see. There's the life-sized Santa, sled, and reindeer. Oh, and the—"

Cici held up his hands in a stopping gesture. "I don't want to hear the rest. It will depress me." Resigned to his fate, he shook his head, and we got to work opening boxes.

A few minutes later, Blane pulled in. "Angi said you might need a hand with the yard ornaments." Pointing his index finger, he began counting the boxes and started chuckling. "She said you went a little crazy buying stuff. But this, Dawn?"

Fisting my hands on my hips, I glared at both of them. "I want to make this Christmas special for Angi and Sophie. Have you got a problem with that?"

Blane shook his head, "No, ma'am. I'm on it. Did you get any outdoor lights?"

"Crap. I knew I forgot something."

Cici opened another box. "Blane, don't worry about the lights tonight. Help me with all these inflatables. Tomorrow we can pick up the lights and come back over."

Cici bent over an open box, glanced up, and pinned me with a look. "You owe me big time. I want chicken and dumplings tomorrow and a lemon meringue pie."

My chin lifted, and an eyebrow raised. "Fine. Chicken and dumplings."

An hour and a half later, with the three of us working, we got all the inflatables set up in the yard. The task wasn't difficult; we just had to plug them in, and they inflated themselves. There was another yard ornament, not an inflatable, which required assembling and was kicking their behinds. Two snowmen sat atop a teeter-totter, which moved up and down. The snowmen lit up, or should, once Cici and Blane figured out how to assemble it or resorted to reading the instructions.

Gravel crunched on the drive as Angi's car appeared. She sprang from the car amid squeals. I didn't know if her excitement was for the decorations or the sight of Blane. She hadn't seen him in over a week.

Blane closed the distance between them, picked her up, and swung her in a circle. Her delighted laughter cut through the crisp air like the tinkling of wind chimes.

"This is wonderful," she said. "I've never seen anything like it before. Not in real life."

I stole a glance at Cici and saw him grinning. I leaned over and whispered, "See, Mr. Scrooge—so worth it."

He cut his eyes to me and tried to look like a hard ass, but just couldn't pull off the look.

***

Wednesday morning, I bounded out of bed at 6 a.m., no alarm needed. I was excited about the painting for Tony, and I had to go to the grocery store to pick up the fixings for Friday night's party. My mood was elevated with my renewed sense of purpose. *Caring for others feels so good, so revitalizing.*

I marveled at my emotional healing. The loss, although still there, no longer consumed me. It was as if the ache had been packed away. The emotion wasn't gone, but the pain was no longer like a piece of unwanted furniture in the middle of a room. No longer an emotional tripping hazard, I could traverse my grief and focus on the wonderful memories I had of Gracie and Mike, and the love I still felt for them. I said a silent prayer of thanksgiving and prepared for the upcoming evening of decorating with the gang. *I hope the guys can conquer the snowmen.*

21.

Falling

The Moment You Know

The rest of the week blew by like leaves on a blustery fall day. It was Friday already. Apple cider warmed on the stovetop, releasing a cinnamon fragrance, and the soft notes of Christmas melodies helped to set the mood.

As I hung the last stocking on the fireplace mantel. The driveway announcer signaled an arrival, and I wagered it was Jasper. Tapping my chin with my index finger, I surveyed the living room and made my decision—the tree would stand in front of the picture window.

I opened the front door and hollered at Jasper. "Leave the tree in the truck until Cici and Blane get here. They'll show up any minute."

He grinned and made his way into the cabin. "Lord, but it smells good in here!"

I retreated to the kitchen with Jasper on my heels. He snagged a cookie from a platter, and after he finished the cookie, he popped a piece of fudge into his mouth. With a wistful glance at the sweets, he swiped the back of his hand across his lips. "I think I'll wait outside so I don't ruin my supper."

The driveway announcer chimed a couple of times in succession. I came out of the kitchen and heard a scuffle at the front door. Jasper hollered at Cici and Blane, "Ain't y'all never brung a tree in a house before? Back 'er up boys, turn 'er around, and bring 'er in backside first." He winked at me as he chuckled and continued to bark orders.

After a few awkward maneuvers, Cici and Blane managed to turn and push the back end of the tree through the open doorway without breaking anything. Resplendent in its natural beauty, the boughs obscured the view out the front window. A red felt tree skirt from my youth draped around the bucket that housed the root ball and lent an air of nostalgia. Just then, Diane, Steve, and Katie breezed through the door laden with trays and containers.

Sophie, suspended in the swing, kicked her legs and watched everything from the doorway of Angi's room.

Angi brought in an armload of boxed ornaments and set them close to the tree.

"Hold on, Angi," I told her. "We've got to get the lights on the tree first."

I observed the room with delight. The gang was all there except Tony. A wave of disappointment engulfed me, but I let the disappointment go. *No time for that.* "Hey, everybody, why don't we eat first, decorate the tree, then have dessert?"

The group nodded in agreement.

Diane and I set the food out buffet style, and as we sat down to eat, the driveway announcer sounded again. At once, all eyes were on me. "What?" I asked as I peered around the table.

Diane's eyes widened, and she shook her head. "Nothing."

Her response was a little too quick, the headshake a little too emphatic. Everyone diverted their gaze and looked everywhere else but me. However, they couldn't stop grinning. Only Jasper looked as baffled as me. Halfway to the door, I heard the doorbell and opened the door to a smiling Tony. "I thought you were in New York!"

He sauntered through the door and wrapped his arms around me, enfolding me in his warmth and intoxicating scent. His lips brushed my ear as he whispered, "I couldn't leave my best girl dateless when she's hosting a Christmas party."

"Your *best* girl?"

He pulled back so he could look me in the eyes. "Okay," he chuckled, "My only girl." Surprising me further, he cupped my face in his hands, and in a slow, deliberate motion, he brought his lips to mine. The heat of his intent reached me before his lips. His hooded eyelids lowered, then closed as his lips touched mine in a soft greeting that conveyed a need and desire that pierced me to my core.

I felt as though I was suspended on a precipice… a moment in time where I was poised to leap from a cliff, and then I did. For an instant, it was as if I hung in the air before my rapid descent. That was when I knew. The kiss ended amid clapping, whooping, hollering, and whistles from the group.

I turned to see the faces of all my guests lining both sides of the doorway of my kitchen in cartoon fashion. I blushed, which I did every time Tony was near.

I leveled a counterfeit glare at them. "You all knew about this, didn't you?"

"I didn't, dang it!" Jasper said in mock disdain. "I guess this means I ain't got no chance." Then he shot me a wink and a grin.

The room erupted in laughter. Tony steered me towards the kitchen. "Come on, I'm starving."

Amid the laughter and light banter of conversation, I was almost overwhelmed by my emotions. Then they leveled out, and I was at peace… content. Confiding in Angi had opened me up to feeling again. My entire being resonated with all the emotions I hadn't experienced the past year.

Tony's eyes lingered on me.

"What?" I asked

He leaned over and whispered, "You're glowing."

From the other end of the table, Blane noticed Tony whisper to me, and he grunted, "Get a room."

I rolled my eyes. We finished dinner and moved to the living room, where Blane explained to Angi the sequence of decorating a tree. It was time for the ornaments. I sat back and watched as Angi and Katie decorated. Blane held Sophie and stood near the tree so she could be a part of the excitement.

I grabbed my camera and took the last of the pictures I planned to give Angi as part of her Christmas present. I had captured many of Sophie's firsts since they had arrived in Chance.

With the tree decorated, I encouraged everyone to empty their stockings and invited them all to another party next year. Jasper raised an eyebrow with an unspoken question.

"Yes, Jasper, that means you, too," I said.

Fidgeting, he asked, "Is it okay if I bring some apple pie moonshine next year?"

"Yes, but only if you'll spend the night."

***

Tony and I stood on the front porch waving as Steve, Diane, Katie, and Jasper left. Blane was in the cabin with Angi and Sophie.

I grabbed the blanket from the porch swing. "Let's sit in the swing for a bit." We wrapped up in the blanket. I gazed at the manger scene illuminated by the light bulb that showed through the cutout Star of Bethlehem. Tony drew me close. We sat in comfortable silence, looking at all the lawn ornaments. Tony broke the silence. "You went all out to make this special for Angi, didn't you?"

"Tony, she's never had a tree or Christmas before."

"You don't have to explain or justify yourself to me. All of this," he nodded to indicate the yard, "what you did for Angi, these are a few of the many things I love about you." He leaned over and kissed me again. The kiss was more intense than the soft touch of his lips earlier this evening. There was an urgency and need that quickened my breath and my heartbeat. I felt a heat in my core that spiraled outward. And just like that, I felt overwhelmed and drew away.

"Too soon?" he asked.

"I'm not sure. It's hard to explain. For almost a year, I couldn't feel anything except anger, grief, and sadness. But in the past several months, since Angi has been here, I've started to open up, started to feel again. But tonight? It's like I've been feeling every emotion known to man. I'm on sensory overload."

He kissed the top of my head. "I get it. I've been where you are. In fact, I took longer to get there. Grief consumed me for several years. I ran from it, but I came to the realization that you can't outrun misery. The despair follows you like the tail of a dog.

"I'm not going to rush you. When you're ready for more, I'll be available. I'm going to my house in Tulsa tomorrow morning, and I'll fly back to New York on Sunday."

I felt an immediate sense of loss. I wasn't ready for him to go, but my emotions were such a jumble. Maybe his departure was for the best.

We stood, and he held me close. I felt his longing as it joined my own, as if we were two broken pieces of pottery that needed repairing—glued together. Taking a step back, he gathered both of my hands in his. "I'll be back for Christmas. Take some time to sort your emotions, then give me a call." He squeezed my hands. "Goodnight, Dawn." He turned and walked to his car.

"Goodnight, Tony."

***

Later, as I laid in bed replaying the events of the evening, a thought occurred to me: *That Tony, he is one smart man.* He knew how to read people, how to reach them through their own desires. Never pressing, just giving little hints. Kind of like planting a seed, then leaving it up to the person to nurture that seed and let it grow or not. Once there was an awareness of the desire, just the smallest inkling, he backed off. A person would be drawn in, would pay more attention. Like, hey, wait a minute. I was just exploring something, and you're going to leave? Just leave me hanging—wanting more?

Oh yes, Tony Rossi was a very smart man.

My thoughts drifted to Gracie and Mike. As sleep pulled me under, I felt a familiar dip in the mattress. I knew Mike was there.

I smiled and opened my eyes. Like before, Gracie was with Mike. He took my hand and stood, bringing me to my feet. Gracie stepped to my other side and took my free hand. Together, they led me into a bright light. I had to squint at first, but once my eyes adjusted, I saw that we were in a field of green grass drenched in sunlight. There were trees on the periphery. A slight breeze moved the branches, casting dancing shadows. As we got closer, I saw a lone figure relaxing in the grass. I knew this place. We were on the parade field of Fort Gordon, and that figure was Tony. He chewed a long blade of grass and was oblivious to our presence.

Mike turned to me, and a flower magically appeared in his hand. The bloom was a red chrysanthemum. He smiled lovingly as he handed it to me. Then a sprig of Arborvitae appeared, then some sweet basil, butterfly weed, pink carnation, white chrysanthemum, Goldenrod, and lastly Myrtle.

I held the beautiful bouquet of flowers and greenery, then Gracie gently took them from me and placed them in a crystal vase. Before handing them back to me, she made a show of nodding towards Tony. She then handed the heavy vase of flowers to me one-handed—her right hand. She leaned in and kissed my cheek. Mike kissed my other cheek. They clasped hands and walked backward in the direction of Tony, obscuring him from my view. They waved to me and slowly became translucent, then filmy until they disappeared like a veil of smoke. I was left looking at Tony. He raised his hand and waved in greeting, and then I woke.

I sat on the side of my bed, head in my hands, overcome with the sweetness of the moment. *The flowers, they mean something.* I turned on the bedside lamp and grabbed a pencil and piece of paper. I wrote down every detail from the dream while it was fresh in my mind.

I listed the flowers and the sequence of the events. I was wide awake, so I grabbed my laptop and started looking into the meaning of flowers, and was surprised to find that there was a language of flowers from the Victorian era. Flowers have different meanings from around the world, but I focused on the meanings from the Victorian era.

Mike smiled and handed me a red chrysanthemum. Hmm. There. A list.

Red Chrysanthemum: I love you
Arborvitae: Unchanging friendship
Sweet Basil: Good wishes
Butterfly Weed: Let me go
Pink Carnation: I will never forget you
White Chrysanthemum: Truth
Goldenrod: Good fortune
Myrtle: Good luck and love in marriage

Gracie nodded her head at Tony and handed me the vase of flowers with her right hand. *Let's see... here it is, in the online Old Farmer's Almanac:*

"In the Victorian era, flowers were primarily used to deliver messages that couldn't be spoken aloud. In a sort of silent dialogue, flowers could be used to answer 'yes' or 'no' questions. A 'yes' answer came in the form of flowers handed over with the right hand; if the left hand was used, the answer was 'no.'

Hmm, so Gracie nodded at Tony and handed me the vase with her right hand—meaning, yes?

It couldn't be any plainer than that. I read my list again, and I was filled with a euphoric sense of encouragement, bittersweet goodbyes, new beginnings, and above all, love and acceptance. Tears streamed down my face. I took a shuddering breath, then heard a faint noise at my door.

"Miss Dawn. What happened? I had another dream and now this wonderful feeling but—you're crying. I don't understand."

She sat beside me, put her arm around me, and tears streamed down her face, too. "Oh, you're happy. You're crying because you're happy."

We started laughing in unison. We were doing it again.

"Was your dream about Mike and Gracie taking me to a field of grass and handing me flowers?"

"Yes! What does the dream mean?"

I grinned at her. "Well, it just so happens I can tell you. At least, I can tell you what I think the dream means."

I read the list and explained the symbolism, and Angi's eyes glowed with understanding.

"I know that's what the dream means. I can just feel the meaning."

I glanced at the clock; the time was close to 1 a.m. "I think I'm going to try to get some sleep now."

Angi nodded. "Yeah, me too."

I fell into a deep sleep, then woke up refreshed. "Oh, my gawd, there are only eleven days till Christmas. I've got to get a move on." I threw back the covers and headed to the kitchen for coffee. I made a mental list as I looked for paper and a pencil.

"Morning," Angi said as she covered a yawn with her hand. She placed Sophie in the bouncy seat and joined me at the table. "What have you got planned today?"

"I've got a bunch of errands to run. Do you realize that Christmas is just eleven days away?"

"I know, right?"

***

I sat at the printing kiosk at Walmart and studied the pictures I had just downloaded from my phone. I wanted to capture the chronological history of Angi's new life in Chance. Printing the pictures took me a couple of hours. There were so many photos, and of course, I had to edit them to make them perfect.

Hmm, should I put them in the album for her? Nope. She should have the joy of doing that herself.

As I shopped, I thought of the painting I was working on for Tony and decided I needed to add something to it. I'd have to start on the painting as soon as I finished my errands.

Shopping for just the right gift for each person, I felt light in my spirit. There was a tingling in my bloodstream. Energy and determination filled me, and I couldn't stop smiling.

***

After arriving home with all my treasures, I worked on the painting for Tony. Standing back from the easel, I surveyed my work with a critical eye, and it pleased me. However, at 10 p.m., fatigue held me in its grip. With supplies put away and the door locked, I walked out into the moonlight. The wintry night air was overlaid with the scent of burning wood. The stars ignited the sky. The front door of the cabin opened, and Angi stepped onto the porch carrying two mugs.

"Hi," she called. "I was just coming over to bring you some hot chocolate. You want to sit on the porch swing so we can gander at all this beauty?"

Rubbing the back of my stiff neck, I took the proffered cup and joined her on the swing. "This is a perfect way to end the day. Sophie asleep?"

"Yep." She met my gaze. "I don't know how I got so lucky. The first eighteen years of my life were…." She looked away. "They were hard. But now, I have the perfect baby, a great guy, good friends, and you." She ducked her head. "You mean so much to me. You're my family."

Wrapping my arm around her shoulder, I pulled her near and kissed her forehead. "Angi, it's mutual. You and Sophie saved me. There are no two ways about it. I had slipped into a well of despair that was so deep, I couldn't have crawled out on my own. You and Sophie came along, and it was like you threw me a lifeline. I can't begin to tell you how much you mean to me. I agree, we are family."

Her face lit up, and she jabbed a finger towards the sky. "Look, a shooting star!"

The steam from our mugs, barely visible in the moonlight, drifted into the cold night air. And like the ebb and flow of a gentle tide, our swing lulled us into companionable silence. A coyote's cry pierced the stillness, an answering call rolled in from the distance, and Angi giggled. I followed her gaze to the snowmen on the teeter-totter.

"What are you giggling about?"

"I was just thinking about the night Blane and Cici were setting up all the Christmas decorations and how much trouble that teeter-totter gave them. Being here, in Chance, it's been magical."

We continued our repose until our mugs were empty, then we made our way inside and said our goodnights.

***

The next ten days shot past, leaving an echo in their wake. I framed the painting for Tony. All the presents were wrapped and strategically placed under the tree. The baking was done, and the house was bursting with Christmas décor and cheer. The big event was almost here.

22.

A New Family Born!
A Surprising Possibility

Stretching in a languid motion, I lay in bed and replayed the previous night, my first Christmas Eve with Tony. True to his word, he made it back to Chance in time for the holiday. We shared a quiet evening with Blane, Angi, and Sophie, here in the cabin. We played Dominoes and discussed the meaning of Christmas for each of us. Angi's excitement was evident.

Tony hadn't pressed me or even called me after the tree decorating party. I took his suggestion to sort out my feelings first, and then I called him.

The dream—visitation—from Mike and Gracie made everything so much easier. I felt their approval and encouragement to pursue a relationship with Tony. I was able to be in the moment when Tony kissed me. And that man could kiss.

A glance at the clock startled me. Tony and Blane would be here in an hour and a half. *I'd better get in gear. It's Christmas!*

I smelled coffee as I made my way to the kitchen and saw that Angi had gotten the French press coffee maker out. "What, no Keurig coffee this morning?"

"A special day deserves special coffee, and we deserve special coffee."

I chuckled at her exuberance. "Merry Christmas, Angi. May this be the first of many wonderful Christmases for you."

I sipped my coffee and put the breakfast casserole together. After popping the dish in the oven, I headed to my bathroom to get ready.

Hmm, what to wear? Okay, bright red tunic sweater, black leggings, and black boots. I threw my hair onto hot curlers and started on makeup. I had become a minimalist in regard to makeup. I found, since I was of a certain age, less was more. Taking out the rollers, I shook out the curls, giving the long layers a waterfall effect that cascaded down my back. Next, gold hoop earrings.

I surveyed myself in the mirror. "Tony Rossi, look out. Ready or not, here I come."

My self-evaluation was interrupted by the doorbell. My stomach clinched, and my heart skipped a beat. Angi opened the door to Santa Tony, who carried a burlap bag full of gifts. My hips swayed to a silent rhythm as I entered the room and was greeted by a low wolf whistle emanating from his lips.

I paused. *Let's see if I can remember how to do this.* I gave him a seductive smile and a little wink as I sashayed over to place a light kiss on his lips. I backed away, hoping to leave him wanting more. Two could play that game.

I was pleased to note that he looked utterly gobsmacked. *Oh, this is going to be fun.*

Tony placed the bag by the tree, and the doorbell rang again. Blane had arrived.

"Okay," I announced, "how do we want to do this? Should we draw out the anticipation by eating first and then opening gifts? Or should we just dive in and open gifts?"

We all looked at Angi. "What are you looking at me for?" she asked.

I grinned. "It's your first Christmas, so you get to decide."

"Oh." She paused. "Let's eat first."

***

With breakfast out of the way, we gathered around the tree and sat on the floor. I took out the camera I had bought for

Angi and started taking pictures. "Angi, why don't you root around under the tree and find your and Sophie's gifts?"

"But what about you all?"

Tony smiled at her. "Angi, I think we all want to watch you enjoy your first Christmas."

"Yes," I added, and when you're finished, you can relieve me of camera duty and take pictures of us opening our gifts."

Sophie watched from her swing that was placed by the tree. She gurgled and reached towards a shiny ornament.

Angi, on her hands and knees, inspected the name tags on the gifts and squealed when she found her first present. She created a pile of hers and Sophie's gifts, then she gleefully ripped into Sophie's presents just like Diane had shown her at Sophie's birthday party.

She oohed and awed over all the clothes, toys, books, and stuffed animals, and held them up for Sophie to scrutinize. Then she moved on to her gifts. She paused and put her hand over her heart. Her eyes glistened, and she took a shuddering breath. "You have no idea how much this means to me."

She held up the painting first and burst into laughter. The watercolor depicted Sophie at her two-month birthday party, sprawled in her bouncy seat with the hint of a smile. Deep in slumber, the wisps of her staticky hair stood on end. "Oh, Miss Dawn, I love it."

Next, she opened two small boxes from Blane. One contained a gift certificate for a spa in Skeeter. The other held tickets to the Warren Theater in Tulsa for a movie and dinner on New Year's Eve.

From Tony, she received a generous Amazon gift card.

She opened the photo album next and hugged it to her. "Oh, I needed this so bad. The one I have is old and falling apart."

"Good. You're also going to need the album for your next two gifts," I said.

"You need to work on your math skills; there's only one more gift." She opened the box that contained all the pictures of her time in Chance, and her face contorted as she tried to contain her emotions. "It's perfect. Everything is just… perfect!"

"By the way," I said, "I know how to count just fine." I handed her the camera. "This is the second gift."

"O.M.G., O.M.G., O.M.G.! How did you know I wanted a camera? I mean, I have my phone camera, but it's not the same. Now I can get close-ups and do telephoto…." She trailed off and grabbed me in a tight hug. We both started giggling as we rode the endorphin rush of our combined emotions.

I went over the basic operations of the camera with her. "I have the instruction manual and warranty in my room."

She looked at Tony. "I know what I'm going to use that Amazon gift card for. I need a tripod and some other camera gear. This is so cool."

Tony, Blane, and I started to open our presents.

A gasp escaped from Tony. "Dawn, this is magnificent!"

He placed the painting on the floor and leaned it against the wall across from us so we could all get a good look.

I was proud of it. The picture showed Tony lounging on the parade field, chewing on a long blade of grass with a lazy smile etching his face—a hint of mischief. The light filtered through the leaves of the trees and highlighted his hair. I had added myself to the scene. I was seated in tailor fashion across from him. An easy smile shaped my lips. I was able to capture the look of admiration that I felt that day, as well as the first inkling of our romance on that parade field.

He crossed the room, put his arm around me, and pulled me close to his side. "I had no idea you were so talented."

I smiled and whispered, "I'm a woman of *many* talents."

He cleared his throat. "Oh, look. You're holding my gift to you."

In my hand was a small package. Inside, I found a folded piece of paper which stated *whether wiping tears of sorrow or joy, you will use one of these.*

The confusion was clear on my face. "I don't understand."

Angi announced, "It's a treasure hunt."

I peered at both. "Why do I get the feeling there was a little collusion going on here?"

I repeated the clue. "A handkerchief or a Kleenex?" I searched the room and saw a box of Kleenex.

I rushed to the box and pulled out a small card and read, *The opposite of top.* "Bottom?" I turned the box over and found another envelope taped to the bottom. *One might drink this on New Year's Eve.* "Champagne?"

I rushed to the kitchen to find a bottle of champagne in the fridge. A notecard dangled from a small string that was looped around the neck of the bottle. *Go where you can fast-forward and rewind.* "The safe room."

All gift openings had ceased as Tony, Blane, and Angi followed me on my trek. Blane carried Sophie, and Angi took pictures of everything. The anticipation and mystery were so intriguing.

I ran to the bookcase and made my way to the security camera viewing console. I found another envelope. *"Wakey, wakey?"*

I had to think for a moment. "Oh!" I pressed the spacebar, bringing the computer monitor to life. Live footage from the security camera covering the back of the house displayed a small, wrapped package dangling from the kitchen doorknob.

I ran back upstairs with my entourage close behind. I whipped open the door and grabbed the box. Inside the box were two more envelopes. I opened the first. "A meal and wine pairing at the Polo Grill in Tulsa. Wow, I've heard it's fabulous, but I've never been."

Angi bounced on her toes and tried to look over my shoulder. "What's in the second envelope?"

I pulled out a pair of tickets. "They're tickets to a New Year's Eve party at the Mayo Hotel and a two-night stay in a king suite."

I was thrilled and overwhelmed at the same time. "Tony, this is too much."

Blane couldn't contain himself. "When I said to get a room—you went all out."

Tony leveled his gaze at Blane. "The room is for Dawn. I have a house in Tulsa, remember?"

He pulled me close and whispered, "No pressure, just a fun weekend."

I was almost disappointed, but at the same time, I was relieved. I marveled at how well this man understood me… how he let me pick the pace.

***

We finished opening gifts and cleaned up the mess. We were going to Steve and Diane's for Christmas dinner later that evening, but were relaxing until then.

Angi retrieved her old photo album, and as she passed by me, several pictures fell from a frayed page that jutted out from the album. Gathering the photos, I noticed a picture of four young men with devilish grins and rakish good looks. I was stunned. I knew those young men. However, they were no longer young.

"Angi? Where did you get this picture? How do you know these men?"

"Let me see." She took the picture from me. "Oh. One of those men might be my grandpa."

With mild confusion, I asked, "Might be? Which one?"

Lowering her eyes, she said, "I don't know which one. I don't know who my father is either, but he told my mom that one of those men was his father. Mom didn't pay attention. She didn't remember which one. She hooked up with my father when she was nineteen. He was on a quest to find his biological father and was just passing through town. Mom met him at a bar, and he stayed with her a week before moving on, leaving this picture behind. A couple of months passed before she realized she was pregnant with me. She didn't even remember his name."

A lot of things connected for me. Our bond. The sense of familiarity when I first saw her. Our shared gifts.

"Angi, why was your dad on a quest to find his father?"

"It's ironic. His mother met a guy in Telluride, Colorado, who was working on the wheat harvest. They hooked up while he was there, and he was long gone by the time she found out she was pregnant. So, the guy that is my dad had never met his father and was trying to find him."

"That is ironic." I handed her the picture and excused myself. Tony gave me a curious look as I grabbed my coat and cell phone.

"I'll be back in a few minutes. I want to take a walk."

Outside, I checked the contacts in my phone and selected the number. The call rang once, twice, and was answered on the third ring. I was greeted by a familiar voice.

"Well, hello, stranger!"

"Well, hello yourself, stud muffin," I said.

A chuckle ensued. "I haven't been a stud muffin for a lot of years."

"I have a question for you. When you worked the wheat harvest, did you hook up with a gal in Telluride, Colorado?"

"Dawn, it's been, what, over forty years since I went on that wheat harvest? But yeah, there was this sweet gal in Telluride, and she could—"

"I don't want any sordid details."

"It's not sordid. I was just going to say she could make a guy forget his loneliness. The trip was my first time away from home. Exciting as the adventure was, I got homesick. Why do you ask?"

"Well, congratulations. It's a boy... and a girl... and another girl."

"Dawn, what the hell are you talking about?"

"I'm talking about the son you fathered in Telluride. And then while he was looking for you, he fathered a daughter that he doesn't know about. You have a son, a granddaughter, and oh yeah, a great granddaughter, too. Your granddaughter, Angi, has been living with me for several months. I just saw a picture of you and your three friends that went on the wheat harvest. She said her father told her mother that one of the men in that photo was his dad. Her mother couldn't remember which one. I haven't seen Angi's father, but Angi has a strong resemblance to your daughters. When I first saw her, she looked familiar, but I knew I'd never met her before. And she has gifts."

"No shit! When can I meet her?"

"I don't know. Let me talk to her about the possibility of you being her grandpa and see if she is up for meeting you."

"Hell yeah! Man, I can't believe it. I mean, I can, but it's… it's just crazy. I may have a son I didn't know about, and a granddaughter, and a great granddaughter."

"Let me talk to Angi. I'll call you back in a little while."

I put my cell phone in my pocket and contemplated how I was going to broach the subject with Angi as I walked back to the cabin. *I should just come right out with it.*

A soft click sounded as the cabin door eased shut, and I removed my coat. "Angi, I think I know who your grandpa is."

Her eyes darted at me. "What? How? Who do you think he is?"

I held out my hand. "Let's take another look at that picture of the four men."

She sat beside me on the couch. I held the picture and pointed. "That is Jim, this is Guy, there is John, and that handsome devil right there," I said as I pointed to the young man with the blond curls, aristocratic nose, dancing eyes, and roguish smile, "that's Kurt, and I believe he's your grandpa."

Angi took the picture from me and studied the faces. "How do you know all of them, and why do you think he's my grandpa?"

"Because Angi, he's my brother, and those are his friends. I just spoke to him, and he did hook up with a young woman in Telluride almost fifty years ago. You resemble his daughters when they were your age. You being Kurt's granddaughter would explain everything else. Like, why you looked so familiar to me the first time I saw you. Like, why you and I have such a strong bond. How our gifts work together. How you share my dreams."

"If he's your brother, that means—"

"I'm your biological aunt. Great Aunt."

Her excitement battered me. "What's the next step? How do we know for sure?"

I chuckled. "I'm fairly certain already, but if you want, we can do a DNA test to prove it. Also, Kurt wants to meet you. Are you up for that?"

"Yes. OMG, I can't believe it. You may be my real aunt!" She grabbed me, and her euphoria washed over me.

"Would you like for me to call him and invite him down today? He lives in Broken Arrow, but he could be here in a little over four hours. I can call Diane. I'm sure she won't mind an extra person for dinner. I'll explain the circumstances. I know she'll want to meet him."

"Yes, yes, yes!"

I pulled out my phone and called Kurt. "Hey, what are you doing right now? Do you want to drive down here and go to Christmas dinner with us at my adopted family's get-together? You and Angi can meet and visit a little, then we can eat dinner?"

"Absolutely! Can I bring Mona?"

"Sure, I haven't seen Mona in ages."

I got off the phone, and Angi wrung her hands. "Who is Mona? Are they coming?"

"Mona is one of Kurt's daughters. His other two daughters live out of town. Yes, Kurt and Mona are coming."

Next, I called Diane and told her what had transpired this morning.

Diane chuckled. "Wow, life is stranger than fiction. I can't wait to meet him. Is his wife coming too, and is he anything like you, Dawn?"

I laughed out loud. "My entire family has always been known as the wild bunch, and he is a little… extra, if you know what I mean. And he won't be bringing a wife. He's divorced."

"This is going to be a good party."

"I have one suggestion, Diane. Hide the tequila."

Five hours later, the driveway announcer sounded. Angi bounced up from the couch. Her hand flew to her heart, and she paced while she kept an eye on the door. I opened the front door as Kurt and Mona drove up. I hadn't seen my brother since Mike and Gracie's funeral. He grabbed me and gave me a hug. "How ya doing, Sis?"

"I'm doing great. Come on in."

Mona grabbed me next. "Aunt Dawn, I've missed you so much."

"I've missed you, too. I've been a self-centered ass, but that's over now. Come on in."

I arrived just in time to see Kurt staring at Angi. "Oh my God. Mona, who does she look like?

A little squeak escaped Mona. "Good Lord. She looks just like Terrie at that age."

Angi's head swiveled from one to the other, not knowing what to say or do. Kurt ate up the distance between them in a few long strides and hugged her. "Baby girl, I don't need a test to know you're one of mine." He held her out at arm's length. "Look at you. Just look at you. You're the spitting image of your Aunt Terrie."

Mona joined them. "Hi, I'm Mona. I'm a hugger and I hope you are too." And with that, she held Angi in a loving embrace.

Next, Kurt eyed Sophie and asked, "Who's this little munchkin?" He bent down in front of the swing, and Sophie flashed him a smile. "Oh wow, Dawn. She looks like Gracie."

He grimaced after he said it, like he wasn't sure how I'd handle the mention of Gracie. I smiled and nodded.

"It's okay, Kurt. I'm better than I've been in a year. Angi noticed the resemblance months ago when I was showing her baby pictures of Gracie."

Turning to Angi, he asked, "Is it okay if I hold her?"

Angi looked pleased and rushed over to lift Sophie out of the swing. She handed Sophie to Kurt, and he started making faces at her. Sophie cackled and hit him on the nose.

Mona didn't wait long. She stole Sophie from Kurt. "Hey," he said, "I wasn't finished making her laugh."

"Too bad, old man, snooze you lose."

Angi stood beside me and, in a low whisper, said, "I like your family."

"Ha. You don't get off that easily. They're your family, too."

***

Later, at Steve and Diane's, we all congregated around the dining table after dinner. Diane looked at the photo of Kurt and his three friends. She got an ornery glint in her eye as she glanced at Kurt, then back at the picture. "So, Kurt, you were a hottie back in the day. Ooh, look at those eyes, that smile, and those curls. What was the nickname Dawn called you? Oh yes, Stud Muffin."

To Kurt's credit, he didn't even blush. At seventy, gone was the lean, well-defined physique of his youth. But he still had a great smile, nice eyes, and a full head of hair. Not to be outdone, he shot Diane a mischievous grin and asked, "Sugar, you wouldn't be flirting with me now, would you? Cause I still got a—"

"Kurt, stop right there," I interjected to a chorus of laughter.

He raised his hands and shrugged. "You can't blame a guy for trying."

"Diane, remember me telling you he's a little extra? This is just a hint of what I'm talking about."

His grin continued to spread. "Hey Diane, you got any tequila?"

"No!" Diane and I chorused.

"So," Diane looked from Kurt to Angi, "are you going to get a DNA test?"

Kurt shook his head. "Don't need one. She's one of mine." He reached across and patted Angi's hand. She glanced at their hands as a sweet smile crooked the corners of her mouth.

Not to be deterred, Diane continued. "Well, here's what I'm thinking. You know your son was looking for you twenty years ago. With all the advances that have been made with DNA testing and the companies like Ancestry and 23andMe out there, I'll bet he's done a DNA test. If you do one, the test results could link you all up. He could find his father, Angi could find her father, and you could find your son."

A hush fell over the room. Angi was the first to speak. "Even if you don't want to do one, Kurt, I want to. I never considered the possibility of finding my father before. It would be wonderful for Sophie to know who her grandpa is. I wish I had known you my whole life.

Kurt took Angi's hand in his. "Baby girl, if it's important to you and that little munchkin, I'll do it. I just meant I don't need a test to prove to me that you're one of mine. But if we want to use the test as an investigative tool, I'm all in."

I could feel her excitement. It hammered me. "How do we do it?" I asked.

Diane rubbed her hands together. "I love this kind of stuff. How about I do a little research and order the test kits? I suggest starting with one company. Kurt and Angi will get confirmation of their family relationship and maybe find Kurt's son. If you don't get a hit from the first test, order a kit from another company. Chances are, Kurt's son did one already. And I'd go with the two most popular companies. I'll do all the paperwork, too. What do you think?"

Kurt nodded his consensus. "Call me when the tests come in, and I'll come back down."

23.

Happy Feet
The Dance Begins

The day before New Year's Eve, I slumped at the kitchen table with a cup of coffee in hand. My eyelids strained to stay open. Being a part of Angi's first Christmas celebration had been enchanting yet exhausting. Discovering the possibility that she could be my niece was an emotional high point, but the holiday gatherings and cleanup had caught up with me. I felt lethargic.

I would be driving to Tulsa later that day and checking into the Mayo Hotel in preparation for my dinner date and to avoid that long drive on New Year's Eve. While contemplating the upcoming date with Tony, I was infused with excitement and renewed energy. Who knew that at this age I could be so affected by the mere thought of a man?

Angi giggled as she scuffed into the kitchen. A sheet wrinkle creased her cheek, and Sophie's hair was raised in staticky threads as she perched on Angi's hip. "I don't know what you're thinking about, but your energy is great. I need it this morning. Can you bottle that, please, so I can have some for later?"

"I was just thinking about my trip to Tulsa."

"The trip, or maybe a certain hot gentleman?"

"That too."

***

The dresses in my closet had all been worn with Mike and I wanted this weekend to be about Tony and me, so I had

172

bought new outfits. Before zipping the garment bag, I stopped to admire my new purchases. The dress I ordered from Amazon for New Years Eve was a perfect fit with the right party vibe. The outfit for the Polo Grill came from a trendy little boutique in Skeeter.

***

I slid the side door of the van shut and turned to hug Angi and kiss Sophie goodbye. "I'll see you on New Year's Day. Have fun with Blane and don't do anything I wouldn't do."

She smirked. "So, you're giving me permission to misbehave?"

"Are you serious? You know old people don't… misbehave." Opening the driver's door, I paused to catch her giggling and gave my version of the queen's wave before starting my adventure.

As I pulled onto the highway, the sun's rays broke through the clouds, penetrating the windshield and warming my chest and hands even though the temperature was cold outside. I tuned the radio to a classic rock station. Before long, I surprised myself by singing along.

***

About three that afternoon, I arrived at my room at the Mayo Hotel. However, *room* was a vast understatement. The suite was enormous and contained a generous sized bedroom, luxurious bathroom, kitchenette, and an expansive sitting area that boasted views of downtown. Soft music played on the sound system. I felt tremendously spoiled.

As I stashed the empty suitcase in the closet, a subtle rapping at the door interrupted the tranquility of the suite's atmosphere. Through the peephole of the front door, I viewed a uniformed man in a rigid stance exuding a sense of purpose. I opened the door and was greeted with a genuine smile.

"Hello, ma'am. I am Anrea. Mr. Rossi asked me to make this delivery soon after your arrival."

"Hi, Anrea. Please, call me Dawn." I opened the door wider and stood to the side. He maneuvered a linen-draped cart to the kitchenette and transferred a bud vase containing a single red rose, a black box with a Dom Pérignon logo on it, and an ornate silver ice bucket to the counter.

I reached for my purse, and he put his hand up in a stopping gesture. "All gratuities have been taken care of, ma'am. Mr. Rossi is a generous man." Then, with a smile and a nod, he whisked the cart out the door.

Turning back to the counter, I noticed a large envelope propped against the ice bucket. Retrieving the envelope, I slid out the contents. My breath caught at the sight of the yellowed photo. The picture was taken at Tony's going-away party at Fort Gordon and captured Tony's expression as he gazed at me from across the room that day. He was surrounded by several of his buddies, who vied for his attention, but at that moment, he only had eyes for me.

A vivid memory surfaced of Tony and me in my barracks room that night after the picture was taken.

Lying tangled in the sheets of my twin bed in our afterglow, I felt his heat, the rise and fall of his chest as his breath calmed, and his sweat drying on my skin. His murmured words were seductive. "Johnson, you're different than I thought. Softer. Not as tough as you pretend to be."

As the vignette faded from my thoughts, I noticed the card and read: "I have kept this picture stashed away over the years. I just couldn't part with it. Dawn, you have always held a special place in my heart. I look forward to spending the evening with you. If you need anything before I arrive, call the front desk and ask for Anrea. He will take care of you."

***

I wore my hair straight for a sleek look. It had taken a ninja move to maneuver into my one-piece pantsuit and get the back zipper closed. The form-fitting outfit was black with three-quarter length sleeves, a boat neck, and straight leg pants, which made me feel sophisticated and somewhat wicked. My earrings were a simple, thin silver bar for each ear and complemented the silver bangle bracelets I wore. Stepping into red leather stiletto heels, I surveyed my reflection in the full-length mirror. *I need lipstick... fire engine red is in order tonight.* Taking one last look in the mirror, I thought, *That'll do.*

A soft knock sounded at the door. I paused, took a calming breath, and lowered my empath shield. I wanted to feel Tony's reaction.

Opening the door, I stepped back to invite him in. He paused at the sight of me, his eyes dilated, and I felt a surge of excitement and positive energy. A wolfish grin appeared. "Oh yeah," he said, as he shut the door with his foot, took me in his arms, and pressed his lips to mine. He teased my lips with a gentle tug from his. His hands slid down my back and grazed over my hips. Sliding his hands back to my waist, he stepped away from me.

"You look stunning."

It was the reaction I hoped for.

He helped me into my coat, and we took the elevator to the lobby. A black limousine waited at the curb. The driver opened the back door for us.

Shaking my head, I asked, "A limousine?"

Tony shrugged. "It's a wine pairing dinner. I didn't know how much we would drink, so I didn't want to worry about driving. I hired the driver for the evening. It's not like I own a limousine."

I slid across the leather seat and marveled at how extraordinary Tony made me feel.

The dining experience was amazing, the food sumptuous, and the ambiance warm and inviting, but everything paled in comparison to Tony. He was attentive, delightful, self-deprecating, and so handsome.

We took our time, enjoyed each course, each wine, and each story told. I was swathed in my infatuation. When dinner was over and we were in the limousine, he asked the driver to take us to look at Christmas lights.

Back at the Mayo, Tony asked the driver to return at eleven, then he turned to me and flashed his dimple. "I want to show you something special."

A suggestive smile tugged at my lips. "Oh?"

He laughed. "A place." He led me to the elevator, and we ascended to the twentieth floor. "Have you ever been to the Rooftop Bar?"

I shook my head. "No, but it sounds delightful."

"It has an unobstructed 360-degree view of downtown Tulsa, and there's live music," he said.

I couldn't contain my excitement. "Oh, Tony, let's get coffee with Irish cream before taking in the view."

While we waited for the drinks at the bar, the rhythm of the music had me swaying in time. "I think I'm getting happy feet."

Tony braced me in his arms and moved in a slow, rhythmic waltz while we waited for our drinks. I touched my cheek to his and whispered, "I love your spontaneity." Then, in an orchestrated move, I brushed my face across his cheek. The stubble of his whiskers chafed my skin, sending a frisson of excitement throughout my body. My lips grazed the corner of his mouth as I pulled away from him. I heard a sharp breath and met his appreciative gaze with a flirtatious smile.

He shook his head, a grin forming at the corners of his mouth. "You are such a tease, Johnson."

"Tease?" I chuckled. "I mean business, Buster."

Our drinks arrived. I retrieved mine and sashayed out the door to the rooftop. A cold gust of air slapped me, whipping my hair. I wrapped my hands around the mug and scurried to the stone wall that overlooked downtown Tulsa. The view was spectacular. The lights of the buildings, Christmas decorations, people scurrying to the clubs, and the headlights of the cars penetrating the darkness all exuded the city's energy. A symphony of sound, color, and movement pierced the night and tantalized my senses.

"This isn't just special; this is amazing. Thank you for this. All of it." I turned to meet Tony's gaze. "This entire evening has been incredible."

His eyes lit up. "Well, that's a relief. I would have been disappointed if you weren't duly impressed."

We both laughed. Setting his mug down, he stepped behind me. Wrapping me in his arms, he pulled me close. We stood in comfortable silence and absorbed the scene below us for a few minutes. Then we walked the circumference of the entire rooftop before heading back inside and snagging a table.

"You still have happy feet?"

"You know it, and now that I've had coffee, I have wide-awake, happy feet."

Nestled in each other's arms, we danced in perfect rhythm. Then Tony glanced at his watch. "I'd better get you back to your room. The driver will be back in fifteen minutes to pick me up."

Disappointment nagged at me as we exited the bar and made our way to the elevator. Tony followed me into the suite and closed the door.

"Dawn, this entire evening was enchanting. Thank you."

I couldn't disguise my longing. "You could stay…"

Placing a finger on my lips, he kissed the bridge of my nose as if to soften the blow. "We're going to have a late night tomorrow, and I don't want to rush anything." He brought his mouth to mine. His lips parted as he pulled my upper lip between his. Releasing my lip, he kissed me again with more urgency and sucked on my bottom lip. My mouth parted, a sigh escaped, and he inhaled my breath. For the second time that night, he placed his hands at my waist and backed away, leaving me breathless.

"I'm looking forward to tomorrow," he said and gave me a quick wink.

I took a deep breath and arched an eyebrow. "Who's the tease now, Rossi?"

His answer was a knowing smile.

***

I laid awake in my luxurious bed, the events of the evening replaying in my head. Sleep eluded me. The coffee didn't help but neither did Tony. I'll say it again, that man can kiss. So, he didn't want to rush things. I knew what I wanted. There was no need to wait. A plan was formed. *I will call Anrea tomorrow morning and enlist his help.* As I continued to scheme and make plans, I relaxed and drifted into a deep sleep.

24.

The Epiphany of Love
A Reason to Celebrate

Yawning, I stretched, rubbed the sleep from my eyes, and smiled. A sense of joy filled me. It wasn't quite seven. Throwing on my workout clothes, I headed to the fitness center and completed a full exercise routine.

Back in my suite, I called Anrea. "Good morning. I need your help with a surprise for Tony. I'm not used to this level of customer service, so if this is too much to ask, just tell me it is." I told him what I wanted and gave him my credit card number. He assured me it wasn't too much to ask, and he would enjoy fulfilling my request.

"Have you had breakfast, ma'am?"

"No, I haven't. I just finished up in the fitness center."

"Please, allow me to bring you something."

"Sure. Surprise me. If coffee is involved, anything else will be a bonus. Give me about twenty minutes."

"Yes, ma'am, I'll be up in twenty."

My hair was wrapped in a towel, and I was swathed in a plush hotel robe when Anrea arrived. He placed the covered dishes on the table, removing the lids with a flourish. "We have lox and bagels—the lox is superb—a medley of fruit, and a pot of fresh coffee with cream and assorted sweeteners. Will there be anything else?"

"I'd like to review our plans for tonight. Tony will pick me up by seven this evening. Can you get everything done between then and ten-fifty tonight?"

"Yes, no worries."

"Thank you so much, Anrea."

His demeanor softened. "I'm a romantic at heart," he said with a wistful sigh as he departed.

After breakfast, I blew out my hair and skipped makeup. I was going on a quick shopping expedition to pick up a toothbrush, toiletries, and a change of clothes for Tony—I had a plan.

***

The earlier shower was just to freshen up after the workout, but it was time to indulge myself before the New Year's festivities. I wanted to soak in a bubble bath and take my time grooming. I rolled my hair on hot curlers and eased under the mounting bubbles. My mind wandered to the coming evening, and my anticipation heightened.

As the water soothed me, I admired my new frock where it hung from the hook on the back of the bathroom door. The entire gown was scarlet. The cap sleeves were off the shoulder and more a strap than a sleeve. The bodice was covered in red lace, ruby-like crystals, and beadwork. A plunging sweetheart neckline with a built-in bra added drama. An A-line skirt of asymmetrical layers of chiffon began above the knee in front and trailed to mid-calf in the back. The back of the dress made a sharp V from the off-the-shoulder sleeves to just below the waist, exposing most of the back. The dress was over the top for me, but hey, it was for New Year's Eve and Tony.

Bath completed and nails polished, I began the arduous task of applying makeup so that it looked natural yet alluring.

Six forty-five. Almost showtime. Removing the rollers, I shook out my hair and ran my fingers through it to separate the curls. I slipped into my dress, stepped into gold stilettos, and added simple gold jewelry. There was a knock at the door. My heart skipped a beat, then raced.

I took a calming breath and willed my heart to slow down. Upon opening the door, I was struck by how devastatingly handsome Tony was in his suit. He looked at me with an appreciative gleam. "I want to see how this skirt moves." Taking my hand, he twirled me. "Yes, a great choice for dancing, and you are ravishing."

I yearned to wrap myself around him—yes, I'd climb that tree—but instead I leaned in and gave him a suggestive kiss full of unspoken promises, then pulled away in a move meant to convey allure. "You ready?"

He gave me his mischievous look. "More than ready."

"We'll see," I said while pulling him out the door.

We began the evening in the hotel restaurant and ordered from a pre-selected menu that gave us three dinner options. We sipped our wine and chatted in shared comfort. I brushed the toe of my stiletto up the back of his calf and flashed a deliberate smile. His eyes widened.

The food was wonderful, but I kept from overindulging because I wanted to dance tonight. Tony took notice. "Not feeling like a lumberjack tonight?"

I raised my eyebrows and chuckled. "Not in this dress, I don't."

After dinner, we were ushered into an adjoining room. There were name cards on the cabaret-style tables along with party hats, horns, and empty champagne flutes. As luck would have it, our table was right next to the dance floor.

Tony and I seldom left the dance floor all evening. I breathed in the scent of him, that mixture of his cologne and his essence that formed the unique fragrance that was singularly Tony. As we flowed to a romantic song later in the evening, I pressed myself against the length of him. He slid his hands to my hips and pulled me closer as we swayed rhythmically, and I whispered, "Are you about ready to blow this Juke Joint?"

Puzzled, Tony pulled back to scan my face. "Are you not enjoying yourself? It's not even midnight."

"I'm having a great time, but it might be more fun to welcome the New Year with fireworks," I said with a wink.

"Fireworks?" His posture straightened.

"Yes. There's a fireworks display over Tulsa starting at eleven-thirty. The grand finale will be at midnight. We'll have a magnificent view from my room."

"Oh," he muttered, sounding disappointed as we left the dance floor and headed to the elevator.

Inside the suite, the open drapes revealed a wall of windows that framed the backdrop of the Tulsa skyline. The furniture had been moved so that the couch and coffee table were in front of the windows. Candles cast a soft glow around the suite. The bottle of Dom Pérignon chilled in the ice bucket on the coffee table flanked by two champagne flutes. A charcuterie board graced the table, and the Righteous Brothers' sultry voices added to the ambiance. I was pleased with Anrea's handiwork.

At the bank of windows, I looked out over downtown. Tony was reflected in the glass as he drifted up behind me. Leaning down to nibble my bare shoulder, he laid a trail of kisses to my neck, where he nuzzled me. Folding me in his arms, he pulled me into him, my back to his front. I could feel his heartbeat and sensed his intense longing. I was on fire.

Images and emotions from our first coupling, a lifetime ago, flood my senses. I recalled how much I liked his quiet confidence, his easy smile, and the way he listened to me as if everything I said was important. His calm nature had grounded me, soothed me. His laughter reminded me of water rippling over stones in a creek bed.

Then, there was the physical attraction and the heat. The memory of his going-away party surfaced, of how his eyes roved over me, how his look warmed my skin and caressed my body. The electricity danced between us. I thought everyone at the party must have sensed it. And later, sneaking into my barracks room, the fear of being caught added to the excitement of our first intimacy.

Gazing at the skyline, I was at peace, secure in my desire. Tony nipped my earlobe and drew me from my reverie. There was a sense of homecoming, and I was consumed by desire.

Tony murmured, "That day on the parade field was when I glimpsed the authentic you. Before then, I thought you were this competitive, hard-ass female who could do more situps than everyone else in our company and more pushups than most. You could put any guy in his place with just a few words or a withering glance, yet you were liked and respected by everyone. Your energy, intelligence, and love of life were captivating. But that day on the parade field, it was as if a veil had been lifted, revealing your sensitivity. There was a delicacy to you I had never seen before. And the night we made love—there was a tenderness and an unexpected vulnerability that enthralled me. I fell in love with you that night."

I had no doubts, and I could wait no longer. Taking his hand, I led him to the bedroom. A diffused glow reflected off the folds of the satin sheets which emanated from the candles placed in strategic locations around the room.

Beside the bed, I caressed his face and claimed his mouth as I ran my hands over his chest and fumbled with the buttons on his shirt.

He captured my hands, effectively stopping me. "Are you sure?" His breath quickened. "I don't want to rush you."

"I've never been surer of anything in my life, Rossi. Stop stalling."

Releasing me, he lowered his hands to skim my waist until he found the fastener of my gown. Unhooking the closure, he applied a gentle pressure to the zipper, drawing it downward in a gradual, measured descent while ravaging my mouth. Our heat escalated. Releasing my mouth, he stepped back and observed as he eased the sleeves of the dress off my shoulders. I held my breath in anticipation as the dress slithered the length of my body in a seductive caress before pooling at my feet.

Tony cleared his throat. "That was better than I imagined. I've been undressing you all evening."

I stepped forward reclaiming the space between us. With methodical dexterity, I unbuttoned his shirt, and the tension mounted. His chest, smooth and toned, was beautiful. The years had been kind to him. Gone was the lean, angular body of his youth, replaced by the mature physique of a man who took care of himself.

Feathering my fingertips over his chest, I traced the muscles of his abdomen down to the line of silken hair at his waist. He breathed in sharply as I unbuckled the belt and unfastened his trousers. In a slow, deliberate pace, I eased his slacks down while gliding my lips along his inner thighs, alternating between their sculpted beauty.

We slid into bed and explored each other in the languid dance of lovers, and the anticipation mounted. Our coupling was different from our first time years before. The fire was still there, but the frenzied heat was replaced with a slow, intense burn.

We tasted each other, nuzzling, touching, caressing. We expressed our longing and reveled in our discoveries. I was dizzy with need as Tony filled me with his passion. When we came together in our ritual of love, we were indeed one. Our hearts beat in a synchronous rhythm while our souls collided and entwined. We were poised on the precipice of our climactic release when the last vestige of control disappeared and sent us tumbling into an abyss of pleasure.

I snuggled into the comfort of Tony's body. He lay on his back, my leg and arm splayed across him. With my head nestled on his shoulder, I spoke into his neck. "Wow, that was way better than I imagined."

I heard the rumble of his laughter through his chest. The fingers of his hand traced circles on my upper arm, and he leaned down to kiss the top of my head. "I have loved you for over forty years. If you allow me, I will share my love with you for the rest of my life."

Excitement encompassed me from head to toe and all parts in between. So much emotion swept over me that I found myself in a desperate attempt to avoid tears. Elation poured into me and filled the void of loss that had tortured me for so long. I was whole in that moment. Although the pain wasn't eradicated, the sharp edges of it were somehow smoothed by the tides of joy and love that washed over me. There would always be ripples caused by the loss of Mike and Gracie because I continued to be a captive of that past trauma. But I was no longer held under the crashing waves of despair that threatened to drown me.

I raised my head and looked him in the eyes. My lips trembled and my vision blurred with unshed tears. "I can't think of a better way to spend the rest of my life than loving and being loved by you."

An expression flashed across his face as if he'd had a stunning idea. "Wait a minute." He scooted to the side of the bed and leaned down to grab his slacks that lay crumpled on the floor. In the process, his exquisite derriere became the object of my focus. He rolled back over, and clutched in his hand was a petite, black velvet bag with drawstrings, which he handed to me.

"What's this?"

Smiling, he nodded at the bag. "Go ahead, open it and see what you think."

I plucked the bag from his fingers and caressed the velvet. Loosening the delicate drawstrings, I peeked inside. A beautiful vintage ruby ring beckoned me. Gasping, I took the ring from the pouch. The ruby was surrounded by small round diamonds and blue sapphires and set in rose gold. I was speechless.

Tony peered up at me from his lowered head as if he were a shy boy. "I bought that ring a few days after seeing you at Diane's house. I knew then that I wanted you in my life for the rest of it. I have carried that ring every day since, waiting for the right moment."

When I found my voice, I asked, "What kind of ring is it?"

"It's an emerald-cut ruby."

"I know that, you goober. I, uh, don't know what the ring means."

"For now, it means I love you. It can be a promise ring—as long as you know that I'm promising to love you and marry you whenever you're ready. What do you say?"

I took a shuddering breath, and as the tears fell, so did the last of my walls. "Yes."

He retrieved the ring from the palm of my hand, placed it on my finger, and crushed me to his chest. "I think we missed the fireworks show," he mumbled into my hair.

A sly smile stole over my face as I murmured, "We may have missed the show, but we didn't miss any fireworks."

Chuckling, he released me and said, "We need to celebrate. How about I open that bottle of champagne?"

I pulled on a robe and threw one to him.

Lounging on the sofa, Tony poured the champagne and gave a toast, "To new beginnings. Happy New Year, Dawn."

25.

The Morning After
No Pill Required

The tantalizing sensation of skin on skin registered as I woke. Tony laid on his back. I was sprawled across him, my head on his chest. His arm was a weight across my shoulders, anchoring me to him. The rhythmic beat of his heart and the rise and fall of his chest against mine felt so natural—so right.

I marveled at how we had found each other after all these years, but I knew we didn't just find each other. We had been brought together. "Thank you, God," I whispered.

"I was thinking the same thing," Tony said as he tightened his arm around me. "I know I said I wouldn't rush you, but I could get used to waking up like this every morning."

I snuggled a little closer. "I'm not going anywhere, Rossi. This is too right to mess up." I nuzzled his neck and laid my lips against the scruff of his jaw.

He pulled me closer. "What would you like to do today?"

"You," I stated as a matter-of-fact.

"Well, that's a given." He squeezed me. "But afterward, what would you like to do?" Tony rolled me to my back and gazed at me with desire flaring in his eyes. "I was thinking we could order room service then head to my house, so I can change clothes, then we can do anything you like."

"Nope."

His brow furrowed. "Nope?"

"Nope, we don't have to go to your house for a change of clothes. I might have done some shopping for you yesterday, so you could avoid the whole walk of shame thing today."

"Johnson, I do believe you executed a flagrant plan to take advantage of and seduce me."

"First of all, Rossi, you can't take advantage of the willing and, secondly, somebody had to make the first move."

"I've got the second move covered," he said as he dipped his head and caressed me with his lips…

***

We lingered over our coffee after breakfast. Tony was dressed in the clothes I bought for him the day before. "I was right."

"I'm sure you were. Care to elaborate?" he asked with a smirk.

"The color of that shirt really brings out the blue of your eyes. You are still a hottie, Rossi." Surprised embarrassment flashed across his face, and his cheeks began to color. "Oh my. Tony Rossi, are you blushing?" I cackled and slapped my thigh.

"What's so funny?"

"It's just that ever since seeing you at Diane's, I have blushed more than my entire previous life. Turnabout is fair play, and I like it."

Tony's gaze warmed. "Me too."

"You know what else I like? I like you. I mean, sure, I love you, but I like you, too. Everything about you. And this ring… I like this ring." I extended my hand, and wiggling my fingers, I watched the light refract off the gems. "It's perfect. It's so me."

"I'm glad you think so. I agonized for days over what to get. I selected that ring because, like you, the ring is vintage—classic yet contemporary, a rare find, and exquisite."

"Wow, *that* was way more elegant than *it's so me*."

Chuckling, Tony asked, "So, what are we going to do the rest of the day?"

"Let's go to Steve and Diane's New Year's Day football party. I'm not going to say anything; I want to see if Diane notices my ring." I was gripped with a sudden pang of insecurity. "I mean, are you okay with that? Do your kids know about this? Will they be okay with… us?"

He slid around the table and pulled me into his arms. "I haven't told them yet, but you're already part of the clan. They love you. I can't think of anything that would make them happier than to see their old man in love and happy. Especially with someone they have already adopted."

A sigh of relief escaped me. "Woohoo! Let's get this show on the road, Rossi." I gave his backside a squeeze before I pulled away and headed to the bedroom to finish packing.

26.

The Announcement
Changes all Around

Tony and I drove to Chance in separate cars. He had a few more weeks until his retirement started, so he planned to drive back to Tulsa the next day. I wished we could've made the drive in the same car. I missed his closeness.

I tuned to an oldies station and Peaches & Herb's *Reunited* played. *Well, that's appropriate.* I chuckled. Tony's blinker winked about the same time I saw the rest stop up ahead. Following him, I parked, rolled down my window, and received a blast of frigid air just before the warmth of his lips. When the kiss ended, I struggled to catch my breath. "What was that for?"

Tony grinned. "I missed you."

"You keep that up, Rossi, and it's going to be a long drive to Chance. Since we're here, I'm making a pit stop."

"That was my second reason for stopping."

"I'm glad we have synchronized bladders."

***

We arrived at Steve and Diane's two hours later. It was just after three, and the party was in full swing. Football was on the big screen, and fans of both teams were in attendance, making for a raucous gathering full of banter, jeering, and popcorn throwing.

I joined Diane in the kitchen, where she was busy assembling snacks. After washing my hands, I reached for a towel on the counter in front of her. She grabbed my wet hand. "Oh. My. Gawd! Is that what I think it is?"

I flashed a jack-o-lantern grin and nodded. A squeal exploded from the depths of her lungs and reverberated off the kitchen walls. She crushed me in a tight embrace. "Yes!" She grabbed my hands and swung me around in a joyful dance. Laughter bubbled up from deep within my soul and overflowed.

Tony and a multitude of faces, who, mere moments before, had been engrossed in the game, lined the doorway and gaped at us.

"Well, that didn't take long," Tony quipped. "Does that mean you approve, Diane?"

Diane ran to Tony and threw her arms around him. "Yes, Daddy, I approve. I knew there was something special between you two at Thanksgiving when you winked at her, and she blushed. I asked her the next morning if I should call her 'Mom,' and she threatened to whip my ass."

The gaggle of onlookers started slinging questions. Tony walked over, put his arm around my waist, and raised my left hand to show off my ring. "Dawn and I are…" He paused and focused an expectant gaze on me.

"We're engaged!" I interjected.

The room erupted with shouts, whistles, and way more enthusiasm than I had anticipated. Covering my ears, I shouted, "How much beer have you all had?"

Angi popped into the kitchen. She and Blane had just arrived. "What's going on in here? We could hear you all clear out on the driveway."

I held out my left hand for Angi to see. Her mouth dropped open, and her excitement pelted me. She bolted across the room, squashed me in a teddy bear hug, and whispered in my ear, "I'm so excited for you!"

"Me too," I whispered back.

For the remainder of the party, I tried to wrap my head around the fact that I had announced we were engaged. When Tony placed the ring on my finger, it had been a *promise* ring.

Sure, we would be engaged eventually, but I had been on the fence, trying out the whole promise/engagement thing. But when Tony paused and looked at me, it just flew out of my mouth.

My brain assaulted me with a myriad of questions. When will we get married? Where will we marry? Where will we live? What about Angi and Sophie?

An hour later, I glimpsed the pinched features of my reflection. Tony strolled across the room and smoothed the worry lines between my eyebrows with a finger. "Relax. We can take all the time we need to figure out logistics and timing. Right now, it's enough knowing you want to marry me."

"Have you been holding out on me, Tony? Are you psychic, or am I just that transparent?"

He chuckled and shook his head. "You look a little shell-shocked. I don't have to be psychic to figure out what's going through your head. I have until the fifteenth before I retire. I want you to take the next couple of weeks and just think about things. We're not going to talk about our concerns until then. I just want you to get used to the idea of getting married and make a list of things you want to discuss, and I'll do the same. Are you okay with that?"

Dazed, I nodded. "Do you want to spend the night with me tonight?"

"I'd like that very much," he said. "I'll head back to Tulsa tomorrow. I'm going to be on the road the next two weeks."

And just like that, he worked his magic. He calmed me. "Alright, handsome, you go finish the game, and I'll let Angi know that we're having a house guest tonight."

***

The following morning, Tony left, and with him some of my calm. My anxiety resurfaced. Was I ready to marry again? I didn't have doubts about Tony as a partner or his feelings for me. I was unsure of myself. I was still in the process of discovering who I was now. Was I emotionally stable enough to be a good partner... a wife? Then there were all the details associated with a wedding and moving in together. I still hadn't gotten justice for Mike and Gracie. Maybe if things just stayed the same for a while…. I was lost in my thoughts, a cup of coffee growing cold in my hands, when Angi peeked into the kitchen. "Am I interrupting anything?"

"No, come on in. You just missed Tony. Have a seat, and I'll fix you a cup of coffee."

Angi took the proffered cup. Setting the coffee down, she fidgeted with the cup. Her features tightened, and she avoided eye contact. "There's something I need to tell you."

"Go ahead. What's on your mind?"

She hesitated and took a sip of coffee. A mixture of emotions crossed her face and bounced off of me before she met my gaze. "Well, Blane is moving to Tulsa. He will be traveling a lot for his new job, and travel will be easier for him if he's living near the airport."

"And?"

Her face glowed. "Cici told me I can have the apartment over the café when Blane moves out. I've never lived by myself, and I'd like to. I mean, I've loved living here with you, but… I… Just… Well—"

I raised my empath shields to block Angi from my inner turmoil. "Say no more, Angi." Conflict warred with my emotions. I was proud of her personal growth, but I feared the emptiness her departure would create. I had become dependent on her presence. Focusing on Angi and Sophie had pulled me out of my depression and given me a new purpose. Was I using her as a crutch? My selfish side wanted her to stay. For her development, she needed to go, and she needed my support. "It's the natural progression of things. It's healthy for you to want your independence. I get it. Really, I do. I am always here for you. I'm going to miss our morning talks. I guess I'll start going to The Last Chance for my second cup of coffee again. And I'd like to watch Sophie from time to time."

The wrinkles on Angi's forehead smoothed, her mouth formed an easy smile, and her posture relaxed. "Great, because

I'm going to need sitters." Her smile broadened, and her excitement pelted me. "I want to go to the junior college in Skeeter and take some photography and web design classes."

"I'm so thrilled for you and proud of you, Angi." And I was, but the change was unsettling. My stomach ached. I looked down as I blinked back tears, and I realized my breathing had become shallow.

She ducked her head and smiled. "If it were just me, I don't know if I'd go to college, but I have Sophie to think about. I want more for her than what I had growing up. She deserves it."

"Yes, she does, and so do you."

"I've always felt guilty about wanting things for myself. But I can do this for Sophie."

"Yes, you can, and you should."

Rising from the table, she said, "I need to get ready for work." She stopped and hugged me, "Thank you. I couldn't have done any of this without you. Oh, I'll be late tonight. I'm going to help Blane pack, and we'll eat out."

I waited till Angi left for work, then retrieved a bottle of Baileys Irish Cream to flavor my coffee. Perhaps the coffee flavored the Baileys since there was little coffee left. I filled the remainder of the cup with Baileys. And that was just the beginning.

I laid awake after a day and evening of binging on a variety of alcohol. My stomach gurgled, and my brain raced from one disjointed thought to another. *Angi and Sophie are leaving. Mike and Gracie are dead. The monster hasn't been punished. What if Tony gets tired of me?* All my fears and insecurities surfaced and squirmed as if they were maggots feasting on my psyche.

During times of stress, I tended to self-medicate with alcohol. I should have known better than to start drinking. If I'm happy and have a drink, the good feeling intensifies. One drink was all I needed. Conversely, if I were stressed, one drink wouldn't do. Then it was two, and if I had two, I'd have several more to chase the high that couldn't be captured. So, there I laid.

Remorse gnawed at me. After what felt like an eternity, I drifted into a fitful sleep accompanied by angst-fueled dreams.

I awoke with a sigh of relief. The night was over, and I had an entire day to create an attitude adjustment. If only it were that simple.

As I suffered through the hangover, I slogged to the shop to exercise and refused to take ibuprofen—self-imposed punishment… if you do the crime, you've got to do the time. Thoughts of Mike and Gracie plagued me. I rolled up the yoga mat. My heart hammered, and I struggled to breathe. *Not now!* I sat on the floor, hugged my knees to my chest, and fought the oncoming flashback. Forcing a deep breath, I asked myself, "Where are my feet?" I focused on the feel of the cool concrete beneath the soles of my feet. "Where is my ass?" I felt the discomfort of the hard surface under me. I continued to take deep, measured breaths. It was working; I was grounding myself in the present. The tingling in my hands and feet subsided, and my vision cleared. I stood and began to pace. I retrieved my phone and placed a call.

William answered on the first ring. "Dawn? It's been a while. Are you doing okay?"

"No. No, I'm not. Please tell me there has been some progress."

William paused. "We're still following leads, and it's still an active investigation, but there's no new evidence yet. Don't lose hope. I won't give up."

Remaining silent, I pressed my fingertips against my lips, and tears coursed down my face as I rocked in place.

"Dawn? I can be there this afternoon."

"No. I'll be okay. It's just a bad day. Call me if there is any change." I ended the call, left the shop, and trudged back to the cabin. I had some tough decisions to make. I needed to talk to Tony. I dreaded the course of my thoughts.

The following morning, I felt much better. After finishing my workout, my phone rang. I knew it was William without checking the caller I.D. My heart skipped a beat, and I experienced a moment of exhilaration, wondering if his call concerned new evidence. The moment was short-lived. "Hi, William. What's up?" As soon as the phones connected, I knew something was off. William was off.

"I wanted to make sure you're alright. You worried me yesterday," he spoke softly. His voice was subdued, and emotional pain radiated from him.

"I'm fine. I just finished a workout, and it's a brand new day. How are you?"

William ignored my question. "How do I know you're not just saying you're fine, and you're not really okay…when was the last time you took a bath?"

"It's been a while, but I took a shower yesterday, does that count?"

"Oh. Okay." He sighed, and then he was silent. His anguish was more pronounced. His heartache hurt me, and I rubbed my chest.

"William, what is going on with you, and don't tell me nothing. You know I can feel your pain."

There was more silence. Then he sniffed and cleared his throat. "Tomorrow is Libby's birthday. She would have been sixty this year." And there it was, our shared grief for our lost loved ones. We sat in silence for a few moments. Then I said, "Tell me about her. What made Libby special?"

More silence, then, "She was light. Energy. Laughter. She was everything. People were drawn to her. She understood me, and she made me better. You may find this hard to believe, but I'm awkward at social gatherings." I chuckled. He continued. "It's because my brain won't shut off. I get in my head, and I'm trapped there thinking about a case or how to fix my leaky faucet. And because of that, I miss the thread of conversation. But when Libby was there, she could touch me and say my name, and it was like she short-circuited my brain. I could let the problem-solving go and be in the moment. She even got me to karaoke once."

I laughed out loud at the mental image of a stoic William standing at attention to sing karaoke. "And how did Libby manage that?"

William chuckled. "She got me drunk. We were on vacation, and our hotel was next door to a Korean restaurant. We were the only customers. The waiter asked if we liked to karaoke, and Libby immediately said yes. The waiter told us if we bought beer, we could karaoke for free, so Libby told him to bring us two beers. Then she told me the last one to finish had to sing first. She acted like she was chugging her beer, so I downed mine. It was weird; there were only the restaurant owner, the waiter, and us, but they locked the front door and took us through a doorway into their karaoke room, where the four of us drank beer, sang, and danced until midnight. That experience was one of the most fun I've ever had." His heartache was ebbing, and the warmth of love was flowing in. He was regaining his emotional footing, and so was I. "Thank you, Dawn."

"My pleasure, karaoke king. What are you doing tonight?"

"I think I'll have dinner at a Korean restaurant–one without karaoke."

"Sounds good. Hey, I need to go. Are you going to be alright?"

"Yes. And Dawn… take a bath."

"You smartass," I said, right before I hung up on him.

27.

The Move
A Diversion is Created

After William's call and my pity party day of drinking, I worked on accepting the changes in my life. There were no more days lost to overindulgence in alcohol. I reminded myself that although growth was sometimes uncomfortable, even painful, it was essential. Angi's move was necessary for both of us, and four days later, we paused in front of the door of Angi's apartment. She stood beside me with Sophie perched on her hip. Angi's excitement radiated from her, and she bounced on the balls of her feet. "Close your eyes," she said. I complied, then heard the high-pitched whine of hinges as the door swung inward. She took my hand and led me inside. "You can open your eyes now."

The décor, although faded and dated, was cute and organized. The windows gleamed. The fresh smell of cleaning products almost covered the rising aroma of lunch from the café below. Her eyebrows and shoulders raised, "Well, what do you think?"

"I think the lunch special must be meatloaf," I grinned. "Angi, the apartment is perfect."

A smile darted across her face, and her head swiveled as she looked at her new home. "It's not perfect yet, but I have a lot of ideas."

"Tell me your plans."

Angi told me her intentions for the apartment, from color scheme to theme. Inspiration took hold of me.

"Do you mind if I help you decorate? I have a few things in storage that would work well with your colors and style. And I know some affordable consignment shops. We can achieve a new look for this space and do it on a budget."

"That sounds great except I have zero budget right now."

"Angi, my dear, you keep forgetting, I have money I haven't spent yet."

I looked forward to the distraction. Tony would be here in ten days, and "the talk" loomed ahead of me. I threw myself into the redecorating project like a fast-pitched baseball. We painted the walls and tore up the ratty carpet that concealed a rich wood floor. The planks were cleaned and polished into submission, then adorned with an area rug. Key pieces of furniture were added. The project proved to be a much-needed reprieve from my thoughts.

The renovation was completed, and my respite was over. Tony would get into Tulsa that night and be here the next day. I'd have to confront the reality of a new life with Tony, and it scared the shit out of me. *I can't do this.*

The Reckoning
Hearts in Turmoil

There was a knock at the door. My pulse quickened, and my heart held the ache of dread. I opened the door to a jubilant Tony who swept me into his arms. I held on tight, not knowing if it would be the last time. My breath hitched, and I stifled a sob as I tightened my arms around him.

"Dawn, what's wrong?"

Still, I clung to him, not knowing how to begin. I didn't fully understand myself. I sobbed and spoke into his neck, "I can't do it, Tony. I can't marry you."

He pulled away and looked at me. There was no anger, just concern. He led me to the couch. Flames blazed in the grate of the fireplace. His hands cupped the sides of my face, and his thumbs wiped away my tears. "Talk to me. What's going on?

All my insecurities surfaced and tangled into a balled-up mess with no means to unravel them. "I don't know. It's nothing and it's everything. I can't make sense of it."

"Do you love me?" Tony asked.

Startled at the starkness of his voice that was devoid of emotion, I blurted, "Yes!"

A sigh escaped him. "Then that's enough. You're enough."

"Tony, did you hear what I said? I can't marry you."

"Yes, I heard you. You also said you loved me. Will you keep seeing me? Will you keep loving me?" The earnest quality of his voice soothed me, but his lack of anger confused me.

"You still want to see me after I just broke our engagement?"

He did the unexpected. He laughed.

What the hell?

He searched my eyes and asked, "Do you think you're the only one with doubts?"

Wait, what? "You're having second thoughts too?"

"Yes. Not about us, but about getting married, and about the timing. At least for now. Remember, I said we should both make a list of things to discuss. As I made my list, I became overwhelmed. Dawn, if it were just the marriage, I wouldn't be so overwhelmed, but I've just retired. That's a major life change. I don't know what I'm going to do with myself in retirement. I'm still coming to terms with abandoning my children and grandchildren the past five years. I have a lot to make up for. I'll be selling my house. That's another stressor. Your turn. What's been happening here? What has gotten you so upset?"

Angi moved out. I spent the day binge drinking. I started fixating on Mike and Gracie's murders. I want the freak that killed them to be held accountable. I don't just want justice, I want retribution. I want that sick bastard punished. I don't know how I can find closure and move forward without that. It's as if I'm fractured, and I can't find all the pieces to reconstruct myself. And what kind of marriage would that be?" I handed him the black velvet bag containing the ring. "But mostly, I'm afraid of losing you. I'm a complete mess."

"Come here." He pulled me onto his lap. "We are a mess, aren't we? See how much we have in common?"

I rolled my eyes.

Tony gave me a quick wink and a lazy smile. "We've traversed from dating to engagement to breaking the engagement in all of two months. Why don't we take a breather? Not from each other but from the stress."

He handed the pouch back to me. "I want you to hang on to this ring, it's *so you* after all. Wear the ring or don't wear it. Call it a promise ring or an engagement ring. It doesn't matter because the way I feel about you hasn't changed. I love you, Dawn, and I want you in my life for the rest of my life, but that doesn't mean we have to get married. Have your feelings for me changed?"

"Yes!" I bawled. "After today, I love you even more, and I didn't think that was possible."

"We're good then?"

I leaned into him and nestled my head between his neck and shoulder. "We're better than good." A sense of sanity seeped in, followed by calmness.

"Binge drinking? Was table dancing involved?" he asked.

"It wasn't that kind of drinking. It was more the snot-slinging, bad dreams, fitful sleeping kind of drinking."

"Should I hide the liquor?"

"No, I'm good. I took back control of myself the next day and dried out."

My stomach growled. "I know it's early, but I could eat. You want to get some fried catfish?"

Tony glanced at his watch. "It's almost eleven. Let's go." We grabbed our coats, and I headed for the back door.

"Dawn, I'm parked out front."

"I haven't lost it completely, Rossi. I know where you're parked. I'm leading you to the best fried catfish in Oklahoma. Walk with me."

We stepped onto the deck. I took his hand and led him to the edge of the cliff that overlooked the lake, then showed him the stairs and railing that led down the face of the cliff. We walked single file down the stairs till we reached a sandy beach below. Hand in hand, I led Tony down the shoreline a short distance to a lakeside café.

Reminiscing, I asked, "Remember the day we sat at a picnic table across the lake, and I pointed out my house? You asked if I owned the dock. I told you I didn't. The man that does own it, Amos, also owns the combination bait store, café, and gas pump. His fried catfish has the crispiest crust and an unexpected zing of flavor that I've never tasted anywhere else. Wait till you try it."

The floating dock was weathered but still in good condition. The café looked faded and worn outside. Tony pulled on the screen door, and we were greeted by the warble of a stretching spring. He struggled to open the main door that had swollen in its frame due to the dampness of the season. The screen door slapped shut behind us, announcing our arrival.

Amos peered out from the pass-through window of the kitchen. An affable grin revealed a gold tooth.

"Ya'll have a seat. I'll be right with you."

We slid into a booth. Amos approached, moving with an athleticism that belied his age. He handed us menus and waited for our order. His pristine white apron contrasted with the hazelnut color of his skin. A crown of tight gray curls highlighted a face dusted with freckles.

Tony glanced at the front of the menu. "The name of the café is the Not So?"

A chuckle flowed from Amos on a lilting note. "Yeh, as in the *Not So Famous Amos*."

"Amos," I interjected, "I'd like you to meet a long-time friend of mine, Tony. Tony, this is Amos, the proprietor of this fine establishment."

Amos offered his hand to Tony, then glanced at me. "From what I hear, Tony is a little more than a friend."

I felt heat rising to my face. "It doesn't take long for that kind of news to make the rounds, does it?"

"Not in Chance. So, what are you two having today?"

"I don't need a menu. We'll take two catfish baskets and lemonades, please."

He strode to the kitchen to work his culinary magic, and Tony's head swiveled as he took in every detail. Decorative fishnets hung on the walls as a backdrop to old fishing poles, street signs, car tags, and rusted advertising signs. The bait shop was on one side of the open floor plan, and the café on the other.

Several minutes later, Amos delivered the aromatic baskets of food and pulled up a chair at the end of the booth.

"Mind if I join you a few minutes before the lunch rush starts?"

"Please do," I said and gestured toward the seat.

He propped an ankle across a knee and lounged in the chair. A thoughtful expression crossed his face before he spoke. "You look good. It's been too long. I've been worried about you, but I see things are better for you now."

My eyes stung at the warmth of his words and the compassion that rolled off him. "Thank you, I've been making some changes and will be making a few more."

"Me too. I've been thinking about selling this place. I can't keep good help, and it's just getting to be more than I want to do. I like cooking, that's always been my passion, but the dock, bait shop, gas, and managing everything? Then there's the fixing up that needs to be done, and I just don't want to invest that kind of money at my age. I don't know what I'll do with myself if I sell. All I know for sure is that I don't want to keep managing all of this." He made a swirl with his hand to encompass the entire building.

We were interrupted by the stuck door being shoved open.

"That's my cue. Come on in, folks. Sit wherever you like."

Then to us he said, "Dawn, Tony, I'll talk to you later."

Tony took his first bite of the fish, and his eyes widened in surprise. "You weren't kidding. This is the best catfish I've ever had." He ate a few fries, then sampled the coleslaw, too. "It's all great." Tony's excitement ramped up. "You know, with a little sprucing up—nothing that would change the small-town charm of it—and the right advertising, this could be a hotspot year-round."

29.
A Plan for Retirement
Not

Tony and I stood in front of the cottage under a gray sky just down the beach from the Not So. Water dripped off the bare limbs of the surrounding trees, and a fine mist fell. Tony had a contract to sell his house in Tulsa. The closing would be in a month, and he was interested in buying the quaint home in front of us.

"Oh, Tony. I've always loved this cottage. I didn't know it was for sale."

He crossed his arms and rocked back on his heels as he studied the Victorian cottage with the charming wrap-around porch. "I've been working with a realtor, Neal Baker. He called me before listing the cottage because he said it was just what I was looking for, and the estate wants a quick sale." The white paint was chipped and peeling, exposing weathered boards. The front steps listed to the side, and one of the shutters hung at a precarious angle. "The interior and exterior need some work, but renovations will give me something to do," he said. "Neal said he'd leave a key under the mat. Shall we go in?"

Although the outside looked forlorn, the inside was tidy and had been emptied and cleaned. The subtle, old-world charm reeled me in. "It's an absolute treasure."

Tony nodded. "It has potential. Would you be up for helping me decorate after the renovation?"

"Yes. I love to decorate, and I don't mind helping with the renovation either."

"I'm going to hire someone to do the restoration because I have additional plans."

I could hear the excitement in his voice and felt his energy swell. "What are your additional plans?"

"I want to buy the Not So and keep Amos on to cook and manage it. I'll manage everything else until I get a handle on things. I want to renovate the boat docks and café and make the complex a showstopper for the area. There are moneyed people on this lake. I can add a few more slips for yachts and larger boats and keep the smaller ones for fishing boats."

"That doesn't sound like much of a retirement."

"I know, but it is. The past five years, I have traveled and worked nonstop. Just being able to stay in the same town in my own home is like retirement to me. I'll have you and my family close. This venture will ease me into retirement, and once it's set up, I can hire people to run the place for me. I have someone in mind. The thought of having nothing to do terrifies me."

"Have you pitched your idea to Amos?"

"Not yet. But either way, I want this cottage."

He pulled out his phone and called the realtor. "Neal, it's Tony. I'll take the cottage and pay the asking price."

Neal must have agreed because Tony uttered a few yeses, then hung up.

"You don't mess around when you want something, do you?"

He held my eyes with his as he spoke. "Exactly." A slow grin spilled across his face, punctuated with a wink.

Inside the cottage, I hopped up and sat on the countertop in the kitchen. "Who do you have in mind?"

"In mind for what?"

"You said you had someone in mind to run the dock for you."

"Oh. Blane. Cici and I are worried about him. Do you know that Blane has Post Traumatic Stress? That his girlfriend was killed during a mission that they were both on?"

"I know about as much as you just told me, but I don't know any details."

Our voices echoed off the walls of the empty space.

"None of us do. He won't open up about it. From what I understand, he was in bad shape when he arrived home. He stopped in at the Last Chance to see Cici when he got to town. A busser dropped a tub of dishes, and Blane dove for cover and had a flashback. Cici was able to get through to him, talk him down, but he couldn't convince Blane to get help. The busboy quit soon after. Cici hired Blane and mentored him as much as possible.

"With the stability of a job and the support of our family, Blane began to heal. But we're worried this security job is providing triggers and opening old wounds. And with all the travel, his support system is long-distance now. Cici and I want to bring him home, get him involved in some veteran groups."

My respect for Cici grew as my concern for Blane did as well. "From what I know about Blane, you won't be able to force the issue. He'll have to think it's his idea."

Tony lifted an eyebrow, and a smirk tugged at the corner of his mouth. "Well then, it's a good thing I'm an expert negotiator, isn't it? He'll never see it coming. He'll think he's helping me out of a jam. He'll ask me for the job."

I shook my head as I hopped off the counter. "That sounds more like manipulation than negotiation, Tony Rossi."

He shrugged. "Tomato, tomatto…"

We ambled down the beach and took the sandstone stairs to the Not So. Amos looked up from cleaning a table as we entered the café.

Tony cleared his throat. "Amos, you got a minute? I have a proposition."

30.

The Reveal
Hide This Will You?

Two weeks later, Diane invited Kurt and Mona down for the NFL Conference Championships. Instead of the usual huge party, she hosted a smaller, more intimate gathering, which was puzzling.

Blane came down and brought Angi and Sophie. We seldom saw Blane as his job kept him on the road so much. He was withdrawn. I suspected his job and associated travel were putting a strain on their budding relationship.

Tony and I brought a smoked brisket to make slider sandwiches. Diane and Steve provided an array of side dishes. Cici showed up with a bag of kettle corn and a large container of ice cream. Little Katie danced and twirled with barely-contained excitement.

Pregame chatter from the television provided background noise as we pushed back from the table.

"Anyone ready for dessert?" Diane asked.

We moaned in unison. I held up a hand. "I need these sliders to slide down further before I pack anything else in here."

Diane started stacking plates. "Fine, I'll just clear the table."

I lumbered out of my chair. "I'll help." As I entered the kitchen, I spied a cake box. "Ooh, bakery dessert. I want to see." I reached for the lid, and Diane slapped my hand away. "It's a surprise. Don't you dare peek."

"Okay."

We had just finished putting the food away and tidying up when Katie ran into the kitchen. "Mommy, Mommy, Mommy! Is it time yet?"

Diane shushed her. "Not yet, sweetheart, but soon."

I narrowed my eyes and leveled my gaze at Diane. "Time for what?"

Hand on her hip, she glared back at me. "Stop asking so many questions. I told you there was a surprise. Grab the dessert plates and forks."

She loaded the cake box, ice cream, salt shaker, bowl of limes, and a fifth of tequila on a beverage cart. As I questioned her about the tequila, she ignored me and we paraded out of the kitchen, Diane in the lead, me just behind, and Katie bringing up the rear.

After setting the cake box and ice cream on the table, she moved to Kurt and set the limes, salt, shot glass, and tequila in front of him. A grin split his face.

"Sugar, you're speaking my language. Now this is what I call dessert!"

My mouth fell open, and my eyes bugged. "Diane, I warned you about Kurt and tequila."

"Lighten up, Dawn. He's earned it." Then she patted Kurt on the back and poured him a shot. "Go ahead, Kurt, slam that baby."

Licking the web of skin between his thumb and index finger, he then sprinkled it with salt and licked it off. He held the glass up in a mock salute, downed the tequila, bit into a lime wedge, then shook his head. "Man, that hit the spot."

Diane moved the cake in front of Angi. "I received the results from the DNA test," she said as she lifted the lid to reveal a message on the cake.

Angi read the beautiful script icing, took a shuddering breath, and burst into tears.

Kurt, at the other end of the table, couldn't see what was written on the cake. Panicked by Angi's tears, he asked, "What? What does it say?"

Blane cradled Angi against him, turned the cake toward himself, and read aloud, "Happy Re-birthday, Angi. Welcome to your family."

My eyes overflowed. *Angi is my great-niece.*

Crusty Kurt wiped his eyes right before he took another shot. "Damn, that means somewhere out there, I've got a son."

Angi glanced up and wiped her nose. "And I have a family."

Glancing at Diane, Kurt asked, "I don't suppose that test linked me to my son, did it?"

Diane shook her head. "No, but we only did one test. We can do another with a different company."

Positive energy charged the air. Kurt even handed the tequila back to Diane. "Hide this, will you? I'm a great grandpa now. I've got to be responsible."

Kurt scraped back his chair as he stood, strode to Angi, and held his arms open wide. "Baby girl, give your grandpa a hug." As she stood, Kurt embraced her in a fierce hug. "Welcome to our mess. I knew you were one of ours."

My empath shields were down, and I was almost overcome by everyone's emotions. The strongest were from Angi. I felt a sense of belonging and joy emanating from her. From Kurt, love and pride were foremost. Everyone was on an emotional high.

That news put the wheels in motion for Angi's future journey. I sensed changes coming.

31.

The Unexpected
A Change is Coming

I stood in the doorway of the Not So. Amos had jumped at Tony's offer to buy the business. A circular saw buzzed, and sawdust swirled in the interior of the café. "What happened to the door?"

Tony stood spraddle-legged, arms crossed over his chest as he surveyed the flurry of activity. "I'm replacing it and the doorframe, so our customers don't have to fight to get inside."

"What does Amos think about your vision for the place?"

"He said if he could have two weeks off to visit his sister and her brood in Florida, and he didn't have to do any of the renovations, he was a-okay with any changes I want to make. He said managing the café and cooking without any other responsibilities would feel like retirement. He's bringing a nephew back from Florida to train in the kitchen so he can take more time off, too.

You know, I was just going to add a few more slips at the dock and freshen up everything else." Tony strolled to the window and looked towards the shoreline. Placing his hands on his hips, he glanced back at me. " But now, I think I want to put in a couple of cabins, too."

He was a man on a mission. I shook my head. "This hardly seems like retirement, but if you're happy, then I'm happy for you. I'm going to leave you to it. I'll be at the cabin if you need me for anything."

***

Back home, I propped my socked feet on the coffee table, watched the flames weave a seductive dance along the logs in the fireplace, and warmed my hands with a cup of hot cocoa. I marveled at the shift in my reality. *Shift* wasn't the right word; it was more like a transformation or a metamorphosis. I still had bad days when I couldn't stop thinking about the injustice of Mike and Gracie's deaths. On occasion, I felt guilty for moving forward with my life. But I took solace in the fact that although I was moving forward, I hadn't moved on. My strength and hunger for life were returning—reawakening, if you will. I no longer merely existed. I was enthralled with living. Even though I struggled emotionally, new prospects excited me instead of creating anxiety. That day, all was well, until it wasn't.

My hand hesitated over the phone; I knew without looking who was calling. Glancing at the incoming caller ID confirmed it. WAC. In the beginning of the investigation, William Arthur Curtis called me almost obsessively, but after I moved and the investigation stalled, his calls became less and less frequent. Since our last call several weeks ago, I didn't expect to hear from him unless he had news about the investigation. Just the sight of that caller ID set me on a downward trajectory. Past disappointments from previous calls had diminished any hope of good news.

Mike and Gracie are dead. The loss was a physical pain that cut through me. How could I enjoy my life when my loved ones had been denied theirs? The ringing jerked me into past trauma. The grief was like a weighted blanket that anchored me to the couch. My heart skipped a beat, and my entire body tensed as it filled with dread. The phone continued to ring.

Wayne Beck Mason was a *person of interest* in Mike and Gracie's murders, but there was no doubt in my mind or William's that he had killed them. Due to a lack of evidence, he still hadn't been charged with their murders. However, during the investigation, law enforcement uncovered that a year before their murders, Wayne illegally possessed a firearm while being an unlawful user of a controlled substance. That gun wasn't the murder weapon, but those unrelated charges led to his arrest and detention while investigators continued to search for enough evidence to charge him with the murders.

I thumbed the screen to answer the call. "Hello, William. Do you have good news for me?"

"We've got him, Dawn. There is evidence that proves Mason bought a gun the month before the killings. We don't have the gun, but there are shell casings from the seller's gun range where Mason bought and test-fired the gun. They match the shell casings at the crime scene. It's just a matter of time before he's formally charged. I wanted you to know. I'm sure the found evidence will make the news tonight. I figure the press will be hounding you once the word is out."

"Wait, what? He's going to be charged… without the murder weapon?"

"Yes, the shell casings are a direct link. The casings tie him to the purchase of the weapon, and they link his gun to the murders."

I felt lightheaded. I struggled to comprehend what he was saying. "Why did the man wait over a year to come forward?"

"The seller lives out of state. He didn't see Wayne's photo in connection with the murders until watching a true crime show last week. He called the tipline and identified Wayne as the buyer of a gun he sold, and told the tipline about the shell casings. He has paperwork that proves the sale, and he has records of the test-firing incident."

"Oh my God, William. I can't believe it's happening after all this time."

We talked a few more minutes, then said our goodbyes. As I set my phone aside, I thought about the relationship William and I had established in the months following Mike and Gracie's murders and how he saved me. Grateful for his friendship, I also appreciated his expertise. I wondered where we went from there and how the case would develop.

32.

Onward and Upward
Ambition Wins Out

I lounged in my booth at the diner. Since Angi's move, I had reverted to my previous habit of people watching at the Last Chance. Angi paused at my table to refill my coffee.

"Aunt Dawn, would you watch Sophie for me tomorrow night? I have class."

"I love when you call me Aunt Dawn, and of course, I'll watch Sophie. Stop by early, and I'll have dinner ready for you and we can catch up. I've missed you."

"That would be great. I need your advice."

The bell over the front door jingled, and she left to seat the new arrival. I wondered what advice she needed.

***

The quiche sat cooling on the stovetop. Tony was working late, overseeing renovations of the Not So. There would just be Angi and me for dinner. I was putting the finishing touches on the salad when I heard the driveway alarm. The thud of her footsteps sounded as she bounded up the stairs. Excitement and youthful energy radiated from her.

"Give me that baby." I suspended Sophie in the air while I made monster noises and tickled her belly with my mouth. Sophie giggled and fisted her hands in my hair while Angi carried the playpen to the kitchen. Once Sophie was absorbed with her toys, we filled our plates.

"So, tell me about school."

"School is great. I registered for the mixed media class because I was interested in the photography portion of the course. I figured getting exposure to additional media in the syllabus couldn't hurt, and I could see if something else appealed to me. But the web design course has been a surprise. I didn't realize how much I'd like it. I can see making a business out of combining both."

"Did you want my advice about school?"

Her excitement dimmed. She lowered her eyes and took a deep breath. "No, not school. I need advice about Blane. I don't know what to do. As much as I care about him, I just don't know how we can make a relationship work. I mean, his job keeps him traveling most of the time, and when he's not traveling, he's in Tulsa. I'm a single mom working full time and now I'm in night school. It's like the timing is all wrong. I'm afraid if I talk to him about how I feel, I'll lose him and regret it the rest of my life. He's great but... what should I do?"

"I can't tell you what to do, but let me ask you a few questions. What's your number one priority?"

She answered without hesitation. "Sophie, of course."

"And why are you taking night classes?"

"To get an education so I can provide a better life for Sophie and me.

"Why do you think Blane took the security job?"

Scrunching up her face, she thought for a moment. "I think he's kind of lost. Like he's trying to figure something out."

"Angi, I think you're right. Perhaps he feels the same way you do, but he's afraid of having the conversation. Maybe he's afraid of losing you, too. For a relationship to work, both people need to know what they want and commit to it. What do you want, Angi?"

"I want to be able to take care of Sophie and me on my own. I don't want to be trapped in a situation because I can't take care of myself. Once I know I can do that, that's when I want to have a relationship."

"It sounds like you answered your own question. If you explain all this to Blane, how do you think he'll react?

"I don't know. I think, maybe, he'll be relieved? I think breaking up will give him time to figure out what he wants." She gave me a smirk. "You did it again."

"What?"

"You gave me advice without giving me advice."

I gave a nonchalant shrug. "That's the way I roll."

33.

Hard Truths
Nothing Difficult is Ever Easy

A week after William called me, he appeared on my doorstep. He was right about the reporters. As soon as the news broke that Wayne Beck Mason had been charged with two counts of first-degree murder, they started circling. I was doing my best to avoid them. A few had shown up in Chance, but they hadn't found my cabin.

William and I sat in my kitchen nook. My back was to the French doors and deck beyond. He sat across from me. My hands, captured in his strong, warm ones, were centered on the table. His emotions swarmed around me. There was excitement, anticipation, longing, and tenderness.

"What is it, William? Why are you here?"

His excitement escalated. "We have the murder weapon. The district attorney is seeking the death penalty."

I had a vague awareness of the French doors opening behind me, but my focus was on William. My vision blurred, and a knot formed in my throat. "What... How... When?"

William looked behind me. Still holding my hands, he rose in a protective gesture. I glanced over my shoulder to see Tony paused in the open doorway, his eyes fixed on our clasped hands.

"Tony!" I pulled my hands free. "It's alright, William." I walked up to Tony and gave him a quick hug. "Tony, I want you to meet someone very dear to me. This is William, the lead

220

detective on Mike and Gracie's murder investigation. William, this is Tony Rossi."

Both men sized each other up, then clasped hands in a firm handshake.

From William, I felt a mixture of disappointment, regret, acceptance, and then approval. Tony's relief registered next as he nodded and released William's hand.

"Tony, join us, please," I said. "William just told me they have the murder weapon, and the DA is going for the death penalty. He was about to give me the details when you walked in."

We all took a seat. Tony sat next to me and rested the palm of his hand on my thigh. William faced us.

"So, how did you find the murder weapon?" I prompted.

William cleared his throat. "Wayne's brother, Aaron. Wayne took the gun to him the night of the murders. He didn't tell Aaron what he'd done; he just told him that someone had given him the gun, and, due to his record, he couldn't be caught with it. Aaron lives in Arkansas, and there wasn't as much in the news there about their murders. When he learned that Wayne had been charged with murder, he walked into a local police station in Arkansas, turned the gun in, and told them he suspected the gun was used in a murder. Ballistics confirmed the gun is indeed the murder weapon."

I was speechless. Tony pulled me to him and pressed his lips to my forehead.

William hesitated, then continued, his tone gentling. "Dawn, you'll have to testify."

I sat up straight in my chair. "I'll be happy to testify against that monster. He is going down."

William shifted in his chair. I felt his discomfort. "There's more. There's something you don't know."

He paused, and the silence became awkward. "Dawn… the two murder charges will be amended to three. Gracie was pregnant. She was twelve weeks along. The pregnancy coincides with the timeline of the last reported abuse by Wayne, and the subsequent protective order that was issued against him."

The room began to spin, and I pressed my hands to the table to steady myself as the realization sank in. "He raped her," I said. "Why, William? Why didn't you tell me before?"

William lowered his head and rubbed the back of his neck. "I'm so sorry. I couldn't. In murder investigations, key evidence is withheld to help identify suspects. But more to the point, Dawn, I didn't think you could handle knowing this a year ago. The baby was Wayne's. If he knew this, the detail could be an additional motive. It strengthens the case against him."

Shuddering and rocking in my chair, I was overcome with a mixture of anger, grief, and loss. I was bereft. Tony tried to console me, but I was inconsolable. I hammered the table with my fists before gripping the edge of the table and forcing myself to take a calming breath. Minutes crawled by without a word spoken. Then, I nodded my head. "Okay. I need to be alone. I need to process this and prepare. He will pay."

William placed his hand over mine. "You'll have plenty of time to prepare. This is a capital case, which means it's not unusual to take one to three years before going to trial."

"What? What do you mean *one to three years?* What the hell is a capital case?" My hands clenched, my respiration increased, and the room began to swim again.

Tony sat in patient silence, providing support while William continued.

"A capital case is one in which, if the defendant is proved guilty, he or she will face the death penalty. There are specific guidelines for the defense counsel in death penalty cases to ensure the defendant's constitutional rights are not violated."

I knocked my chair over as I jumped up and began pacing. "His constitutional rights? As far as I'm concerned, he has one right—and that's to die."

William's calm voice continued. "Additionally, the process includes *discovery*, which means the State's evidence is sent to the defense to be reviewed by the defense team, and then they go over the evidence with their client to form a defense and strategize the case. The case is then negotiated. Hearings have to be scheduled. All of these steps take a tremendous amount of time."

I grabbed handfuls of my hair, then threw my hands in the air. All my frustration, anger, and rage were expressed by a roar. I didn't think I had ever made such an animalistic sound. "I feel so damn helpless!"

Helpless, but not hopeless. My heart rate slowed as I got a grip on my emotions. To their credit, neither man said a word nor made a move. They traded glances then watched me as I righted the chair, dropped into it, and crossed my arms over my middle with a scowl plastered on my face.

Tony raised one eyebrow and looked at me as if he were studying a mongoose preparing to fight a cobra. "Better now?"

"No. But I will be. And I'm serious, guys, I need some alone time. I won't be good company today."

Rising, Tony looked at William and nodded toward the back deck. "We'll give you some space."

Tony opened the back door, and William followed him out. I heard the murmur of their voices from outside—no words, just the low rumble of their conversation. I could feel the waves of concern flowing from each of them. They shared a common goal now. I hoped they could bond because they were the two most important living men in my life.

Never again did I want to feel the anger, pain, and absolute hatred that I felt for Wayne Beck Mason at that moment. I had to find a way to harness that hatred and direct it into constructive action. I would testify and hold him accountable in that courtroom. I would look him in the eyes in front of everyone and tell them what he did. If the evidence weren't damning enough, I would hammer the last nail into the coffin of his defense with my testimony. I would be so compelling that everyone would know he was guilty.

Tony opened the back door and leaned in. "Hey, I know you're upset, and you have every right to be, but..." He eased through the door, bringing William with him. "There are several positives to focus on, too, like the murder weapon being found and the DA going for the death penalty. So, I was thinking, it's Saturday. I'd like to get to know your *Dear William,* and maybe we should realign our attitudes. Let's have a party tonight and celebrate the progress in the case. *Dear William,* can stay and meet everyone. You won't have to do anything. I'll take care of the food and call everyone."

Tony gave William a pointed look.

William, ordinarily dominant and authoritative, looked awkward and unsure. "Oh, uh, yeh. What he said. And uh, I'll help."

I stared at them, bewildered. I felt like I'd just been catapulted from a slingshot—pulled back into despair, then launched into party mode. I couldn't form words. I just stared.

"What? Too soon?" A charismatic grin lit Tony's face.

I glanced at William, who sported an enigmatic smile. He raised his hands in surrender, gave a slight shrug, and looked uncomfortable.

I couldn't help it. I started laughing. "*Dear William?*"

William, bless his heart, looked as if he wanted to crawl under a rock.

***

At dusk, we gathered around a campfire in front of the shop. A warm evening for February, but typical of ever-changing Oklahoma weather. Tony kept the meal simple. We roasted hot dogs on sticks over the open flame. Smoke permeated our clothes and hair, but added that extra flavor that made food cooked outside taste so good.

Steve crouched behind Katie and helped her roast her dog. Thank God Tony invited Diane, or the food would have consisted of hot dogs, chips, and beer. Diane contributed chili, baked beans, and macaroni salad. Cici was building s'mores to be roasted next.

Angi sidled up with Sophie and an attractive young man who exuded a sophisticated metro vibe. Striking, he looked out of place at a cookout dressed in khaki slacks and a polo shirt.

"Aunt Dawn, I'd like you to meet my friend from college. This is Thomas."

I took his proffered hand. "Welcome, Thomas. It's nice to meet you."

Angi led him away to continue introductions.

Blane was absent, and my heart ached for him. It hadn't been that long since his and Angi's breakup. She recovered quickly. *I thought she didn't want a relationship.*

I was still reeling from the events of this afternoon. Although so out of character for me, I relinquished control of the party to Tony. I leaned back in a camping chair, sipped on a bottled beer, and watched the performer in Tony emerge. He motioned for William to join him. William looked over his shoulder to see if Tony meant someone else. Tony motioned again. "Come on up here, Wac."

William stood from an ice chest on which he sat, grinned in spite of himself, and sidled up next to him. Tony threw an arm around William's shoulder in a bro hug. "Everyone, I'd like you to meet Detective William Arthur Curtis, my new best friend and the lead detective on Mike and Gracie's case. Go ahead, Wac, tell them the news."

Standing next to Tony as *Wac* in front of these strangers, William appeared unsure of himself, awkward even. Then I felt the shift in his demeanor as Detective William took charge. "There was a break in the case." He addressed the group in a succinct, concise manner, as if they were officers at roll call, and relayed the details he'd told us earlier.

The group was overjoyed. Diane left her food and dashed to William. "Wac, welcome to our motley crew." He offered his hand, but she batted it away. "No, sir, I want a hug."

And that was how William Arthur Curtis was brought into the fold.

34.
Lost but Not Forgotten
A Child Remembered

Baby Patterson deserved more than I was capable of dispensing. A lifetime more.

I leaned against Tony near the foot of Mike and Gracie's graves. The twitter of birds formed a melody, and the dew-soaked grass dampened my shoes. An ache filled me as if I were wounded, and indeed I was. How was it possible that I felt so much for this child that I would never meet during my lifetime?

It had taken six months for the monument to be created. I had ordered it the week after I learned of Baby Patterson's existence and murder. Rather small, the monument wasn't ostentatious in the least. Instead of a standard granite or marble headstone or footstone, I commissioned a sculpture of a sleeping baby with wings to be laid on the center of Gracie's grave.

The artisan had adapted my illustration, and the sculpture was a stunning portrayal of a bare infant that appeared to have been captured in a deep slumber atop a plush throw. There was a pout on the delicate, rosebud mouth. Tiny eyelashes fanned out over her cheeks. The knees and elbows were dimpled and drawn into a fetal position as she lay on her side. A halo of soft curls

226

surrounded her angelic face. The stone had been transformed from its rough, virgin state, so that the skin of the child appeared soft and supple, and the blanket as if it were velvet. On the face of the blanket, where it draped over the support base, the etched inscription appeared to be embroidered and simply read, *Baby Patterson.* And below that, *SOAR!*

William arrived and took my hand. I was buoyed by my two best friends.

I decided to have a graveside service in the hopes of gaining closure, choosing early morning for the service because it was August and promised to be a scorcher.

The minister stood in front of the headstones. "Will anyone else be attending?"

"No," I answered. This loss was too personal. I didn't want to discuss it or have my other friends try to console me. I wanted to grieve privately with my two best friends.

There was a wall of clouds overhead impeding the sun and casting a shadow over our entourage.

As the minister cleared his throat and opened the bible, a ray of light pierced the clouds and illuminated the effigy of Baby Patterson. Then, a vibration of energy entered through my chest and spread outward, creating an unexplainable sense of joy and peace—closure.

35.

The Trial
Pushing the Envelope

*"Fate whispers to the warrior, 'You cannot withstand the storm.'
The warrior whispers back, 'I am the storm.'" —Unknown*

I lived in an emotional haze while awaiting the trial. I went
through the motions of living, but events passed me by without
registering. Tony was the one constant in my life. He threw
himself into creating Rossi's Landing and provided an emotional
landing pad for me on the days I needed it. Eighteen months after
the memorial service for my grandbaby, and two years since
William told me about the murder charges, the first day of the
trial arrived and so did my renewed purpose.

Tony and I stood before the deputy, who was drinking
coffee at a raised podium in the lobby of the courthouse. The
gold nameplate on his uniform indicated he was Deputy
Michaels. Setting down the Styrofoam cup, he asked, "May I
help you?"

I nodded. "Can you tell me where the Patterson murder
trial will be?"

"Yes, ma'am. That will be in District Judge Tankersley's
courtroom on the third floor. Jury selection begins in thirty
minutes." He studied me for a moment, then asked, "You're Mrs.
Patterson, aren't you?"

"Yes, I am."

"I'm sorry for your loss, ma'am."

"Thank you, Deputy Michaels."

Soon after settling into a seat in the courtroom, anxiety kicked in. The unease I felt wasn't from the discomfort of the bench, which resembled a wooden pew from an old country church and emitted a squeak every time a body shifted. Nor was it the uncontrolled thermostat which regulated the warm and stuffy air, periodically dispensing enough chilled air to raise goosebumps. What made me uneasy was the proximity of the murderer—seated mere feet from me—on the other side of a waist-high wooden partition. I chose to sit on the defense side to convey to Wayne Beck Mason that I wasn't afraid of him. I was coming for him. But that didn't mean I enjoyed being that close to the monster.

I had never been in a courtroom before. I wanted to see the trial from the beginning, at least, I thought I did, so we arrived just before jury selection, which began at 9 a.m.

The entire spectator area was filled with the jury pool. Twenty-three people were called by name from that pool to the jury box. I watched the faltering approach of an old man who smiled and nodded to the gallery as he shuffled by. I wanted to hug him, but I wasn't sure I wanted him as a juror. Likewise, when a skinny young man in tattered jeans and a stained T-shirt ambled by with a nonchalant gait, and a pregnant woman who looked as if she were due last week took her spot, I questioned the quality of the candidates.

The young prosecutor, Jared Bigley, buttoned his jacket, squared his shoulders, then ran a hand down his tie in a smoothing gesture. He moved to the podium with the confidence of an all-star athlete entering a football stadium on game day. His confidence was comforting, at least as much as I could be comforted in that situation. Grasping the sides of the lectern, he paused and made brief eye contact with the potential jurors. His smile appeared genuine.

"Good morning. Thank you for appearing here today." He glanced at his notes. "I will be asking questions that may sound silly or unimportant. I assure you, they are not, and the honesty and candidness of your answers are important. The questions are designed to determine if you are prejudiced against one side or the other. Also, to evaluate if you can determine guilt or innocence based solely on the facts without being swayed by opinions of others."

After Prosecutor Bigley questioned every juror, the defense took their turn.

Seasoned Defense Attorney Charles Westerfeld, a lion of a man with a commanding presence, drew a hand through his white mane that curled just below his collar. He approached the podium at a slow and graceful pace, his eyes moved over the potential jurors as if he were stalking prey. "The prosecution referred to my client as the defendant. It is prejudicial and done by design. My client has a name. Wayne. Beck. Mason. Wayne is an innocent man until proven guilty, and the burden of proof is on the state."

He left the podium to stand behind his client, then rested a hand on Wayne's shoulder in a show of solidarity. "Unless the prosecution can prove otherwise, Wayne is, and will remain, an innocent man."

I clenched a tissue in my hand. *He is not innocent!* My breathing became labored as air gusted in and out of my nose. My head pounded, and my eyes burned. *I will not cry. Not yet.*

As far as I was concerned, Mr. Westerfeld was grandstanding and came off as an egotistical bully. I glanced at the jurors and wondered what they thought. Stone-faced, they gave no clue, and I could not discern their feelings. My empath shields were firmly in place. There were too many people, too many emotions in addition to my own. The combination would hit my sensitivity like a blitzkrieg, and I knew it.

Westerfeld ceased his monotonous rhetoric, returned to the podium, and questioned each individual in the jury box. At the end of the interviews, nine people were released. The remaining jurors were a cross section of race, gender, and professions. Among them were a college professor, an architect, a nurse, and an airplane mechanic. I felt good about the mix. The twelve jurors and two alternates were sworn in. Afterward, we broke for lunch.

***

The pungent aroma of garlic and yeast assailed me when Tony and I entered the Italian restaurant across the street from the courthouse. He placed his hand on my lower back and guided me to a booth. I was incapable of small talk, so I picked at a grilled chicken salad, but my stomach rolled, and what little I ate threatened to come back up. After what felt like an eternity, Tony laid his hand over mine. "Dawn, we can wait outside the courtroom until you're called to testify. Seeing him has to be—"

"I have to be in the courtroom. Before the break, I was questioning whether I could stick it out. But I just have to. Mike and Gracie deserve justice. I want the jury to see me sitting in that courtroom. I want Wayne to see me. I will not abandon my family."

Tony raised an eyebrow, a corner of his mouth lifted, and he nodded. "That's my warrior. Come on, let's head back."

***

Approaching the entrance to the courtroom, I made a decision, "Tony, let's sit on the other side of the room. This courtroom isn't set up like the ones in the movies. I couldn't see everything, and I don't want to be so close to Wayne."

"Okay. Lead the way."

We sat in the second row on the far side of the room and waited for the proceedings to reconvene. From my new vantage point, the judge would be visible and centered at the front of the room, the jury against the wall to my left, and I could see both the prosecution and defense teams.

Judge Tankersley gave the jury instructions followed by the prosecutor's opening statement. A haze of melancholy settled over me while a band of anxiety held me tight in its grip. I didn't want to listen to the states' accusations or the horrendous description of the murders.

Slated as the first witness, I would have to resurrect those hideous scenes in gruesome detail—here, in front of Mike and

Gracie's killer and all these strangers. I could not relive those details multiple times and retain my sanity. So, I leaned my head on Tony's shoulder and zoned out, the prosecutor's voice became muffled and the words indistinguishable as if spoken in a barrel.

Seeing the defense approach the lectern, I sat up straight and reengaged. Wayne slouched into the chair, his eyes searched the crowd until he found me and sneered before casting his eyes to the floor, *acting* dejected but stoic. Mr. Westerfeld began his opening statement and inserted *innocent* into his soliloquy at every opportunity. I knew Wayne was not innocent, and the insistence of his innocence by the defense was almost more than I could bear. Attorney Westerfeld droned on about the presumption of innocence and the burden of proof beyond reasonable doubt. He said, "You need to evaluate the reliability of evidence. Judge the facts and the evidence, not Wayne."

As if sensing my anger and discomfort, Tony squeezed my shoulder and pulled me closer. It was what I needed. His steady reassurance grounded me and strengthened my resolve.

Defense Attorney Westerfeld then provided a summary of juror responsibilities. "You are individually responsible for your vote. Follow the law, remove emotion, and differentiate between opinions and facts." He finished with a flourish and strutted to his seat.

Prosecutor Bigley approached the podium next, but before he could call me to testify, Defense Attorney Westerfeld rocketed out of his chair to invoke the Rule of Sequestration. This meant that all other witnesses must leave the room before I testified, and none of the witnesses would be allowed back into the courtroom unless they were testifying or until all witnesses were finished testifying. The one exception was William. As the lead investigator, he was allowed to remain in the courtroom.

All of the other witnesses exited to the benches outside the courtroom.

Prosecutor Bigley then announced, "The state calls Dawn Patterson to the witness stand."

I gripped the back of the pew in front of me as I stood. My legs shook and my palms dampened. *I can do this. I can, and I will.* Determined, I walked to the stand, shoulders back, head held high.

William sat at the back of the room. Since we were both witnesses, we ceased all contact. No phone calls, texting, or talking in person. We didn't want to give any reason for a mistrial. On the witness stand, I avoided eye contact with him, too, but knowing he was present was a comfort.

My gaze traveled the expanse of the room and settled on Wayne. *You will pay.* He flashed a dismissive smirk.

Prosecutor Bigley spoke, drawing my attention. "Please state your name for the record."

"Dawn Patterson."

I was then sworn in. My heart raced. I took a sip of water to moisten my parched mouth.

Prosecutor Bigley began his questioning. "Mrs. Patterson, please explain your relationship to the deceased in this case."

I squeaked, so I stopped, swallowed another sip of water, and then cleared my throat. "The three *murder* victims were my husband, Mike Patterson, my daughter, Gracie Patterson, and my unborn grandchild, Baby Patterson." My throat tightened, then my neck and shoulders tensed.

"Mrs. Patterson, please pull the microphone closer. Did you find the bodies of your husband and daughter on the morning of July 17th, 2020?"

I blanched and nodded. A headache was knocking

"Mrs. Patterson, you need to speak your answers for the record."

"Yes. Yes, I found their bodies that morning." An involuntary shudder rattled through me.

"Before we discuss what you saw, Mrs. Patterson, tell us why your husband was at your daughter's house."

"Gracie was moving home. Mike went over that Friday night to help her finish packing. He planned to stay the night so they could load the truck at first light and come home. I stayed home to get her room ready and clear a space in the shop for storage purposes." Perspiration dotted my hair line and a bead of sweat ran down my back.

"I'd like you to identify the people in this picture." Prosecutor Bigley then handed me a photograph.

Gazing at the images before me, a tremulous smile formed, then my eyes stung, and my shoulders slumped. "This is a picture of Mike and Gracie, a selfie that Gracie took."

"Mrs. Patterson, when was this selfie taken?"

I wiped my eyes and sniffed. "The night before their murders. Gracie sent it to me via text, and that's what prompted my call that night."

"And does this photo exemplify Mike and Gracie's relationship and their mood that night?"

I nodded. "Yes." I pointed at Gracie. "Look at the joy on her face. See the adoration on Mike's face? This was typical of their relationship. The picture shows their excitement at the prospect of her moving home."

He took the photo from me. "I offer this photograph into evidence, Your Honor."

Prosecutor Bigley then handed the photo to the court reporter, who documented and marked it as an exhibit before handing the picture to the judge.

"Mrs. Patterson, why was Gracie moving home?" Prosecutor Bigley asked.

"Because," I focused a hard stare on Wayne, "she filed a protective order against the *defendant*, but he wouldn't stop harassing her."

"Objection, your honor, hearsay!" The defense was quick to protest.

Prosecutor Bigley continued. "Your honor, if I may ask a few more questions, I'll be able to establish this is not hearsay."

The judge nodded. "I'll allow it. The prosecution may continue questioning the witness."

Prosecutor Bigly continued, "Mrs. Patterson, did you see the defendant harass your daughter?"

"I saw harassing text messages from him on her phone." My pulse throbbed in my temples. "He threatened many things. He texted that he would slash her tires, and her tires were slashed. He also texted that she would be sorry if she didn't drop the charges against him."

"Your Honor!" Defense Attorney Westerfeld was on his feet again.

I wanted to tell Westerfeld to shut up, but I held my tongue.

Prosecutor Bigley addressed the judge. "Your Honor, the state has supplied copies of the threatening text messages to the defense. If the defense prefers, we will read the threatening texts aloud."

"That won't be necessary, Your Honor," Mr. Westerfeld stated before setting back down.

Judge Tankersly nodded. "Continue."

Prosecutor Bigley asked, "Mrs. Patterson, what were the charges the defendant alluded to in that text?"

I spoke with confidence, "The main charge was aggravated assault. He beat her viciously."

"Objection!" A red-faced Westerfeld was on his feet in an instant. "There was no conviction."

I went hot all over as I sprang up from the chair and blurted, "There was no conviction because Gracie was murdered before she could testify!" My heart pounded and I felt slightly dizzy.

The banging of the judge's gavel penetrated my rage. "Sustained!"

I sat down, and Judge Tankersly peered at me over the top of his glasses, "Mrs. Patterson, you will not address the defense directly unless the defense is questioning you. Is that clear?"

I bowed my head and feigned contrition. "Yes, Your Honor."

I saw the hint of a gleam in Prosecutor Bigley's eyes as he struggled to keep a composed expression before he continued.

"So, your daughter, Gracie Patterson, filed a police report, and charges of aggravated assault were brought against the defendant.

How can I say this? "After suffering a ruptured spleen, broken ribs and nose, and multiple contusions, Gracie filed a police report alleging the defendant beat her."

Attorney Westerfeld appeared to be spring-loaded as he came out of his chair again. "Your Honor!"

Judge Tankersly's eyebrows drew together in displeasure. "Mr. Bigley, you will instruct your witness to answer only the questions asked without elaboration." Then the judge focused the full wattage of his glare on me. "Mrs. Patterson, you're pushing the envelope. You will find yourself in contempt if you continue in this manner. Understood?"

Taking stock of my situation, I mumbled, "Yes, Your Honor."

Prosecutor Bigley continued. "Now, Mrs. Patterson, let me see if I have the sequence of events correct. And please, answer only the questions I ask, without elaboration. Gracie Patterson was assaulted. She filed a police report that led to a charge of aggravated assault to be brought against the defendant. Is that correct?"

"Yes."

"Where did the alleged assault take place?"

"In St. Louis, at the defendant's house."

"When did Gracie move to Oklahoma?"

"Three weeks after her release from the hospital."

"And, Mrs. Patterson, did she continue to receive harassing text messages from the defendant?"

"She did."

"And when did Gracie agree to move in with you and your husband?"

"After the tires on her car were slashed."

"Mrs. Patterson, was a protective order in place?"

"Yes, but she lived in a rural area, and unexplained things kept happening. She was terrified and didn't feel safe." I felt my blood pressure rising; it felt as if my scalp tightened around my head.

"Please explain for the court what motivated you to go to Gracie's house, predawn on July 17th, 2020, where you found your husband, Mike, and daughter, Gracie's, bodies."

My stomach rolled, a rushing sound filled my ears, and I became dizzy. I took a shuddering breath, gripped the edge of my chair, and found Tony's eyes. He gave a slight nod and mouthed, "You can do this."

My heart ached with the remembrance of that happy call—the last time I would ever speak to Mike and Gracie. I rubbed my chest to relieve the pain, then I leaned closer to the microphone. "I called Mike around ten o'clock Friday night, right after I got the selfie from Gracie. He switched the phone to speaker mode, and we all three talked. Gracie was so excited to move home, and we were overjoyed to have her back in the house. The call was great. We were all happy.

"About 3 a.m. I woke from a sound sleep for no apparent reason. Feeling apprehensive, I checked the locks on the doors and windows, then went back to bed. I couldn't get back to sleep so I finally got up and drank tea. I couldn't shake the bad feeling, so I called to check on them and to ask when they would be home. I tried Mike's phone first. The call went to voicemail. I called Gracie. That call forwarded as well. Mike was a light sleeper, so at that point, I knew something was wrong, and I drove to her house.

"When I arrived, it was still dark. The porch light was off, and there were no lights on in the house. I found out later the breaker box was tampered with. I ran up the steps and stopped. The door was open about an inch. I eased it all the way open and… and—"

I gagged. I covered my mouth and rocked. *Keep it together. You can do this.*

Judge Tankersly asked, "Do we need a brief recess?"

"No!" I almost yelled. I wanted this over with. "I… I can finish, Your Honor."

He nodded. "All right, Mrs. Patterson. I can appreciate the difficulty of your testimony. If you change your mind, we can recess at any time."

"Thank you."

I blew my nose and continued. "When I stepped inside, the house was silent—completely still. There was a foul odor. I couldn't see anything at first. When my eyes adjusted, I saw Mike asleep on the couch. I called out to him. He didn't answer. I crossed the room. When I got to him, I saw… I saw—"

I stopped short, keeping a sob at bay. I closed my eyes and took a calming breath, then another, and opened my eyes. My voice grew hoarse as I continued. "I saw a hole in his temple. I dropped to my knees and felt his neck for a pulse. There wasn't one. His skin was cool."

Immersed in the memory, I stopped speaking. I felt Mike's cool skin on my fingertips. The cloying smell engulfed me. My eyelids fluttered, and my cheeks dampened.

"Mrs. Patterson?" Judge Tankersley prodded, bringing me back to the current moment.

In a monotone voice, I continued. "I must have been in shock. I just stared at Mike in disbelief. Then I thought of Gracie. Calling her name, I stumbled to her bedroom."

My world began to spin again. I fought not to pass out before I could finish recounting the horror of that day. "When I reached the bedroom, the sun was coming up, and light began to filter through the blinds. As I peered into the room, I grabbed the door frame for support. There was… so much blood." I shook my head. "So much blood. It was on the walls and… everywhere. The smell was overpowering."

I gagged and covered my mouth, then swallowed. A cold sweat coated my skin. Grabbing tissues, I wiped my face and continued. "The room was in chaos, as if a rampaging bull had been trapped inside. And then…my Gracie. I saw what that monster did to my baby! I ran outside and vomited, then I called 911."

Still on the witness stand, a keening wail erupted from the deepest recesses of my soul. Bent at the waist, I hugged myself and sobbed. A hush fell over the courtroom.

The judge called a recess. I could not move. I struggled to control my emotions. The rustling sound of people leaving the courtroom registered. Tony was allowed to come to me.

"Dawn, it's me. Let's get you out of the courtroom for a few minutes." Tony placed his hand on my shoulder while I calmed myself. Kneeling in front of me, he swept the hair back from my face. "The defense is going to ask you some questions so let's get you ready. William is worried about you, too. He's watching you from the back of the room."

"I know." I hiccupped and regained my composure. "Lord, forget tissues, I need paper towels. I didn't realize how hard it would be to talk about that day in front of a room full of strangers. I need to go to the ladies' room and throw some water on my face."

***

Face scrubbed and somewhat refreshed, I was back on the witness stand, and now the defense would question me.

Defense Attorney Westerfeld began. "Ms. Patterson, isn't it true that Gracie was your only child? That you were jealous of Wayne's relationship with her, and you disliked him because of your jealousy, and that caused you to be biased against him?"

His voice grated on my nerves, and his cocky attitude infuriated me. "No, I wasn't jealous of their relationship, nor did I dislike the defendant in the beginning. What I disliked were the facts I uncovered when I did a background search on him. And as far as bias is concerned, I wasn't biased. I had informed opinions based on facts. Bias would indicate a lack of objectivity or fairness."

It was Defense Westerfeld's turn to blanch. He wasn't expecting that answer. He didn't realize I had done my due diligence. I would not let him intimidate me. *Game on!*

Careful consideration preceded his next question. "Ms. Patterson, did you ever observe Wayne hit, mistreat, or harm your daughter in any physical manner?"

I stalled. I needed some sense of control. I took a sip of water and cleared my throat. "I didn't *see* it happen, no."

He hesitated a beat. "No more questions, Your Honor."

Prosecutor Bigley stood. "Redirect, Your Honor?"

The judge nodded, "Go ahead."

Prosecutor Bigley moved to the lectern. "Mrs. Patterson, you say you didn't see the defendant hit your daughter, but someone did. Someone beat her severely enough to hospitalize her. And according to your earlier testimony, she filed a police report alleging the defendant was the one who beat her. Is that correct?"

Sitting up straight in the chair, I lifted my chin and glared at Wayne. Then, turning back to Prosecutor Bigley, I stated, "That is correct. She filed a police report, and charges of aggravated assault were brought against the defendant."

"Nothing further, Your Honor."

Judge Tankersly announced, "The witness is dismissed. Call your next witness."

Tony moved to the aisle and waited to escort me out of the courtroom.

***

The trial lasted four excruciating days. I went to the courthouse each day and sat on a bench just outside of the courtroom to ensure every juror, without exception, saw me as they entered and exited.

Around 2 p.m., on the last day of the trial, my hip was aching, and as I stood to relieve the pain, Deputy Michaels stuck his head outside the courtroom. "Hey, the last testimony just ended. Closing arguments are next. Judge Tankersley will call for a twenty-minute recess afterwards, before the jurors begin deliberations. After the recess is announced, you'll be allowed back in the courtroom for the rest of the proceedings."

I nodded. "Thank you, deputy."

An hour later, William exited through the door. With a smug expression, he gave me an assured wink as he passed.

I grabbed Tony's arm. "Did you see that? William winked at me. That's got to be good, right?"

36.

The Verdict
A Dog Day Afternoon

"The dead cannot cry out for justice. It is a duty of the living to do so for them." —*Lois McMaster Bujold.*

Once again in the courtroom, Tony and I sat in the same spots we occupied three days earlier, as if we had assigned seating. I prayed the jury would return with a swift and guilty verdict for the murder charges. Too distracted and nervous to engage in a conversation, I occupied myself playing solitaire and word games on my phone.

The bailiff sat as a sentinel outside the closed door of the jury room during deliberations. We waited an hour and a half before the door to the jury room opened and a woman handed a note to the bailiff, then retreated, pulling the door closed.

A flurry of activity erupted. The clerk scurried from the courtroom and returned with Judge Tankersley. Both attorneys were summoned to the courtroom, and Wayne Beck Mason was brought back in. He reclined arrogantly in his chair at the defense table as if he hadn't a care in the world.

Once Judge Tankersley was confident the key players were in place, he spoke to the bailiff. "Escort the jury in."

The jury filed in and took their assigned seats. Studying their faces, I tried to get a read on what they were feeling, but their faces gave nothing away, and my empath shields were still firmly in place.

Judge Tankersley addressed a female juror who clasped papers in her hand. "Ms. Sheridan, are you the foreperson?"

"Yes, Your Honor, I am."

"Have you reached a verdict?"

"Yes, Your Honor, we have."

"Was the verdict unanimous?"

"Yes, Your Honor, the verdict was unanimous."

Judge Tankersley then asked, "If anyone disagrees that the decision was unanimous, please raise your hand." Not a single hand went up. "Bailiff, bring me the verdicts so I can review them for form."

After perusing the three forms, Judge Tankersley summoned Prosecutor Bigley and Defense Counsel Westerfeld to the bench. After reviewing and conferring, the attorneys took their respective seats.

The judge announced that when the verdicts were read, he would not tolerate any outbursts from the gallery, and if there was anyone who couldn't control their emotions, they should leave at that time. He then gave the forms to the clerk.

The clerk read aloud, "Count one, we the jury find as follows—the defendant is guilty of murder in the first degree of Baby Patterson."

I glanced at Wayne; his earlier arrogance appeared to evaporate. He stared straight ahead, devoid of emotion.

The clerk continued. "Count two—find the defendant guilty of murder in the first degree of Michael Patterson. Count three—find the defendant guilty of murder in the first degree of Gracie Patterson."

Gasping, I sucked in air. I must have held my breath during the entire reading of the verdict. My hand hurt, and I realized I was squeezing Tony's hand and had been doing so the whole time. Stunned and overjoyed, my spirit rejoiced. I felt light—buoyant. The verdict was what I hoped for—prayed for—ever since Mike and Gracie's murders over three years ago. The jury would now start the penalty phase, where they would go back over evidence, aggravating circumstances, and mitigating circumstances, to determine whether to impose a sentence of life, life without parole, or death. Once done, the jury would make its recommendations for punishment. There was still the ordeal of formal sentencing. Nevertheless, an immense weight was lifted, and I felt as if I were floating. Satisfied with the verdict, I didn't want to sit through the penalty phase. To learn Wayne's fate, I would have to wait a month for the formal sentencing.

The jury filed out, and a young woman rushed into the courtroom and up to the partition that separated the gallery from the defense table. Leaning over the railing, she handed a folded slip of paper to Defense Attorney Westerfeld. He unfolded the note, and when he finished reading it, he leaned over and whispered to Wayne. Wayne glanced at his attorney wide-eyed, gave an emphatic nod, then pushed himself halfway off the chair and searched the room with quick, erratic jerks of his head.

Attorney Westerfeld stood. "Your Honor, I have a request on behalf of the defendant. His dog has been brought to the courthouse. Will Wayne be allowed to see his dog?"

"Your Honor!" Prosecutor Bigley sprang to his feet. "We don't know anything about this dog, whether it's leash trained, house broken, or attack trained!"

Judge Tankersly raised a hand and motioned to Prosecutor Bigley to sit. "Those are valid concerns."

Glancing at Deputy Michaels, who had entered the room just minutes before and leaned against the wall, Judge Tankersley asked him, "What is your position on the matter, Deputy?"

Coming away from the wall, Deputy Michaels stood at a relaxed parade rest. "I would advise against it, Your Honor. I've seen the dog; it's large and poses a security risk."

Returning his attention to Attorney Westerfeld, the judge said, "You have your answer, Counselor."

A chair shot back and tipped over as Wayne jumped to his feet. "Oh come on! I'm going to die. I just want to see my dog one last time."

Attorney Westerfeld grabbed Wayne's arm and tried to calm him. Wayne shook off the attempt. His chest heaved, his nostrils flared, and his eyes widened as he took on a feral expression. Judge Tankersly yelled, "Security! Remove the prisoner!"

A scuffle ensued. It took three deputies to subdue Wayne and get handcuffs on him. They were still struggling with him when I rose to leave. "Tony, let's go out the side exit. I don't want to see any reporters.

We descended three flights of stairs and exited the door on the east side of the building, the exit closest to the public parking lot. Seeing Wayne become violent disturbed me. I stood just outside the exit and sucked in a lungful of fresh air. A bark drew my attention to the fence on my right, which ran the circumference of the courthouse secured parking area, where prisoners were loaded and unloaded. "Tony, that's Maisy. I wonder if she remembers me." The man holding the leash bore a strong resemblance to Wayne. We descended the stairs, and I walked toward the man and dog. "Maisy? Hi, girl. Do you remember me?"

The man's Adam's apple bobbed as he swallowed, and his eyes darted from Maisy to me.

Maisy's muzzle wrinkled, her lips drew back in what appeared to be a smile, and she strained against the leash as she danced and jumped. I stopped a few feet from them and asked, "Is it okay if I pet her?"

The man shifted from side to side. I lowered my shields, and I could feel his unease. "You must be Wayne's brother. Aaron, right?

He dropped his gaze to his feet. "Yes, ma'am, but I'm nothing like my brother." He raised his eyes to meet mine. "I am so sorry for your loss."

"Thank you, Aaron, I appreciate that." Tony stood behind me and observed while Aaron closed the gap to allow Maisy to greet me. I knelt and Maisy wiggled all over and slathered my face with her wet tongue. "I guess you do remember me, girl." Then I addressed Aaron. "For security reasons, they won't let you bring her into the building."

Aaron nodded. "They told me. That's why I'm here. He'll be coming out the back door." He motioned with his head. "If he gets in one of these cruisers by the fence, he'll at least get to see her. He hasn't seen her in over two years."

"So you've adopted her?" I asked, as I stood.

He shook his head and looked away. I felt his turmoil. "No, ma'am. I never wanted a dog. You see, when we were kids, my dad was mean. He always told us not to bring any animals home. He wouldn't tolerate an animal in his house. When Wayne was about nine and I was eleven, a stray dog followed him home. Mom and I warned him to get rid of the dog. He didn't. When Dad got home, he went ballistic. He made Wayne tie the dog up out back, then Dad went in the house. When he came out, he had a gun. Dad made Wayne shoot the dog."

"Oh, my God," I whispered.

Aaron's eyes looked vacant, as if he were reliving something. "Mom and Dad fought a lot. That night was the worst. Mom was mad about Dad making Wayne kill the dog. Dad locked us in our room. I remember them yelling and hearing slapping, hitting, then… silence." Aaron made eye contact with me. "We never saw our mother again…." Aaron paused, then took a shaky breath. "I never wanted a dog after that, but Wayne was obsessed with having one. I've been keeping Maisy for Wayne until the verdict. But since he… he'll never be able to have her, I'm taking her to a shelter when I leave here. She is a constant reminder of everything bad that happened in my life."

"No." My eyes filled, and my heart pounded. I stroked Maisy's head, and she leaned into me. "I'll take her. Gracie loved Maisy."

Movement caught my eye. The back door of the courthouse opened, and a handcuffed Wayne was escorted out the door. Three deputies surrounded him. There was a cut on Wayne's cheek, and his hair was wild. Aaron turned and walked Maisy to the fence. Tony and I remained in place.

Wayne caught sight of Maisy and called to her. "Maisy girl! How's my good girl?" He spoke to the guards as they neared a police cruiser parked six feet from the fence. "Can't I just pet her through the fence?"

The lead guard fixed him with a bland expression. "No. Now get in the car without a fight, or you'll get more of what you got in the courtroom."

A rear door of the car was opened, and a deputy pushed Wayne's head down as they shoved him into the cruiser. Wayne never acknowledged Aaron. The cruiser backed out of the parking spot and drove away from us toward the exit.

Aaron turned from the fence, his face appeared to have fallen, and his sorrow radiated towards me. When he reached us, he patted Maisy's head in an awkward gesture, then he handed me her leash. "She's yours now. I have her bed and toys in my car."

I shook my head. "Maisy deserves a fresh start. She'll get a new bed—a new life."

Aaron nodded, then said, "At least take her bear. Her favorite game is hide and seek."

A memory flashed of visiting Gracie when she lived with Wayne. Gracie showed me how they would hide the bear, and Maisy would search for it. "I'll take the bear."

Aaron left to get the toy. Tony stepped around me to greet Maisy, and she nosed his crotch. "Whoa, girl," he said as he gently pushed her head away, knelt, and stroked her neck and body. "We're going to be good friends, Maisy."

Aaron returned with the bear, and Maisy barked when she saw it. Tony reached for the toy. "I'll hide this under the blanket in the backseat of my car." Tony rushed to his car with the toy in hand, leaving me with Maisy and Aaron.

I touched Aaron's arm. "You're right, you are nothing like your brother. Thank you for letting me have Maisy." He nodded, then lumbered away.

Maisy strained against the leash, eager to play. Tony called to her. "Maisy. Seek!" She pulled me across the parking lot, jumped into the backseat of Tony's car, and began her new life.

37.

Reflections
Life is What Happens While We Wait

Daybreak announced itself with a subdued, hazy aura backlighting the trees and reflecting off the water in hues of pink and orange that were barely discernible. Although the air around me was still, the top branches of the trees swayed in a languid dance. There was a briskness in the air that April morning that made me grateful for the sweatshirt I donned. A pair of geese released a chorus of honks as they pumped their wings overhead. Maisy lay at my feet, and steam rose from a mug of coffee, dampening my nose. I rested my elbows on the picnic table on the back deck of my home, surrounded by the glory of nature, infused with a sense of peace and tranquility. I reflected on the events that transpired after William shared the news of finding the murder weapon twenty-six months ago. The trial ended just last month. Although I felt as if I were suspended in time, endlessly waiting, the wheels of justice kept turning, and the rest of the world kept moving around me. The end was near.

A disembodied, jaunty tune whistled from an unknown origin and interrupted my reverie. Maisy barked and jumped to her feet. A movement at the cliff's edge caught my eye as the top of Tony's head appeared, and he ascended the stairs. Maisy barked joyfully and dashed to him.

Waving, I hollered, "Hi, sailor, new in town?"

Tony flashed his ever-present charming grin. "Gotta extra cup of coffee for a wayward soul?" Maisy danced at his side, and he ran his hand over her back.

I nodded toward the thermos and extra mug.

He slid onto the bench opposite me and leaned over to give me a kiss. Maisy dropped a wet tennis ball at his feet. He threw the ball, then asked me, "You ready for the sentencing tomorrow?"

"You know, I think I am. I've had an entire month since the guilty verdict to prepare for the sentencing. In some ways, it feels like just yesterday since the murders because the events remain so vivid in my mind. In other ways, it feels like an eternity since the murders. I mean, Sophie is almost three now. And look at the spruce tree from her first Christmas." I pointed beyond the corner of the deck. "It has grown three feet." We had planted the tree to commemorate Sophie's many firsts.

"And Angi," I continued, "she has matured so much. She found her niche in photography and web design."

"She has," he said. "Since she designed that website for the Not So diner and Rossi's Landing, business has been *bustin' a move*."

"You know, she got an A plus for that in her web design class." Talking about Angi brought up thoughts of Thomas and Blane. My mood shifted and was reflected in the worry-lines that etched my face.

Tony took my hand. "Hey, what just happened?"

"I was thinking about Angi and Blane's break up. And how close she is to Thomas. She says they're just friends, but he's very good-looking. I worry about Blane, knowing he's providing security for others while he's still struggling emotionally. I wish he'd get help for his post-traumatic stress."

"Ah. I have a plan to bring him home. I'm going to ask him to manage the dock and handle security of the entire complex for me. I do need the help, and I'll appeal to his protective nature by playing the old man card."

A throaty laugh escaped me. "You? Play the old man card? I thought your motto was 'show no weakness.'"

"That's in business. Family is an altogether different matter."

The mention of family brought William to mind. He was the newest inductee to our Chance clan and proved that family was formed by more than blood. Tony and William, although the consummate odd couple, became fast friends. In fact, William bought a houseboat and kept it at Rossi's Landing. He spent his free time in Chance and renewed his relationship with his daughter, Jenny, who lived in Paris, Texas, just eighty miles due south of Chance. She was divorced and brought her twelve-year-old son, Dillion, up once a month to spend the weekend on William's boat, *Libby*.

"Is William riding with us to the sentencing?" I asked.

Tony shook his head. "No, he'll meet us there. He said he had some business to take care of afterward, and Jenny and Dillion are coming up for the weekend. So, he's going to leave right after the sentencing to take care of business and to make sure the boat is ready for their visit."

I nodded. "Jenny and Dillion have been good for William. Her confiding in William that she wanted Dillion to spend time with him, because Dillion needed a good role model, gave William a renewed sense of purpose."

"It has. And although she asked William, Cici appears interested in the position of role model for Dillion."

"Now that you mention it, Cici does act interested, doesn't he? I noticed he has taken up fishing again, at least on the weekends that Jenny and Dillion are here. I've seen the four of them out on the lake together."

My mind wandered to the murder trial.

Tony squeezed my hand. "Earth to Dawn. Where'd you go?"

"I was just thinking about the trial. How, out of twenty-six months, the trial lasted only four days."

"Yes, and the guilty verdict was worth the twenty-six-month wait. About tomorrow…"

38.

The Sentencing
Freedom

I glanced to my right as we glided past a gray stone building of Greek Revival design that was the Sapulpa courthouse. My heart rate increased, and a nervous energy vibrated within me. I focused on my breathing, filling my lungs, then holding for a count of five and releasing it.

Tony parked the car, then peered into my eyes. "Are you okay? You don't have to do this. We can leave anytime. You just say the word."

I balled up a tissue. "I'm fine. I've got this, but thank you for asking." Looking toward the building, I noticed the sky for the first time–a brilliant blue, and not a cloud could be seen. "You know, this is probably the last time I'll be here. Would you look how beautiful the day is?"

We made our way into the building and cleared security. During the trial, we acquainted ourselves with most of the courthouse staff. Today, they met my gaze and nodded in recognition. I checked in with the clerk, then spoke to the prosecutor and confirmed my intention.

Entering the courtroom, I moved to the far end of the front row, and Tony sat to my right. I kept going over things in my mind. The dense wood of the bench supported me, and the hallowed walls of justice surrounded me. My confidence escalated, and my resolve solidified. I sat erect, the picture of calm, except for my leg, which continued to nervously jiggle, giving away my inner turmoil.

William joined us soon after. He sat on the other side of Tony.

Angi and Thomas entered the courtroom and rushed to me. Angi hugged me before they took a seat in the row behind us, next to Steve and Diane.

I felt eyes on me, which drew my attention to the doorway where Blane stood. He walked toward me with a purposeful gait and embraced me with a warm, silent offer of support.

He looked at the bench behind me and hesitated as if making a decision. I felt his energy ripple as he took in the sight of Angi seated next to the gorgeous Thomas. Blane's chest expanded with a deep breath, and his posture swelled. His eyes riveted on Angi. He forged ahead in her direction, moving like a locomotive in motion as he rounded the bench, slid in beside her, and offered his hand to Thomas. Blane appeared to be staking a claim. I felt a confusing mix of emotions from Blane and Angi.

The bailiff preceded the judge into the courtroom and stated, "All rise." I raised my shields, preparing for the onslaught of emotions in the courtroom.

Judge Tankersly entered and took his seat on the bench. "You may be seated."

I was struck by the ritual and beauty of the courtroom and how the elegance was in stark contrast to the repulsiveness of the crimes tried there.

Prosecutor Bigley spoke, followed by Defense Counsel Westerfeld. Wayne Beck Mason waived his right to the defendant's allocution—his right to speak on his own behalf. Sullen, in an ill-fitting orange jumpsuit, Wayne slouched in his chair. Spotting me, he narrowed his eyes and curled his lip in a sneer.

The very sight of him buoyed my resolve. *I can do this.*

Judge Tankersly surveyed the courtroom. He addressed the prosecuting attorney. "Is there anyone who wishes to present a victim impact statement before I sentence Mr. Mason?"

"Yes, Your Honor. Dawn Patterson is here to speak today."

It was time. Tony squeezed my hand.

My heart thundered. My neck throbbed with the pounding of my pulse. My mouth and tongue were dry. I stood, and as I marched to the podium, my legs felt weak. This was it, my chance to influence the outcome of this sentencing—an opportunity to confront the monster.

I spread out the sheet of paper and pulled the microphone closer.

The judge spoke into his microphone. "Please state your name and your relationship to the decedents."

Meeting the judge's intense but impartial gaze, I cleared my throat and took a calming breath. "My name is Dawn Patterson. I was the wife of Mike Patterson, mother of Gracie Patterson, and grandmother of Baby Patterson.

The judge nodded. "You may begin."

"Your Honor," my voice held a slight tremor, "the impact Wayne Beck Mason had on my loved ones' lives and deaths and my life is immeasurable." I found my pace and stilled the tremor temporarily. "He is not just a murderer, he is also a thief. I suspect he is a rapist, too. I was the one who found my family's bodies after he murdered them. Although murder is too mundane a word to describe how he slaughtered my daughter and her unborn child. His child. I cannot erase the images of that massacre from my mind.

"He stole those three lives, their futures, and the influence they would have on the world. He robbed me of my future with them. He took my ability to be a grandmother to my biological grandchild and future grandchildren. He stripped their legacy and mine.

"There have been days that I struggled just to get out of bed. I have endured nightmares and post-traumatic stress from the images of their lifeless bodies, as well as from the sight and smell of the bloodbath left in my daughter's bedroom. There have been days when all I wanted was to die.

"Up until today, he has held a certain amount of power over me. The anger, hate, and rage I felt for him gave him control over my thoughts, my dreams, and my life. That ends today."

Warring with my emotions, I took a step back and wiped my eyes. Placing my hands on the podium, I locked my elbows, bracing myself for what was to come, and continued. "I stand before this court calmly. I want Wayne Beck Mason to know," I turned my head to make direct eye contact with him, "you don't matter."

He sneered, raised his head subtly, and pursed his lips as if blowing a kiss to me.

I doubled down and met his unremorseful arrogance with a defiant gaze and a knowing smile.

"Go ahead, Wayne, blow kisses, but at the end of the day, I get to go home. Whatever the outcome of this sentencing, whether you get *life imprisonment* or the *death penalty,* you will be caged or dead. I am free. I will thrive. You have no power over me. You are nothing. Wayne Beck Mason, you are dead to me already."

Focusing my attention back on Judge Tankersly, I continued. "Your Honor, please impose a sentence that will justly punish… this." I extended my arm and hand in a graceful, fluid motion to indicate Wayne Beck Mason. "Thank you, Your Honor."

Wayne narrowed his eyes and focused his gaze on me as he gripped the armrest of his chair so tightly his knuckles turned white. "I saw you take my dog! What did you do to Maisy?"

The judge pounded his gavel. "Order! Mr. Mason, any further outbursts from you and you will face contempt charges and possible fines."

In that moment, looking at Wayne, I saw past the monster to the abused, traumatized child who had become an adult. I lowered my shields and was hit by a wall of sorrow that radiated from him, dousing me in his misery. A wave of compassion swept over me, washing away my desire to hurt Wayne—to retaliate. Shocked that I wanted only justice, my shoulders relaxed, and a genuine smile lifted the corners of my lips. Surprised that I felt the need to reassure Wayne, I said, "Maisy is well and will continue to have a wonderful life… with me. She is innocent. Gracie loved Maisy, and Maisy loved Gracie." I gathered my paper and left the podium. Arriving at my seat, I nudged Tony over so I could sit between him and William. Tony's eyes shined, and he gave a quick nod as if to say *well done*. Resting an arm across my shoulders, he lay his other hand on my thigh.

William gave a curt nod, keeping his poker face in place. He sat erect and stared forward, then took my hand in his. The dampness of his hand, the flare of his nostrils, and the clenching of his jaw belied his outward calm. This sentencing was the culmination of nearly four years of William's life. He immersed himself so far into this case that it couldn't be classified as just work. He had a personal stake in the outcome.

The judge cleared his throat. "Mr. Mason, your contemptuous displays of disrespect in this courtroom, your propensity for violence, and your complete lack of remorse are abhorrent.

"These murders were especially heinous, atrocious, and cruel. They were premeditated and committed for the purpose of avoiding or preventing a lawful arrest or prosecution. I find no mitigating circumstance that would change the determination of the jury."

There was an audible gasp throughout the gallery as if the courtroom itself were a living entity responding to the judge's decree. Wayne Beck Mason crossed his arms over his chest, slouched further in his chair, and kept his gaze on the floor.

"Therefore," Judge Tankersley continued, "Wayne Beck Mason, as to count one, you were judged guilty of the crime of first-degree murder for the unlawful killing of Baby Patterson. For this crime, the court sentences you to life in prison without the possibility of parole.

"As to count two, you were judged guilty of the crime of first-degree murder for the unlawful killing of Michael Allen Patterson. For this crime, the court sentences you to life in prison without the possibility of parole. These sentences are to run consecutively.

"As to count three, you were judged guilty of the crime of first-degree murder for the unlawful killing of Gracie Page Patterson. For this crime, the court sentences you to be put to death in the manner prescribed by law."

Death. Justice. Tingling all over, I wanted to laugh and yell and cry. I was finally free.

I stopped listening to the proceedings and became aware of William's reaction. An emphatic *yes* escaped his mouth in an almost silent hiss. A smile lit his face, and he squeezed my hand.

Tony pulled me into a hug and reached for my other hand... my left hand. As he folded it into his, I heard a startled inhalation as he felt the engagement ring on my finger.

Epilogue

The squeaky rattling of a trailer rousted me from my reverie the morning after the sentencing. I peered out the window from my spot at the Last Chance Café. Through the gritty haze raised by the extended cab pickup and trailer, which hauled two four-wheelers, I spotted a magnetic sign on the driver's door. From the sign, a cartoon rendition of a pile of pooh resembling soft-serve chocolate ice cream smiled at me and announced *Meland Co. Septic.*

"No way," I whispered.

Every door of the cab flew open, and four vaguely familiar people sprang out amidst laughter and loud banter. Their boisterous chatter drilled through the closed windows as they headed towards the café.

The door burst open, and their robust energy pummeled me with playful delight. The first through the door was a young woman with sun-kissed, wavy hair held back from her freckled face by a pair of sunglasses. "Where is she? Where is that Jamaica beach bunny?"

I couldn't believe my eyes. "Kelly Plants and Shana Meland!"

Before I could process everything, Kelly hauled me out of the booth into her embrace. Shana was next. The bill of her baseball cap, adorned with a pooh logo, smacked me in the forehead when I was passed to her. Kelly's husband, Mike, and Shana's husband, Joe, fidgeted in the background. I had not seen these two couples in over four years. My Mike and I met these

Iowans in Jamaica on our last trip the Spring before the murders. They were young enough to be our children, but we formed an immediate bond and stayed connected via social media.

"What are you all doing here?" I asked.

Kelly laughed. "Well, Iowa does stand for *Idiots Out Wandering Around.* We heard Wayne Beck Mason got the death penalty, so we drove through the night, and we're here to celebrate."

Joe and Mike cruised forward, each giving me bear hugs that lifted me off my feet. Memories of our last trip to Jamaica flooded in. However, despite the pain that drove me to pack away the photograph of us all, I was filled with joy for the wonderful memories we created and for the friendship forged with these two young couples.

"Anyway," Kelly went on, "we've rented a cabin with a fire pit, and we're throwing a party tomorrow night to celebrate the outcome of the sentencing. Invite all your friends."

"Where's the cabin?" I asked.

"Rossi's Landing. The Phoenix cabin. You know the place?"

"As a matter of fact, I do. I'll tell you what," I said, "there could be twenty or more of us, so you idiots—I mean Iowans— take care of the drinks, and my friends and I will bring the food.

Joe and Mike gave a thumbs up, and Shana chimed in, "The more the merrier."

***

The box lay hidden in the back corner of the closet. Dragging it out, I hoisted the container onto my bed and was rocked by a sneeze from the dust. Upon removing the lid, a joyous expression greeted me—a three-year-old Gracie atop a pony at a pumpkin patch just before Halloween many moons ago. No longer a source of unbearable pain, Gracie's picture comforted me, and I set it on my bedside table. Directly below that picture lay the photo of my Iowa friends posed with Mike and me in Jamaica.

***

Sitting in a camping chair surrounded by the stillness of the afternoon heat, I sipped lemonade and hoped for a cool breeze before the celebration began. I glanced at the photograph in my lap and trailed my fingertips across the smiling faces of the six of us, transporting me to the memory of that day. The photo would be a historical introduction of Mike, Kelly, Joe, and Shana to my eclectic Chance tribe. Hopefully, the picture would prompt questions and stories so the Chance clan could get to know the delightful self-proclaimed Iowa idiots the way I did.

Focusing on the patio, I surveyed the ongoing setup for the party. Amos, Tony, Steve, and William unfolded two long tables on the back patio and covered them with tablecloths for the catfish feast to come. Maisy was in the thick of things, as if she were supervising. Raising her head, she turned her gaze toward me and smiled. During the month she had been living with me, we had become quite close, and she exhibited more playfulness each day. Joe and Mike befriended Bernard while shopping at his liquor store and invited him to the party. The three of them were setting up the bar adjacent to the tables.

Carrying covered dishes, Diane and Katie slipped into the cabin to help Kelly and Shana prepare snacks and dessert.

A vintage pickup truck rattled to a stop just before 5 o'clock. Jasper stepped out of the truck in his formal wear consisting of a clean pair of overalls and a freshly shaved mug shaded by a brand-new John Deere cap. He dug around behind the seat in the truck, while Rags, the tree farm dog, jumped down from the cab, bounded towards me, and placed his head on my lap. His entire backend wiggled with the wag of his tail while I scratched behind his ears. Maisy bounded over, intent on checking out the four-legged interloper. Rags executed a playful downward dog, then rolled to his back, allowing Maisy to sniff him. They both remained by my chair.

Jasper withdrew a brown paper bag from behind the seat.

"Is that some of your infamous apple pie moonshine?" I hollered.

"Yep."

"You're spending the night, then."

"Yep."

"Jasper, you're a man of few words."

"Yep," he responded as he moseyed towards the bar.

Sophie squealed and ran over to greet the dogs. Angi followed her with Thomas and another sharp-looking young man in tow.

"Aunt Dawn, I'd like you to meet Thomas's *friend*, Patrick."

I extended my hand. "Happy to make your acquaintance, Patrick. There is a wide array of drinks available at the bar on the patio. There's even an apple-pie moonshine. Make yourselves at home."

The two men ambled to the bar as Angi hugged me.

Perplexed, I asked, "Thomas's *friend*?"

"What?" Angi asked, feigning innocence. "Thomas is gay. You knew that, right?"

I snorted. "Well, I do now. I've been distracted lately, so fill me in on what's going on with you."

"Well, I'm going to do it. I'm going to search for my dad."

"You are? That's wonderful. I'll help you. I mean, he is my nephew after all."

Another pickup rolled to a stop. "Oh, look," I said. "Blane is here. Does he know Thomas is gay?"

Angi smiled and raised her eyebrows. "Not yet."

I couldn't help chuckling. "You little minx."

She shrugged and strolled towards the bar while Sophie skipped by her side, and the dogs followed as if Sophie were the pied piper.

I should have gotten up and played hostess, but hey, I wasn't the host, and I just wanted to relax.

Blane ambled over, looking like a model fresh from a Levi Strauss photo shoot. An errant curl dipped over his forehead. An open chambray shirt revealed a white T-shirt beneath, and snug-fitting jeans topped hiking boots. Bending down for a hug, he asked, "How goes it, Dawn?"

"It's good. I'm at peace. A chapter has ended. What about you? How's the security business?"

He shrugged his shoulders. "Can you keep a secret? I haven't told Dad yet, but I'm taking him up on his offer to manage Rossie's Landing. I'm moving home."

Bouncing out of the chair, I threw my arms around his neck. "Welcome home." I pulled back to study him. His blue eyes sparkled, and his face was relaxed. He looked happy. What a relief for Tony to have his beautiful boy back in the fold.

We broke apart. With a furtive glance, Blane spotted Angi at the bar with Thomas and Patrick. He shifted with nervous energy while he drank in the sight of her—the soft waves of her hair that fell to her waist, the spring sweater, and skinny jeans that complemented her slim figure.

Nudging him with my shoulder, I asked, "Isn't she lovely? Why don't you get a drink and meet Thomas's new... *friend?*"

Blane whipped his head towards me. "*Friend?* Huh, I think I'll do that."

As he moved at a brisk pace towards the bar, Sophie ran to him. Stopping a few feet before reaching him, she disarmed him with a beaming smile, then looked at her feet. In one swift movement, he scooped her up and made growling noises while nuzzling her neck, pretending to bite her. Sophie cackled, and Angi's expression softened as their eyes met.

Jenny and Dillion arrived next, accompanied by Cici. *Hmm, that's interesting.*

William strolled up beside me. Tilting his head back, he closed his eyes and inhaled deeply through his nose. With his eyes still closed, he stated, "It's over." Opening his eyes, he met my gaze. "It's all... over."

"What does that mean, William?"

His face broke into a rare smile, one that reached his eyes. "I tendered my resignation yesterday after the sentencing. I am retiring."

Speechless, I grabbed him in a ferocious hug, and for reasons I didn't understand, I cried.

Tony trotted to my side and addressed William. "Hey, what's going on here, Buddy? Why is my gal crying?"

I began laughing while I continued to cry. "William resigned yesterday. He's retiring. Isn't that great?"

Frowning, Tony said, "That depends. William, are you going to live on your houseboat and be a pain in my ass?"

William chuckled. "That remains to be seen. I am moving to my boat, though."

The two men embraced in bro-hug fashion.

By 6 p.m. Tony's two sons from Tulsa and their families, along with my brother, Kurt, and his daughter, Mona, arrived. All of our clan were there.

Tony grasped my hand. "It's time."

As we sauntered toward the group, a light breeze lifted my hair and rippled the fabric of my long, floral sundress, hinting at Mike and Gracie's presence. Tony and I approached the patio, where he retrieved a microphone. We turned to face the crowd, and he spoke. "Everyone, I have an announcement."

Jasper ambled up behind us. Sticking his hands in his pockets, he rocked back and forth on the balls of his feet. He looked uncomfortable—out of his element, away from the tree farm, and standing in front of the large group.

As everyone gathered around us, Tony dropped to one knee. "Dawn Patterson, you have resided in my heart for over forty years. Will you do me the honor of marrying me… tonight?"

I knew we were going to do this. We planned the surprise together, but hearing those words spoken aloud thrilled me and erased all my doubts and fears concerning our marriage. The only word I could form was, "Yes!"

Tony then stood amidst thunderous applause, ear-piercing whistles, and cat-calls from the peanut gallery. Reaching for what I thought was a delicate floral centerpiece on the nearest table, Tony lifted a small wreath of fresh flowers interwoven with baby's breath and white satin ribbons which formed streamers. In front of our relatives and our chosen family, Tony arranged the fragrant wreath on my head.

We turned to face Jasper, who withdrew a bible from the bib of his overhauls. Taking the microphone from Tony with a shaking hand, he began. "Dearly beloved, we are gathered here in the sight of God—"

And so, a new chapter began.

The End.

Acknowledgements

First, David, my husband, friend, and the calm in all of my storms.

Nikki Hanna, award-winning author and writing coach extraordinaire, who wields her red pen like a sword to slice away the debris of my writing transgressions.

Amy M Le, my multi-talented publisher and founder of Quill Hawk Publishing.

The Sapulpa courthouse staff, who wish to remain anonymous. You know who you are.

They welcomed me with curiosity and generosity, answering a multitude of questions on law and courtroom procedure, and informing me of courtroom proceedings I wanted to observe.

The Oklahoma writing community, specifically:
> Tulsa Night Writers writing club and host of The Craft of Writing conference
> The Oklahoma Writers Federation Inc. and host of The OWFI writing conference
> WriterCon, host of WriterCon writing conference and multiple workshops

- ➢ Friends of the Tulsa County Library, sponsor of Tulsa County Library Adult Creative Writing Contest
- ➢ eMerge Magazine, giving emerging writers and poets a platform for their creative works
- ➢ Talented authors who offered invaluable feedback and suggestions to hone my craft: Vicki Montoya, Jeanean Doherty, Joan Sandergard, Marty Ludlum, Faith Phillips, Lara Bernhardt, and William Bernhardt

My special friends who read chapters or the entire manuscript. All encouraged me throughout this extraordinary journey: Darla Pfannenstiel, Randy Frost, Ranell Shea, Janet Hanewinkel, and Polly Bright.

Thank you, it seems so inadequate. I am grateful beyond words.

About the Author

Joyce Hanewinkel is an award-winning author. She has numerous awards for her short stories and poetry in the genres of fiction, memoir, and essay. Hanewinkel's writing is rich with humor, inspiration, and strong messages. She has been published in Life's Vintage Magazine, eMerge Magazine, and on the Tulsa  County Library website. Her stories are drawn from a wide variety of life experiences gained from her active-duty service in the Army, playing recreational soccer, and working in healthcare, telecommunications, and manufacturing. She now debuts her award-winning novel, *An Unforeseen Chance*, a deeply moving women's fiction novel lush with drama, recovery, and romance.

www.ingramcontent.com/pod-product-compliance
Lightning Source LLC
Chambersburg PA
CBHW061232310726
48971CB00007B/2031